FAST FEMINISM

SHANNON BELL

AUTONOMEDIA | *New York*

ISBN 978-1-57027-189-2

Autonomedia
PO Box 568
Williamsburgh Station
Brooklyn, New York
11211-0568 USA

www.autonomedia.org
info@autonomedia.org

www.fastfeminism.net

BOOK AND COVER DESIGN
Zab Design & Typography

COVER
Shannon Bell [FF]: S(he)va Phallus
taken on a rowboat in the middle of
the sacred River Ganges, Varanasi,
India. Photo by Monica Frommer.

Printed in Canada

torontoartscouncil
An arm's length body of the City of Toronto

Canadian Federation for the
Humanities and Social Sciences
Fédération canadienne
des sciences humaines

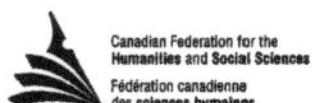

Acknowledgments

Erika Biddle for being the best editor in the
world for FF. Erika's style, precision
and militancy turned *Fast Feminism* into
the fast powerful philosophical-political
thought it is.

Gad Horowitz for his relentless engagement
with FF—the project, text and person.

Canada's leading Executive Editor Virgil
Duff for his belief in the risk of writing and
publishing the risk.

Zab Hobart for bringing her design techné to
FF's words and images.

Rachael Rakes for her insightful
reorganization of chapter one.

Konstantine Stavrakos for his critical eye and
precision editing, especially in chapter 3.

The Ontario Arts Council for a Writer's
Reserve Grant.

The Aid to Scholarly Publications Program
(ASPP), Canadian Federation for the
Humanities and Social Sciences, for a
publishing grant.

FOR

Gad Horowitz – "you are still the best part"

Monica Frommer, girlfriend always

Kath Daymond, best spouse a grrl ever had

Pals: Nicola Short, Tobaron Waxman and Tania Visosevic

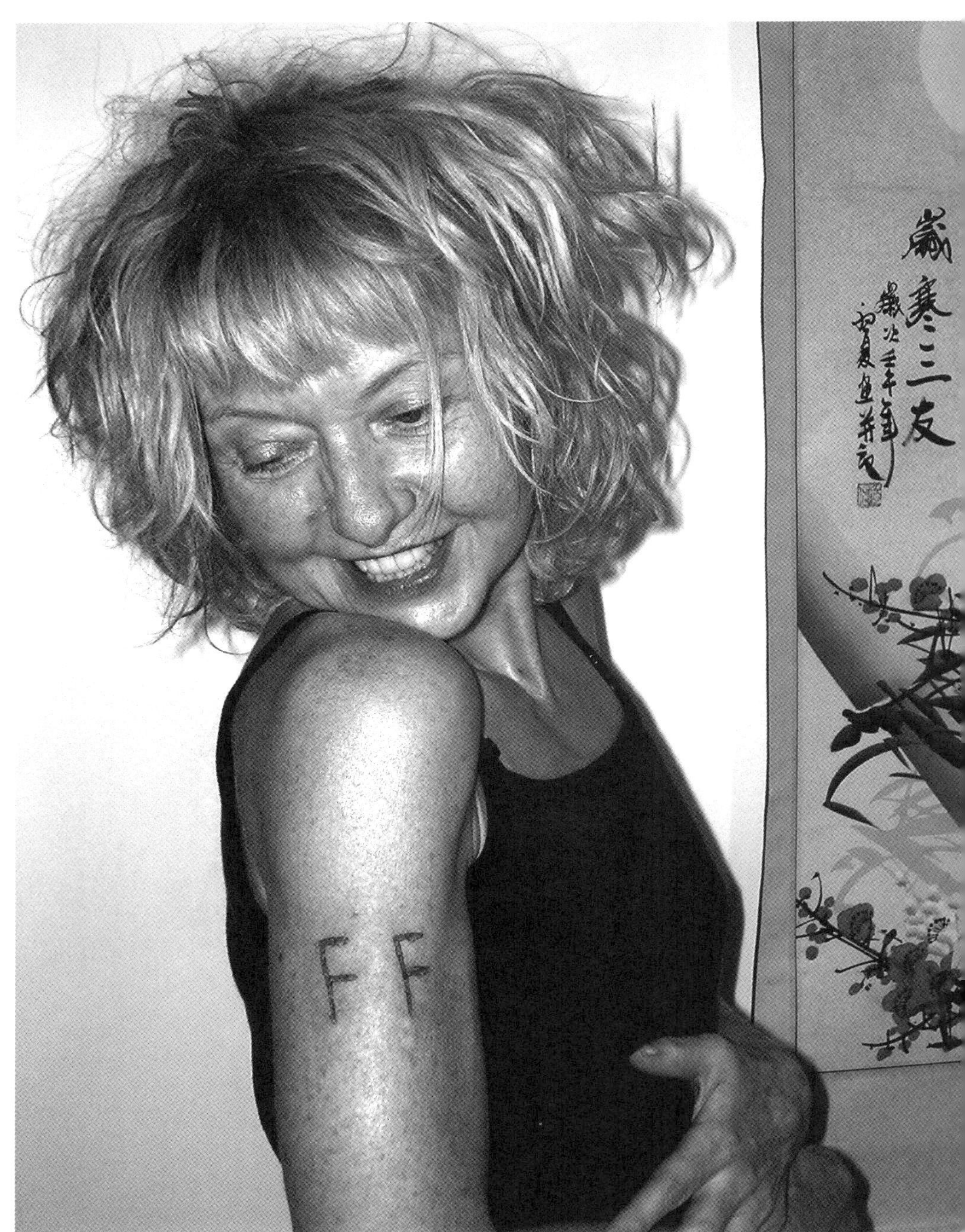

Shannon Bell (FF). Branding by Blair. | PHOTO Blair McLean.

CONTENTS

CHAPTER 5

POSTCRIPT

The
Fast Feminist [FF]
&
FAST FEMINISM

THE FAST FEMINIST [FF]

The fast feminist (FF) is a post-gender provocateur, not so much a gender terrorist[1] as a gender risk-taker going the distance with her body. FF's philosophy is lived. Actions count. One resists with one's body.

The operative principles in *Fast Feminism* are that as FF I never write about anything I haven't done and that I locate the enactments inside a philosophical discourse. The sites of enactment are framed within queer postpornography. 'Postpornography' is a term used to refer to erotic sexual images, films and stories that recode how we look at bodies and sexual acts.[2] If "pornography codes how to look at women,"[3] postpornography queers the gaze, and in so doing destabilizes and recodes how we look at everyone. Postpornography, as the theorists, performers and image producers of *Post/Porn/Politics* (2009) do it, and as FF does it, "involves different strategies of critique and intervention in pornographic representation arising out of the feminist, queer, transgender, intersexed and anti-colonial movements."[4]

FF, however, is first and foremost a philosopher. Her sexual feats are embodiments of philosophy: they are philosophical events. Fast feminism is a philo-porno-political practice, a

pragmatic philosophy and politics, enacted by the pornographic sage fast feminist who moves through the text as FF.

FAST FEMINISM:
Speed Philosophy, Pornography, Politics

Fast Feminism is a work of speed philosophy, pornography and politics. The philosophical discourses that play out in the text are extensive and varied. The underlying contention is that feminism needs to be infused from non-obvious philosophical locations. The most non-obvious site is the work of Paul Virilio, the hypermasculinist philosopher and technologist of speed.

Fast Feminism is situated simultaneously as a complement to speed theory and as the accident of speed theory. *Fast Feminism* applies seven tendencies of Paul Virilio's work: 1) critique the world quickly; 2) deploy speed to interrupt intellectual scholarship; 3) position the body as the basis of intellectual work; 4) write theory as art; 5) do theory from non-obvious points of departure; 6) speed and slowness work together as stability and motion, stasis and velocity, interruption and linkage; 7) use the staircase method for doing philosophy. That is, once an idea is introduced and deployed, jump to linkages with another idea and always, always do violence to the original context. For Virilio, the accident, although an unintended and disturbing consequence, is inherent in and created by the very technology or system it comes out of. Needless to say, *Fast Feminism* is the bastard offspring and "the happy accident, the stroke of luck" [5] of speed theory.

How is *Fast Feminism* both the likely and unlikely accident of speed theory? An accident of any system, whether that system be ecological, technological or philosophical, is the unknown quantity inherent in the original substance. Where is fast feminism inherent in Virilio's speed? Three locations: the fiercely courageous speed style that profoundly critiques the world quickly and breaks intellectual scholarship. The recurrent messianic moment that Virilio never fully hides: "if you save one man, you save the world.... The world and man are identical." [6]

And, in Virilio's positioning of the body as the basis of his work: "I am a materialist of the body, which means that the body is the basis of all my work"[7]; "when I talk about speed, I am talking about bodies."[8] Of course, the material body has always been central in feminist philosophy and practice, but the coupling with speed, this is fast feminism. The corollary question is how does *Fast Feminism* implement Deleuze's imperative of buggering the author's work, in this case Virilio's work, to produce itself as the new offspring? While Virilio's points of departure for speed theory are military history, architecture and aesthetics, fast feminist points of departure are the female phallus, performative action and perverse aesthetics. *Fast Feminism* not only deploys Virilio's speed method to sites he wouldn't envisage, the operative principle of fast feminism—theory as enactment—is precisely what is so obviously missing in Virilio's later work on aesthetics, particularly *Art and Fear*,[9] in which he mercilessly critiques the work of artists he has not viewed.

While Virilio is the main philosopher of influence in fast-feminist performance philosophy, *Fast Feminism* is influenced by the pragmatic techno-philosophy of the international cyber-robotics performance artist Stelarc,[10] who Virilio identifies as a global prophet of posthumanism.[11] Stelarc is a high-risk pragmatic philosopher who continuously puts "the body"[12] (his body) on the line, on shark hooks, on robotic exoskeletons and into cybernetic technology. He has wired his body directly into the Internet and has put microtechnology into his body, all in the name of art, life and new intelligence. Stelarc has been theoretically redesigned by feminist philosophers Amanda Fernbech and Joanna Zylinska as a feminist[13] and a Levinasian pragmatist,[14] the latter due to his openness to allowing the speed of the Internet to drive his body and his hospitality in acting as a body host for virtual entities in the physical world.

Aside from the outright endeavor and originality of Stelarc's work there are two related aspects of his philosophical reflections that directly impact fast feminism. Stelarc always premises his theoretical claims and philosophical pronouncements on his practice. For Stelarc, "the idea is always in the act."[15] New thought

is grounded in action and physiology. A techno-phenomenologist, Stelarc directs his work to disclosing that "philosophy is fundamentally grounded in our physiology."[16] New philosophy, significantly different thought and ideas, come about through radically redesigning the body.

While Virilio and Stelarc are the central philosophers deployed in fast-feminist performance philosophy and performance writing, fast feminism is also strongly informed by George Bataille and Emmanuel Levinas. *Fast Feminism* posits an ethics that dwells where Georges Bataille encounters Emmanuel Levinas, that is, where the risk of the endeavor privileges a particular other: the pervert other. FF's other is the 'pervert widow, pervert orphan and pervert stranger' who arrives theoretically when Levinasian ethics is brought together with Bataille's understanding of risk and excess. For Levinas substitution, putting one's self in the place of the other, is the ethical itself.[17] It is easy to put oneself in the place of Levinas' widow, orphan and stranger. It is not so easy to substitute one's self for the pervert: the publically promiscuous bi-homosexual, the sadomasochist, the pedophile.

The linkages in each of the chapters circulate among Virilio, Stelarc, Bataille and Levinas with minor interruptions by other philosophers such as Gilles Deleuze and Félix Guattari, Jacques Lacan, Sigmund Freud, Marquis de Sade, Sacher-Masoch, Arthur and Marilouise Kroker, Judith Butler and Elizabeth Grosz.

Fast Feminism falls within the performance-writing genre, wherein writing is doing; it is embedded in praxis. Writing is both an outdated medium and as Virilio contends, our only hope: "Salvation will come from writing and language. If we recreate speech, we will be able to resist."[18] Like Helen Cixous' method, fast-feminist writing is undertaken and presented as "a high-speed exercise,"[19] but rather than presenting it as *ecriture feminine*, it is presented as 'speed writing.' It is an homage to the punchy style of Virilio and Kathy Acker and to the gait of Maurice Blanchot. The 'I' of the text is a postidentity recognized by gait, movement and speed. Influenced by Blanchot's textual strategy, *Fast Feminism* propels you through locations. Speed necessitates rigorous control and precision, which surrenders to the failure of

restraint. The work produced is thus simultaneously controlled and unrestrained.

In an interview with Semiotext(e) editor Sylvère Lotringer in 1991, Acker refers to the unrestrained moments in her texts as going "into the space of wonder"[20]:

> ACKER: When you write, are you controlling a text? When you're really writing you're not, you're fucking with it…. What you do, when you body-build, is work to failure… actually I want to work to past failure… and I think you're doing exactly the same thing with the text.
>
> LOTRINGER: What's past-failure for a text?
>
> ACKER: To go into the space of wonder.[21]

Fast Feminism's erotic narratives enter "the space of wonder" and in so doing put a knife to the heart of Western philosophy and pornography. FF adopts Acker's means of writing: "taking the text to be the same as the world,"[22] and "writ[ing] in a way that is most present."[23]

FF's discipline (living and work) is devoted to intensity, speed and energetic chaos. Speed theory is a form of "theoretical art" or "artistic theory,"[24] a *techne* that comes out of the very condition that it addresses: "the age of the bored eye: the eye which flits from situation to situation, from scene to scene, from image to image… with a restlessness and high-pitched consumptive appetite that can never really ever be satisfied."[25] "Lasting interest"[26] lies in the realm of nostalgia. Nostalgic theory, burdened by a teleology and ontology, can't catch the bored I [eye]. What can is Virilio's method of working in staircases:

> I work in staircases… I begin a sentence, I work out an idea and when I consider it suggestive enough, I jump a step to another idea without bothering with the development. Developments are the episodes. I try to reach the tendency. Tendency is the change of level.[27]

Virilio deploys suggestion, breaks, stoppage and rapidity.[28] He states: "I don't believe in explanations, I believe in suggestion, in the obvious quality of the implicit."[29] Virilio notes "the importance of interruption... of things that are stopped as productive.... The fact of stopping and saying 'let's go somewhere else' is very important."[30]

Fast Feminism features a new technology of writing, writing as morphing, which remixes and blends materials from different contexts. It does violence to the original contexts in the process. In this respect it owes its lineage to the modernist practice of collage. However, morphing doesn't surgically cut and transplant as collage did; it genetically crossbreeds, producing a trans-textual chimera, a neo-breed of philosophy, pornography and politics.

Fast Feminism morphs speed with past feminisms— postmodern feminism, postfeminism, cyberfeminism, third-wave feminism—and with neo-beat living and locates this in the blend of Bataille's philosophical treatise, *Inner Experience*, and his feminist pornographic sexual treatise, *Madame Edwarda*. These cross-blend with Levinas' concept of alterity, which shares unsuspected similarities with Stelarc's performative encounter with the alterity of the digital matrix. In turn, this meld operates through a politics that is indebted to the radical feminism of Catharine MacKinnon and the relentless critique of sexism and demands for sexual and social equality of second-wave feminism. Fast feminism is fluid feminism which holds no distinction between academia and activism, the female phallus and male phallus, living and writing, philosophy and pornography.

Fast Feminism is in close proximity to postfeminism of the poststructuralist variety—third-wave feminism, queer feminism, cyberfeminism and feminism 3.0—and shares the most general features of these postmodern feminisms: gender is viewed as performative; there is no essential female/male self; grand referents and feminist ontologies are abandoned; multiple, complex and contradictory subjectivities are acknowledged; philosophy is overshadowed by politics; politics is lived as a realm of contestation, instability and struggle; and ethics is

reconfigured as a situated pragmatics.

Fast Feminism works in accord with the deconstructive tendency of postfeminism. Postfeminism is a term that encompasses both deconstructive feminism that dismantles the phallogocentric paradigm of gender and what has come to be considered 'anti-feminist feminism.' The latter tendency, which is the antithesis of Fast Feminism, is more of a liberal individualism in which personal empowerment trumps critical political analysis and collective action. Deconstructive feminist principles are at play in chapter 2, The Female Phallus: 'Something to See,' in which historical and contemporary texts of female ejaculation are taken apart, and in chapter 3, The Perverse Aesthetic of a Child Pornographer: John Robin Sharpe, where court decisions and trial transcripts are scrutinized and played upon.

Like new wave or what has been termed 'third-wave feminism,' fast feminism is not concerned with fighting men but rather with fighting injustices. Third-wave injustices include economic, racial and sexual inequalities: racism, child abuse, rape, domestic violence, homophobia, heterosexism, environmental degradation, classism, health care and reproductive rights. Fast Feminism is particularly concerned with the injustices meted out to pervert others. The "third-wave feminist assumption of independent female sexuality as a valid part of the public sphere"[31] gives this wave of feminism an in-your-face sexuality that Fast Feminism certainly shares. While I was delighted to be a part of the new-wave collection Jane Sexes It Up, "a book of confessions and kinks,"[32] Fast Feminism, nonetheless, prefers sex when it's crossbred with politics and philosophy. Consequently, I am even more delighted to see my pussyphallus front and center in post-queer philosopher-artist Tobaron Waxman's memorial text, "The first Time he thought he was beautiful: A transmasculine Sublime. In Honor of the Life of Brixton Brady."[33] Waxman includes images of my female phallus and enactment of the artist Louise Bourgeois' Arch of Hysteria (1993), truly one of the most beautiful, powerful, feminist presentations of a female body-in-action. While Bourgeois' sculpture reveals the hysteric's

convulsive thrust as an orgasm, our image adds to the thrusting orgasm the post-hysteric arch of female ejaculation.

Front and center in third-wave feminism, and what draws fast feminism to third wave, is ownership of one's body and respect for sexual diversity. Third wave is about the right to do grrrl and not be written off as a girl.[34] Grrrl reclaims the naughty, kick-ass, confident, loud, assertive, active, curious, prepubescent, joy-for-life tendencies that have been toned down, repressed and castrated in turning woman. The grrrl that FF enacts is, however, closer to Deleuze and Guattari's 'little girl':

> The girl... is defined by a relation of movement and rest, speed and slowness... she never ceases to roam upon a body without organs. She is an abstract line, or a line of flight. Thus girls do not belong to an age group, sex, order, or kingdom: they slip in everywhere, between orders, acts, sexes.... The girl is like the block of becoming that remains contemporaneous to each opposable term, man, woman, child, adult. It is not the girl who becomes a woman; it is becoming-woman that produces the universal girl.[35]

FF likes how in feminism 3.0 the once distinct entities man/woman/adult/child can be relocated on an androgynous avatar that mixes a beard with breasts and pigtails with forehead wrinkles. FF feels at home with her cyber sisters because this remixing of homogeneous gender codes is precisely what she does with her flesh avatar.

If "the body is obsolete"[36] as Stelarc has been stating and proving since the early 1970s, then gender, the dominant body signifier, is also obsolete. 'Gender is obsolete' has been the recurrent claim of cyberfeminism since Donna Haraway wrote "A Cyborg Manifesto" in 1985. "Cyborgs might consider more seriously the partial, fluid, sometimes aspect of sex and sexual embodiment."[37] Haraway's "vision is that the blurring of boundaries between human and machine will... make the categories of male and female obsolete."[38] Gender as a

performance with no original sex is definitive of postmodern feminism and postfeminism of the poststructuralist variety, as it is of queer theory which is premised on the obsolescence of the boundaries of hetero and homosexual practices and the fluidity of sexual orientation.

While *Fast Feminism* operates in proximity to other feminisms, its 'natural' home is in queer theory. Queer gets its meaning and its politics from its oppositional relationship to hegemonic norms. To queer something is to disrupt it, to put it under scrutiny and to attempt to change it.[39] Queer theory is Bataille's heterogeneity enacted through 'bodies and pleasures': "the heterogeneous world includes everything resulting from unproductive expenditure."[40] It is the world of "those who refuse the rule."[41] It's FF's world.

DESTRUCTURE: THE ERECTION OF FAST FEMINISM[42]

Fast Feminism spans twenty years of my performance philosophy (1989–2009). The female phallus and female ejaculation texts (in chapter 2) originated in lesbian cultural space in the late 1980s/ early 1990s. Chapter 3 documents and intervenes in the first and probably the last child pornography trial in the world to use the 'artistic merit defense.' The interactions that take place at a number of Pussy Palaces, in chapter 4, are among biowomen, transmen, transboys and transwomen. The final site of enactment, Chapter 5, is machinic-masochistic. It involves intimate sexual enactments with two of the world's largest performing machinic robots, a seduction between FF and a virtual Prosthetic Head, and finally FF's construction and growing of her own male and female phalluses.

Fast Feminism presents events of FF's world that are simultaneously political and personal.[43] I have participated in these events bodily and performatively: female ejaculation, in which I was one of the first feminists to produce visual and written texts (1989); drag-kinging, on which I wrote one of the earliest performative articles (1993)[44]; child-pornography, where my published work supports intergenerational sex, sexual

images and written texts; Bataillean fucking at the Pussy Palace, Toronto's women's bathhouse; sexual enactment of Sharpe's charged "child pornography" tales in *Boyabuse*, with the very wise, skilled, old-school masochist who wrote it, and posthuman or humachine seduction and sex organ tissue-engineering.

In chapter 2, *The Female Phallus: 'Something to See'* the speculum, the very instrument that originally hid the female phallus from view, is with a turn redeployed to reveal the female phallus. It is this unconventional viewing from the position of ownership of the female phallus that drives the subsequent chapters. *The Female Phallus: 'Something to See'* is interrupted by performative ejaculation events: workshops, a cabaret performance, film and radio documentation, and photo shoots.

Chapter 3, *The Perverse Aesthetic of a Child Pornographer: John Robin Sharpe*, tells "a story 'out of time'"[45]; that is, the story of the literary child pornographer. The focus of the chapter is the 'perverse aesthetic,' or the aesthetics of perversity, an aesthetic trajectory developed through the writings of Dante, Sade, Bataille and William Burroughs, for example.

Chapter 4, *The Will to Laughter: A Fast Feminist Bataillean Narration*, presents Bataille's 'will to laughter' in the context of queer sexual encounters. Bataille's philosophy of risk and his concepts of laughter, sovereignty, heterogeneity and unknowing, set out in his texts *Madame Edwarda*, *Inner Experience*, *Guilty*, *On Nietzsche*, *My Mother* and *Blue of Noon*, are interlinked with lived fast-feminist sex tales. The specific selections of Bataille's texts are a mix of his philosophical work and his pornographic literary work, which applies the philosophical principles. Chapter 4 oscillates from the main Bataillean narrative to three adjunct portals: Portal One is "Paying for Eternity: Time with Mistress Patricia"; Portal Two is "The Pussy Palace"; and Portal Three is "Gender Clearing." The portals can be read either as interruptive narratives or as independent short texts.

Chapter 5, *The Accident of Fast Feminism*, attempts to avoid the integral accident in its refusal to conclude while presenting a dynamic fast-feminist manifesto. The chapter turns to posthuman erotics, seduction and creation. There is a return to the human

in the *Postscript*: "Thank you For Being My Mom," a tribute that FF lived, wrote and presented to her mother, Mildred Alice, at the time of and following her death.

Two decades is a significant period of time for pushing the limits of what a body defined as female can do. I am no novice fast feminist. These days when I do ejaculation demonstrations and nude public performances, what meets the viewer's eye is not just a small muscular femme body, but an *older*, small, muscular femme body; a body that is not supposed to be seen, nor up until now to be sexual and sexualized. The obscenity is in the showing, the obscene seduction is in presenting a hypersexual older powerhouse femmly [female equivalent of manly] body. Of course, one of my political commitments—having as my modus operandi a politics of affect—is to queer the old female body, to fuck with the signs of aging while presenting them. Gesture, movement, style and body composition meet and meld with age spots, knee wrinkles and sagging upper-arm undercarriage. It doesn't matter how many years one has worked out, or how long and how hard each time, time will get you. Perhaps that is why time is my most worthy and best-endowed seducer. Time leaves no gender, no flesh—just pure intensity.

Realizing that I was almost fifty and still doing alternative post-porn public performances, I decided to take bodily affect further. In 2005 I had my birth date, 5755, tattooed on my pelvis. It was a number tag not just to keep me honest but also to mark me as a fast feminist philosopher-king in precisely the body location—the female sex organ—that throughout history has prohibited females from ever becoming philosophers, let alone philosopher-kings. 5755 meshed with another tattooed number, 551, in which the 1 became a 7 and we added a third 5. The 551, records the debt of respect I have for the cadaver, known to me only by her institutional number 551, whose urogenital region I dissected in my work on the female phallus and female erectile tissue. The female erection, albeit ossified in a semi-flaccid state, was present during the dissection.

A couple of months later in Berlin I had a very large yellow Star of David tattoo placed just above my heart as a mark of courage,

the will to endure and love of existence. As a performance philosopher committed to revealing the female body as it has not been seen before, I wanted my bodyscape not just to explode the commonplace perceptions of the aging female body, but also to redeploy through material ownership the subject position advanced by the May '68 movement in France: "We are all German Jews."[46]

Fast Feminism was a long time in the making. A feminist press commissioned it in 2001 and rejected it upon delivery in early 2003. In 2006, a university press accepted it at a Friday afternoon board meeting only for it to be overruled by the president of the press on Monday morning. In 2007, a British Queer Studies series expressed interest in publishing Fast Feminism, only to be blocked by the senior editor on the grounds that the series publisher was "still a tad too conservative" for it. Also in 2007, a Gender and Modern Culture series with a Dutch publisher solicited the book and then refused publication on the grounds that the publisher was "too traditional." Finally, Fast Feminism found a home, or perhaps returned home, with Autonomedia who published my book Whore Carnival in 1995.

What kept killing Fast Feminism?

Read it and see.

All the while, FF has engaged in new endeavors and kept adding these actions to the Fast Feminism text. I have three principles of action: (1) theory must be grounded in action otherwise it is dead; (2) "we are to the degree that we risk ourselves"[47]; (3) never write about what you don't do. The third principle has propelled me through some wonderful experiences. And sometimes FF did actions just so she could write about them.

FF moves quickly through multiple queer and posthuman sites, oscillating between submission and dominance, movement and interruption. FF's politics are affective: to actively produce or effect change at the bodily and cellular levels and to be affected at these levels.

FF has no gender but can do gender in excess if it is in her interest and not at all if interest wanes. She's Haraway's cyborg, the phallic mother, the Sadean woman, Deleuze and Guattari's

little girl and Bataille's female Don Juan, all gone hyper, doing gender as escape velocity not only from woman but even from what feminist philosopher Rosi Braidotti has identified as "post-woman,"[48] getting rid of the postmenopausal culturally positioned waste of time wasteland.

Needles in the flesh body—menstrual blood ends. "Your period won't bother you much anymore," the female acupuncturist claims. "Stick a needle in my heart line," FF says. Intensity speeds through FF in a sobbing scream. That was for the queer bisexual Genet-like Pygmalion who made me: "I love you more than I love any human." "Do the heart line again!" Intensity speeds through and out her body in a cry once known as anguish, now just as intensity: "I love you more than I will ever love any posthuman." Heartbreak is so neat, tidy and quick; psychoanalysis is a waste of time, schizoanalysis is a method now passé; the speed of clean steel entering the flesh fixes what language, "the talking cure," never could.

The crunch of needles going into the forehead is an exhilarating sound. FF begins to laugh, intoxicated by the sound and the miniscule amount of Botox as it enters her flesh. Another needle follows, her laughter increases. Like Bataille, "this intoxication has as its condition that I laugh, principally at myself"[49] and I was laughing, knowing that I just made my body a living Dorian Grey. Right before your eyes the wrinkles now under erasure will reemerge in the not too far-off future. Time's the whore I'm in love with. "Existents"[50] are mere embodiments, of course, "the dialectic of time is the very dialectic of the relationship with the other."[51]

"Stick a needle in where it will give me focus, I need to write!" The female acupuncturist grants the request.

Stasis.

Writing is "a high-speed exercise,"[52] flipped over.

Stasis.

I positioned the autographed poster of Allen Ginsberg taking his picture in a mirror directly opposite my bathroom mirror: mirror-image reflecting Ginsberg looking at himself looking at me. "It'll keep you honest," G., the bearer of the gift

told me. On the poster, beneath Ginsberg's doubled image is his poem "Cosmopolitan Greetings," in which he writes: "Universe is Person." "Mind is Outer Space." "First thought, best thought." As the Botox wears off and the lines of living reemerge perhaps the lines of humanity will deepen: "The face of a neighbor signifies for me an unexceptionable responsibility.... The disclosing of a face is nudity, non-form, abandon of self, aging, dying, more naked than nudity... the skin is with wrinkles, a trace of itself... already a poverty that hides its wretchedness and calls upon me and orders me. Such is the singular signification of an existence deserting itself."[53]

FF sat frozen for an hour staring at Gunther von Hagen's *Skin Man*, the plastinated posthuman male, red-muscle body, white-fat tummy, skin hoisted up on his left arm. His head was cocked towards his skin in congealed contemplation of what von Hagen could not erase, the lines and wrinkles of his life.

> Decay is a considerable impediment to morphological studies. Therefore scientists have been searching for centuries for suitable preservation techniques. With the invention of plastination it has become possible to preserve decomposable specimens in a durable and life-like manner for instructional, research, and demonstration purposes.[54]

What von Hagen's *Body Worlds* is really about is the clear dead beauty of the clean dead body. "Every voluptuous embrace is necrophilic, sinking into a body decomposing and cadaverous."[55] What fascinated FF was the neatly folded skin. "Skin no longer signifies closure. I wanted to rupture the surface of the body, penetrate the skin."[56]

FF opened her floor-length black leather coat, letting it slide off her arms onto the banister railing, revealing her shredded black panties barely hanging onto her boy hips. The skin on her pecs bore bruises from the passion of the previous night. Standing there in her black motorcycle boots, she interpellated the other: "Hey baby, I never want to be away from you long enough for the

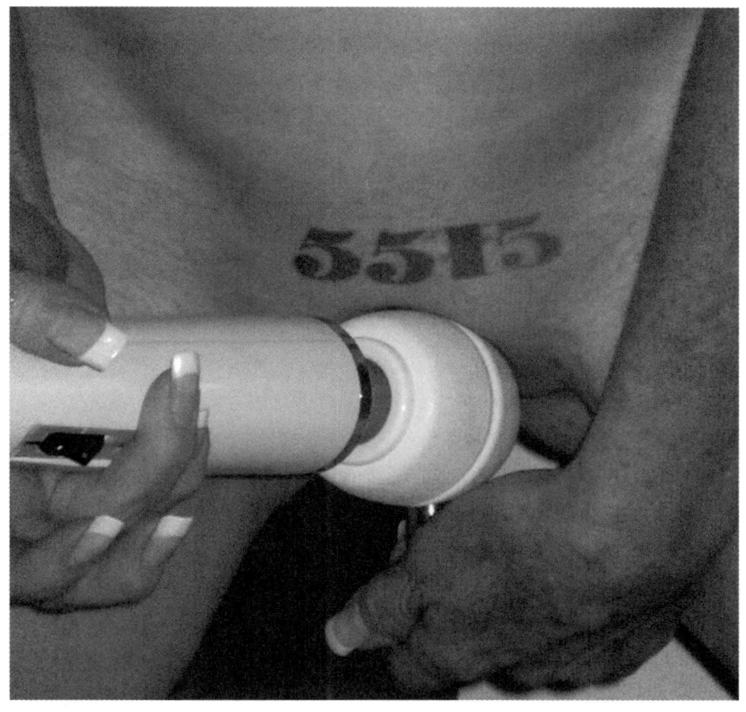

Shannon Bell (FF). Female ejaculation workshop at Come As You Are. | PHOTO Erika Biddle.

bruises to go away: red, blue, green, yellow, the colors of fire, water, earth, air and space; the elemental."[57] As with a lover, one should never be away from feminism long enough for the bruises to go away. "Feminism is for everybody," bell hooks says, and "passionate poitics."[58]

Endnotes

1 According to Del LaGrace Volcano, "a gender terrorist is anyone who consistently and intentionally subverts, destabilizes and challenges the binary gender system." See www.disgrace.dircon.co.uk/page1.html.

2 Shannon Bell, "Post-Porn/Post-Anti Porn: Queer Socialist Pornography" in *New Socialisms*, eds. Robert Albritton, John Bell, Shannon Bell and Richard Westra (London: Routledge, 2004).

3 Catharine MacKinnon, *Feminism Unmodified* (Cambridge, MA: Harvard University Press, 1987), 173.

4 Beatriz Preciado, "Walls, Urban Detritus and Stag Rooms for Porn-Prosthetic Eyes" in *Post/Porn/Politics. Queer Feminist Perspectives on the Politics of Porn Performance and Sex as Culture Production* (Berlin: Verlag, 2010), 42.

5 Paul Virilio, *The Original Accident*, trans. Julie Rose (Cambridge and Malden: Polity Press, 2007), 4.

6 Louise Wilson, "Cyberwar, God and Television: An Interview with Paul Virilio" in *Digital Delirium*, eds. Arthur and Marilouise Kroker (Montreal: New World Perspectives, 1997), 46.

7 Virilo says: "The body is extremely interesting to me because it is a planet.... There is a very interesting Jewish proverb that says: If you save one man, you save the world. That's the reverse idea of the Messiah: one man can save the world, but to save a man is to save the world. The world and man are identical... [T]he body is not simply the combination of dance, muscles, body-building, strength and sex: it is a universe. What brought me to Christianity is Incarnation, not Resurrection. Because Man is God, and God is Man, the world is nothing but the world of Man—or Woman... to separate mind from body doesn't make any sense. To a materialist, matter is essential... I am a materialist of the body, which means that the body is the basis of all my work." [Louise Wilson, "Cyberwar, God and Television: An Interview with Paul Virilio" in *Digital Delirium*, 46–47.

8 Virilio and Sylvère Lotringer, *Crepuscular Dawn*, trans. Mike Taormina (New York & Los Angeles: Semiotext(e), 2002), 56.

9 Virilio, *Art and Fear*, trans. Jacqueline Rose (London & New York: Continuum: 2003).

10 Stelarc, an Australian artist who has performed extensively in Japan, Europe and the United States, fuses the body and technology in his performance work. He has used medical instruments, prosthetics, robotics, virtual reality systems and the Internet to explore alternate intimate and involuntary interfaces with the body. The defining issue that Stelarc has addressed, from his early video documentation of the inside of 'the body' to his first suspension event in 1976, to his more recent performances with mechanical prostheses and robotics, is the issue at the core of Western philosophy: what it means to be human.

11 Nicholas Zurbrugg, "Virilio, Stelarc and 'Terminal' Technoculture" in *Theory, Culture & Society* (London and New Delhi, 1999), Vol. 16, No. 5–6, 179.

12 Stelarc refers to his body as 'the body,' an object for redesign. See www.stelarc.va.com.au/redesign/html.

13 Amanda Fernbach contends that "as Stelarc enters the Web he gives up agency over his body to remote participants, in effect he… undergoes what could be considered a 'feminization.'" [Amanda Fernbach, *Fantasies of Fetishism: From Decadence to the Post-Human* (New Jersey: Rutgers University Press, 2002), 115.

14 Joanna Zylinska uses the Levinasian ethics of respect for the Other to develop what she terms a 'prosthetic ethics of welcome or hospitality' that she sees Stelarc as offering to nonhuman alterity. Zylinska writes: "While differing as to degree and scale in which the body is extended, augmented and transformed, all these performances seem to have been inspired by the idea of openness, of welcoming the unpredictable and the unknown…. By abandoning the desire to master the house of his own body and opening himself to the (perhaps hostile) intrusion of the guest, Stelarc performs the most ethical act of what Derrida terms 'unconditional hospitality.'" [Joanna Zylinska, "The Future is Monstrous: Prosthetics as Ethics" in *The Cyborg Experiments: The Extensions of the Body in the Media* (London: Continuum, 2002), 229 & 232.]

15 Stelarc Interview, Victoria, British Columbia, February 9, 2002.

16 Stelarc, www.stelarc.va.com.au.

17 Emmanuel Levinas, *Otherwise Than Being or Beyond Human Essence*, trans. Alphonso Lingis (Pittsburgh: Duquesne University Press, 1998), xxix.

18 Virilio, *The Politics of the Very Worst*, trans. Michael Cavaliere (New York: Semiotext(e), 1999), 51.

19 Helene Cixous and Mireille Calle-Garber, *Rootprints: Memory and Life Writing*, trans. Eric Prenowitz (London & New York: Routledge), 41.

20 Kathy Acker, "Devoured by Myths: An Interview with Sylvère Lotringer" in *Hannibal Lecter, My Father* (New York: Semiotext(e), 1991), 13.

21 Ibid.

22 Ibid., 22–23.

23 Ibid., 14.

24 Zurbrugg, "Virilio, Stelarc and 'Terminal' Technoculture," 182.

25 Arthur Kroker, "The Image Matrix." Available at www.ctheory.net, Article A105, 7.

26 Ibid.

27 Virilio and Lotringer, *Pure War*, trans. Mark Polizzotti (New York: Semiotext(e), 1988), 44.

28 Ibid., 44–45.

29 Ibid.

30 Ibid.

31 Lisa Johnson, "Jane Hocus, Jane Focus: An Introduction" in *Jane Sexes It Up*, ed. Lisa Johnson (New York: Four Walls Press, 2002), 10.

32 Ibid., 1.

33 Tobaron Waxman, "The first Time he thought he was beautiful: A transmasculine Sublime. In Honor of the Life of Brixton Brady" in *Post/Porn/Politics*, 338–339.

34 Jennifer Baumgardner and Amy Richards, *Manifesta: Young Women, Feminism, and the Future* (Farrar, Straus & Giroux, 2000).

35 Gilles Deleuze and Félix Guattari, *A Thousand Plateaus: Capitalism and Schizophrenia*, trans. Brian Massumi (Minneapolis & London: University of Minnesota Press, 1987), 276–277.

36 James Paffrath and Stelarc, eds., *Obsolete Body Suspensions: Stelarc* (Davis, California: JP Publications, 1984), 8 & 17.

37 Donna Haraway, "A Cyborg Manifesto: Science, Technology, and Socialist-Feminism in the Late Twentieth Century" in *Simians, Cyborgs, and Women: The Reinvention of Nature* (New York: Routledge, 1991), 180.

38 Liza Tsaliki, "Women and New Technologies" in *The Routledge Critical Dictionary of Feminism and Postfeminism*, ed. Sarah Gamble (New York: Routledge, 1999), 83.

39 Bell, Noam Gonick and Dan Irving, "Why Queer? Why Now?" in *Canadian Dimension*, Vol. 43, No. 4, July/August 2009.

40 Georges Bataille, "The Psychological Structure of Fascism" in *The Bataille Reader*, eds. Fred Botting and Scott Wilson (Oxford & Malden, MA: Blackwell Publishers, 1997), 127.

41 Ibid.

42 'DeStructure' is a play on Heidegger's destruction and Derrida's deconstruction.

43 Carol Hanisch "The Personal is Political," Redstockings collection, *Feminist Revolution*, March 1969: 204–205.

44 Bell, "Finding the Male Within and Taking Him Cruising: 'Drag-King-For-Day' at the Sprinkle Salon" in *The Last Sex: Feminism and Outlaw Bodies*, eds. Arthur and Marilouise Kroker (Montreal: New World Perspectives, 1993), 89–97.

45 Ken Plummer, *Telling Sexual Stories* (London & New York: Routledge, 1995), 120.

46 Deleuze and Guattari, *Anti-Oedipus: Capitalism and Schizophrenia*, trans. Robert Hurley, Mark Seem and Helen K. Lane (Minneapolis: University of Minnesota Press, 1983), 363.

47 Bataille, *On Nietzsche*, trans. Bruce Boone (New York: Paragon House, 1994), 72.

48 Braidotti writes: "She, in fact, may no longer be a she, but the subject of quite another story: a subject-in-process, a mutant, the other of the Other, a post-Woman embodied subject cast in female morphology who has already undergone an essential metamorphosis." Rosi Braidotti, *Metamorphoses* (Cambridge: Polity Press, 2002), 11–12.

49 Bataille, *On Nietzsche*, 60.

50 "For the Being which we become aware of when the world disappears is not a person or a thing, or the sum total of persons and things; it is the fact that one is, the fact that there is." [Emmanuel Levinas, *Existence and Existents*, trans. Alphonso Lingis (The Hague: Martinus Nijhoff, 1978), 21.]

51 Ibid., 93.

52 Cixous and Calle-Garber, *Rootprints: Memory and Life Writing*, 41.

53 Levinas, *Otherwise Than Being or Beyond Human Essence*, 88–90.

54 See www.bodyworlds.com/en/plastination.htm.

55 Alphonso Lingis, *The Imperative* (Bloomington and Indianapolis: Indiana University Press, 1998), 148.

56 Paolo Atzori and Kirk Woolford, "Extended-Body: An Interview with Stelarc" in *Digital Delirium*, eds. Arthur and Marilouise Kroker (Montreal: New World Perspectives), 198.

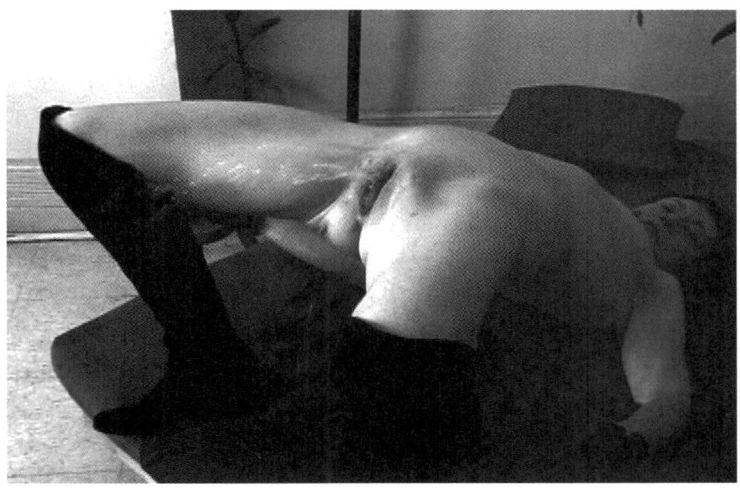

FF, Arch of Ejaculation. | PHOTO Tobaron Waxman.

57 Levinas writes: "Every relation or possession is situated within the non-possessble which envelops or contains without being able to be contained or enveloped. We shall call it the elemental.... The element has no forms containing it; it is content without form. Or rather it has but a side: the surface of the sea and of the field, the edge of the wind; the medium upon which this side takes form is not composed of things." [Emmanuel Levinas, *Totality and Infinity*, trans. Alphonso Lingis (Pittsburgh: Duquesne University Press, 1969), 131.]

58 bell hooks, *Feminism is for Everybody: Passionate Politics* (Cambridge, MA: South End Press, 2000), 118.

THE FEMALE PHALLUS:
Something to See

I'm just looking for my yellow vibrator. [Vibrator switches on.] In order to get an internal erection, one of the best things is a really small vibrator, just to ride on the top of your lips. Just place it between your two lips, sort of just below your clit. What it does is—it feels nice, you get little vibrations—it starts the erection happening inside. The other thing is, in order to ejaculate, you really have to push out. The feeling that a lot of people have when they're making love— that they have to pee—that's usually a sign that you are ready to ejaculate. What you need to do is to push out. We've been training ourselves not to push out, but to hold back because we think we have to pee. If you actually train yourself to push out, you can push the fluid out. It's an incredible high.

I'm going to do that right now.

What I find happening is I can feel fluid building in the glands and ducts surrounding my urethral sponge. I can feel it from the outside. If you put your hands

from where my clit is up to where my ovaries are, you can actually feel the glands and ducts filling up with fluid. Now I normally ejaculate pretty easily. I'm in the scientific group that they call the "easy expulsors": it takes me from one to three minutes at the most. I can usually ejaculate a lot and repeatedly. There's a middle category where it takes women longer before they can ejaculate with stimulation; and there's also a group where it's harder to induce but it's a really powerful ejaculation.

What I am doing here is I am getting somewhat turned on. I'm feeling like I'm starting to have to ejaculate. I can feel internal contractions. Yeeeesss. Pssssssssss ss sss. [Audio ejaculation.]

That was just kind of warming up.

I like to ejaculate on mirrors, it's got this phenomenal sound; you can see yourself ejaculating really well, and it's just very, very beautiful. So I'm going to do that.

What I am doing now is getting ready to ejaculate again. I'm masturbating, the way I normally masturbate. I've got my fingers between my two lips and pulling on my clit, and I am also pushing on the ducts that surround my urethral sponge.

From the outside, I can feel them getting full of fluid. Yeahhhh. Psssss ssss sss ss twang, trickle. [Audio ejaculation.]

The thing about having a penis inside of you and ejaculating is that often the penis is too big and you can't really push out. You have to take the penis out to do it because you need room to be able to push out. I like to have mirrors around so I can see what I am doing.

I also like to ejaculate on mirrors because you can see yourself ejaculating. When the ejaculate dries, you can see that female ejaculation isn't all that different from male ejaculate. It is a bit thinner, of course, because it doesn't have the semen properties. But women do have an equivalent to the prostate gland, so the fluid is there, and if you were to have both side by side you could see that female fluid is a white fluid on the mirror when it dries. It's usually clear.[2]

Since 1989, the ejaculating female has been speaking on her own behalf, presenting images and texts initially inside a queer feminist discourse.[3] I wrote "Q: What shoots and sprays, shoots and sprays, shoots and sprays? A: A Woman," the first how to female ejaculate instructions, as the feature article for the International Women's Day issue of the lesbian magazine *Rites* in 1989.[4] The issue included black-and-white images of me doing two different types of female ejaculation—the spurting gush and the jet stream—and two texts, one which traced the genealogy of female ejaculation and one entitled "The Everywoman's Guide to Ejaculation." Later in 1989, Kath Daymond and I did *Nice Girls Don't Do It*, the first film on female ejaculation.[5] It is a thirteen-minute pastiche of knowledge, porn and instruction, in black and white, in which a beautiful blonde femme sits on my face while I masturbate and ejaculate. I was doing androgynous butch boy in those days, now I am doing hyper or fast femme. It makes no difference. Butch/femme, somewhere in between, we all have the female phallus.

The fast feminist, in addition to her hypermasculine-cum-hyper-feminist genealogy, has another lineage that traces back to the Bitch outlaws of second-wave feminism:

Bitches are aggressive, assertive... strong-minded, direct... hard-headed... competent... independent, stubborn... driven, achieving... ambitious, tough... a Bitch occupies a lot of psychological space... Bitches are... strong... loud... awkward, clumsy, sprawling... Bitches move

their bodies freely rather than restrain, refine and confine their motions in the proper feminine manner. They stride when they walk and don't worry about where they put their legs when they sit... Bitches seek their identity strictly thru themselves and what they do.... The most prominent characteristic of all Bitches is that they rudely violate conceptions of proper sex role behavior... What is disturbing about a Bitch is that she is androgynous. She incorporates within herself qualities traditionally defined as 'masculine' as well as feminine.[6]

In today's speed world, a Bitch is a fast feminist. In 1970, when the *Bitch Manifesto* was first published, a bitch was the opposite of the culturally castrated "Female Eunuch."[7] Almost forty years and a new millennium later, the fast feminist has the female phallus, "the sex of the uncastrated female,"[8] as part of her bio-body and psycho-body. When she wants, she has the phallus—a hard prosthetic cyborg cock. She is part woman, part silicone, part rubber. She straps on the phallus to jack in to fucking: up your ass, in your mouth, in your cunt.

FF has an agenda: to place female ejaculation firmly between women's two lips so that we are in control of ejaculation—we choose whether or not to ejaculate and we squirt, gush, shoot or trickle when and where we want.

FF has endless sister ejaculators who are into the power and fun of female ejaculation. For a number of years at the Michigan Women's Festival there has been an ejaculathon in line with my "Reason to Ejaculate #8" in *Whore Carnival* (1995): "You can have circle jerks, shoot offs with other female ejaculators" or "Who Can Spray the Farthest contests."[9]

The Michigan Women's Festival categories for the ejaculathon include distance, quantity, speed and number of repetitions:

We began with the speed category. A judge yelled, 'Go!' and, at the first sign of ejaculatory fluid, screamed 'Stop!' to the woman with the stopwatch.... A shy, silver-haired,

fifty-something butch prefaced her performance with: 'I only began ejaculating after I turned forty. I don't know what's going to happen, but I'm going to give it a try.' Paired with a complete stranger (one of our generous volunteer 'ejaculation helpers'), she squirted her way to the championship in two seconds, that's right, two seconds. The crowd went wild.

Next up was distance. Red assisted a hot femme wearing false eyelashes to beat out two others with her winning spurt of 27 inches on the tape measure.[10]

The ejaculathon is about body power, politics, skill, fun and the spectacle of female ejaculation; getting female fluid 'out there.' As Australian techno-body artist Stelarc has written, "A body is designed to interface with its environment."[11] Female ejaculation is about marking the territory as the property of female ejaculators. After all, that is what female ejaculation is: the property of female ejaculators.

Malestream sexologists have spent endless time and effort collecting and analyzing the composition of female ejaculate to ensure that it is not urine, only to prove that *it is and is not urine*.

One of most enduringly prolific of these sexologists, 'DoctorG,' Dr. Gary Schubach, Ed.D., A.C.S. got his PhD in Human Sexuality by catheterizing seven women, testing their ejaculate, and publishing the results in articles such as "The G-Crest and Female Ejaculation" and "Urethral Expulsions During Sensual Arousal and Bladder Catheterization in Seven Human Females." Schubach's brilliant conclusion was that female ejaculate is actually "deurinized liquid."[12] Then there is Dr. John Perry, the self-proclaimed 'Dr. GSpot,' coauthor of *The G-Spot and Other Recent Discoveries About Human Sexuality* (1982), which is credited with being the first text to call the G-spot by name. More than twenty years later, Perry and Schubach continue to play off one another's research:[13] Perry links Schubach's watered-down urine in the bladder of sexually stimulated subjects with what he terms his 'beer-piss hypothesis,' referring to colorless expulsions that are

ejected in the lavatories of singles bars.

According to Schubach: "In the past, the assumption has been that the expulsions originated either in the bladder or from the urethral glands and ducts. My study indicated that both may be the case in that a small amount of fluid may be released from the urethral glands and ducts in some instances and mixed in the urethra with a clear fluid that originates in the bladder."[14]

In Schubach's study, urine specimens were collected from the seven subjects prior to stimulation. Then after "they were aroused for a period of at least an hour in whatever manner was preferable to them" a foley catheter was inserted, the women's bladders were drained and the collection was saved for analysis. "The purpose of the catheter was to... segregate the bladder from the urethra and collect vagianl expulsions." "With the catheter in place, the subjects were asked to resume their stimulation of choice and achieved what they (and the medical team) considered to be an ejaculatory orgasm."[15] What Schubach and his medical team found in their tests of pre-stimulation bladder fluid, pre-orgasmic bladder fluid and post-orgasmic bladder fluid was that "the vast majority of the fluid [95 percent] expelled by women during sexual arousal originates in the bladder." "Even though their bladders were drained by the catheter, they still expelled from 50 ml to 900 ml of fluid post-orgasm, drained through the tube and into the catheter bag." Schubach suggests, "fluid which passes through the urethra may be 'deurinized' fluid from the bladder."[16]

The quantity that the seven women expelled [50 ml–900 ml] is quite spectacular. Tested against the pre-orgasmic urine sample, it was found that the "fluid contained... only 25 percent of the amounts of urea and creatinine found in the subject's baseline urine samples."[17] Additionally, Schubach suggests, "In some women and at some time, a small discharge may be added from the female equivalent of the prostate gland." Schubach states, "On five occasions we observed a small milky discharge from the urethra which may mix in the urethra with the fluid from the bladder."[18]

The claim that made Schubach famous in the world of

ejaculation studies is the following: "It is possible that the ejaculatory fluid originates not from either the bladder or the urethral glands, but from both."[19] Schubach believes: "The clear inference is that the expelled fluid is an altered form of urine, meaning that there appears to be a process that goes on during sensual or sexual stimulation and excitement that effects the chemical composition of urine."[20] Female ejaculation as a *process that changes the chemical composition of urine?*

Schubach's addendum theory is "that the hormone aldosterone and/or elevated blood pressure during sensual/sexual activity might contribute to a lowering of urea and creatinine [main properties in urine] levels."[21] It seems that raised blood pressure leads to a conversion of the properties of urea and creatinine into another type of fluid, call it "deurinized liquid." Thus *scientia sexualis* marches on through beer and piss to deurinzed liquid and eventually to 'retrograde ejaculation.'[22]

CUM, BLOOD, URINE

Lying on my back, knees wide apart, I place the magic wand on my vulva, just behind the clit, pressing hard on the urethral opening and on the erection that was beginning to show externally. I switch to sitting on my knees and snap the G-spot attachment onto the head of the magic wand. The hard plastic cock vibrates against my pussy wall. I rotate it, massaging different sensitive spots. I feel a piercing heat, contract my muscles and push out. A flame of water erupts and lands in the catching bowl that I have arranged on the floor four feet in front of me. I estimate about half a cup. I'd better do another one. This time, on my knees, legs wide apart, I use the middle finger of my left hand to play with the spot just behind my clit and in front of my urethra. With my right hand I press on my belly, squishing the fluid in ducts that I can feel from the outside. I tilt my pussy forward. A piercing burning starts. My muscles contract. I press hard on a bulging duct, take a big breath and push out as hard as I can. Bull's eye! I hit the collecting bowl once again, with about 40 milliliters of

fluid. Double bull's eye. This time I orgasm.

I pour the bowl's contents into a beaker, measuring about 180 milliliters, pour what I can into a vial, cap it, and off I go to see my left-wing butch doctor at the neighborhood health clinic. He has agreed, just this once, to test my ejaculatory fluid. He puts both ejaculate and urine through the lab as separate urine samples. Sure enough, my test turns out to replicate the sexology lab tests: ejaculate has a higher pH, more gravity, less urea and less creatinine. The resulting printout also reads: 3+ blood in the ejaculation sample, and a trace of blood in the urine sample. I was in the middle of menstrual bleeding: cum, blood and urine.

Monty Cantsin (Istvan Kantor), the infamous Canadian Neoist performance artist, would draw blood from his veins, throw it on gallery walls, and the rest he collected in vials. A vial of Cantsin's blood currently goes for $250.[23] Shannon Bell, a more-or-less infamous fast-feminist performance philosopher, would spray fluid on the cabaret stage and give vials of her ejaculate, sometimes mixed with her blood, away for free. This was in response to the sexologists and pornographers putting a price on it: normalization at the cost of ownership and control.

Schubach stresses that his concern is to prove that female ejaculate is in some ways distinct from urine and that ejaculating is a "natural sexual bodily function" and therefore, "women could be free of guilt and shame about expelling fluid during sex." [24] But what could possibly be the cause of shame and guilt other than hegemonic heterosexual assumptions about what a female body is capable of and what it should be allowed to do? Schubach suggests, "For women, relaxation and emotional safety are crucial in order to become aroused and stimulated enough so that at orgasm they can ejaculate." [25]

FF removed her knee-high leather boot from her submissive's chest and yanked the chain-linked tit clamps; he screamed with pain. She smiled down at him. He was four-point restrained by beautiful black ropes wound three times around each leg and arm, the rope end threaded beneath each loop and drawn through the final loop. FF struck his adoring face, squatted over it and rode his mouth as her phallus became even harder. Removing his

blindfold, she raised ever so slightly, contracted and precision-shot female cum into his mouth.

As I say in *Nice Girls Don't Do It*: "There is a big difference between ejaculating and being in control of ejaculation, ejaculating when you want to. A lot of women who do ejaculate see it as something that happens, not something that they can take as their own activity and empower it and make happen."[26]

Schubach makes the claim that a benefit of the public recognition of female ejaculation "could be the creation of additional sexual activities that might not just be a prelude to intercourse but an end unto themselves."[27] He deems female ejaculation a source of "new sexual activity" and locates these activities inside what he calls "a pleasure ceremony." How can men and women be together in ways where men can enjoy physical contact and women can feel safe and comfortable?"[28] If we ignore for a moment that Schubach is displacing a radical body action—shooting hot sticky liquid out of one's urethra with great velocity—and locating it inside what Deleuze and Guattari term the 'mommy-daddy-me triangle' of the nuclear family, then non-goal-oriented sexual contact in and of itself is fine. But even this fairly innocuous gesture to body pleasure is situated in the overriding heterophallic assumption that a woman has to be made to feel comfortable in order to ejaculate.

Female ejaculation isn't about comfort: "it is not a maternal soft encompassing experience; it's raw, it's rough and it's going right to the limit."[29] Ejaculation is a biological function of the female body, and like its male counterpart, it is a body's right.

Schubach contends that the G-spot, "the area on the upper wall of the vagina" is "erroneously" named and would be better named "the G-crest."[30] This is for two reasons: "the search for a 'spot' on the anterior wall of the vagina, as opposed to searching for the urethral glands through the anterior wall"[31] could contribute to the difficulty of locating the G-spot and therefore, create doubts about its existence. "Crest" is a more adequate description because "the swollen female urethral glands feel more like a protruding ridge than a spot."[32] Although Schubach wouldn't say so, the swollen protrusion actually feels more like a cock.

Catharine MacKinnon contends: "Anything women have claimed as their own—motherhood, athletics, traditional men's jobs, lesbianism, feminism—is made specifically sexy, dangerous, provocative, punished, made men's in pornography." [33] And, I would add, in sexology. At one end of this malestream continuum are males who demand one ejaculation or many in their face as evidence of a hot sexual encounter. At the other extreme are those who have 'emotional issues' with ejaculation—they can't stand the mess, odor or power and tend to restrict female ejaculation to a designated area, such as the shower, a perfect location for "deurinized liquid." The sexologists analyze the fluid, invent gadgets for sighting the erect urethral sponge, produce cross-sections of the urethral glands and its ducts and rediscover the female prostate. Not surprisingly, what they won't do is see and acknowledge the female phallus.

Female ejaculation is no longer a secret, in fact, in the decade between 1995 and 2005 there was a knowledge explosion that can be situated in four discourses: sexology, spirituality, pornography and feminism.

POST-PORN CYBER FUCKERS

As of 2010 there are over a thousand female ejaculation videos on YouTube. The videos provide information and instructions by sex educators, male and female alike, porn performers and the general female ejaculating public. They are mainly verbal and simulated demonstrations with sex toys, a favorite being the rubber vagina tutorials of "1stop4femaleorgasm." While YouTube keeps it educational, on Xtube and YouPorn there is a burgeoning subgenre of fifteen-second to five-minute female squirt videos. The videos usually come in under two minutes and zero-in on the female money shot. In particular, this is a significant turn in heterosexual porn, which the Monochrom activist performers so aptly describe in *pr0nnovation?* as having the end goal of "putting sperm on a female's body in a more or less Jackson-Pollock-esque way. Pumping sperm into the outside

world represents the climax of pornographic narration."[34] The female ejaculation videos on Xtube and YouPorn are often spectacular. The amateur "Sploosh" series has a devoted following. In the words of one Xtube fan: "The sound of your wet pussy is so exciting and it just pushes me over the edge to see you squirting."

With user-generated websites such as Xtube, YouPorn, Milkboys (the queer teenage-boy blog) and especially the now defunct *ssspread* for "hot femmes, studly butches and lots of genderfuck," there is the possibility to produce what I term postporn. By this I mean nonrecuperable pornography—films, images and stories—that are an excess to what Bataille might call the 'homogeneous' genre of porn. The problem with this, as MacKinnon points out, is that the porn industry is always ready to absorb anything new that sells.

In "Post-Porn/Post-Anti Porn: Queer Socialist Pornography" (2004), I set out six criteria of nonrecuperable porn: 1) it involves lots of genderfuck; 2) it is queer, that is, it disrupts and changes the actions and genders it depicts; 3) the labor producing the images is self-determining life-activity enacted by nonprofessional actors and writers; 4) the content is collectively determined and produced as an interactive process between those acting in and shooting the scenes; 5) the material posted on the website is interactive, with discussion forums for viewer feedback; 6) the material is made from the position of control and sovereignty of action which I identify as the position of the Sadean woman.[35]

There is a distinction between the pornography that, in the words of Angela Carter, "remains in the service of the status quo"[36] and "codes how to look at women [in a way that] reinforces the prevailing system of values and ideas in a given society"[37] and the pornography that works to take apart the prevailing system of values and ideas. Carter identifies the latter as "moral pornography"; it functions as "a critique of current relations between the sexes."[38] She claims:

> The moral pornographer would be an artist who uses
> pornographic material as part of the acceptance of

the logic of a world of absolute sexual license for all the genders, and projects a model of the way such a world might work. A moral pornographer might use pornography as a critique of current relations between the sexes. His [/her] business would be the total demystification of the flesh and the subsequent revelation, through the infinite modulations of the sexual act, of the real relations of man and his kind.[39]

It is this idea of moral pornography that informs my idea of nonrecuperable pornography. A nonrecuperable politics of representation is located in what Kobena Mercer terms the "perverse aesthetic."[40] As I point out in Chapter 3, *The Perverse Aesthetic of a Child Pornographer: John Robin Sharpe*, the perverse aesthetic is the territory of the pervert who "resists oedipalization" and "has invented other territorialities"[41] to operate in. It is the territory of "a body that is incapable of adapting to family life... to the regulations of a traditional sex life"[42] and it is fast-feminist territory.

Some years ago, I did a post-porn ejaculation interview with *ssspread* in which we captured the first-ever image of ejaculating while a speculum was inserted inside the vagina. What was brought to view is the erect female phallus pushing out as liquid shoots from the urethra.

My position in producing postpornography was, in this shoot and as always, as a Sadean woman. For me, this means I simultaneously occupy the position of desiring subject and freeze the object of desire outside the realm of hegemonic desire. There is never a gap, a space left in which the viewer is invited to "stick his[/her] hard cock inside my pussy."[43] I do this in at least three ways: 1) by publishing images with didactic porn text; 2) using codes of dominance (in this case, leather driving gloves and thigh-high dominatrix boots); 3) owning and occupying my own anatomy. In the *ssspread* images, some of which are published in the *Post/Porn/Politics* interview with Tobaron Waxman, my body is occupied by a gold kegelcisor, then a speculum is used to display the internal female erection as similar and different

to the external male erection. I produce an ejaculation shot with the speculum inside to bring the female sex organ to outside view. This functionally achieves a physical and visual redesign of the female body's sexual anatomy. Finally, I produce, with my own body, a re-inscription of the artist Louise Bourgeois' erotic bronze sculpture *Arch of Hysteria*. I re-encode the piece as the arch of ejaculatory orgasm and place female ejaculation inside the redefined hysteric image as a comment on Freud's linking of female body fluids with hysteria.

Historically, the question defining modern female sexuality, from Sigmund Freud to Sheri Hite, was whether the vagina or the clitoris was the primary female sex organ and the main site of female genital pleasure. The question defining post-female sexuality concerns the existence of female ejaculation and the female prostate. The ejaculating female body is the postmodern female body *par excellence*: it engages in non-gender-specific body action, makes the ontological categories of woman and man obsolete, and allows female and male bio-body difference to blur into body sameness.

THE GENDER GAME

Female ejaculation, the expulsion of sexual fluids from the female body through the urethra, is the foundation for a new view of the female body in which both male and female bodies are phallic bodies with "equivalent genitals and equivalent sexual response."[44] The discovery of female ejaculation and the female prostate, urethral sponge or female phallus (my preferred term) exposes gender as a cultural hallucination done with variations according to time and place. Gender is a highly invested hallucinatory game in which players who do it too well die as part of the process. *Sati* [widow death] in Hinduism and what I call "slut death," in which a jealous male partner or ex-partner kills as punishment for infidelity, are the opposite extremes of this process. In other cases, players who don't quite do it well enough to pass as the presenting gender die for it:

male-to-female transsexuals are attacked and killed by hegemonic males for not quite passing as female, or for not being femme enough, and female-to-male transsexuals are killed for the inverse, for not quite passing as male or for remaining too femme.

Gender is a game, a deadly game, in which some of the players know they are "just gaming" [45] and others are oblivious, just doing it without awareness. My understanding of gender as a game has been critiqued by those invested in maintaining gender categories even if their purpose, such as that of Judith Halberstam, is simply to indicate the degree to which manifest gender is produced as much by those with discordant sex organs as it is by those with culturally appropriate sex organs. Judith/Jack Halberstam contends that masculinity is "a construction by female- as well as male-born people" [46] and that "what we call 'masculinity' has also been produced by masculine women, gender deviants, and often lesbians." [47]

In *Female Masculinity*, Halberstam criticizes me for using a drag-king workshop to make a game of gender. Halberstam contends: "Bell plays gender like a game precisely because her gender normativity provides a stable base for playing with alterity." [48] Judith/Jack is partly correct. I do play gender as a game, but not because of any privileged normativity, but rather, because I know that like Socrates, as the poison hardens my body into the rigidity of death, I too will die with an erect phallus. In death, the game of gender reveals its unimportance. As postmodern philosopher Jacques Derrida said: "Sexual difference does not count in the face of death." [49] Or, as phenomenologist John Caputo claimed, "Flesh makes... sexual differences... melt into each other." [50]

In *The Drag King Book*, Halberstam observes: "Bell represents gender as something that is essentially fluid and as a... series of acts." [51] That is correct. However, Halberstam is wrong when he goes on to contend that FF simply hops between the two poles. Halberstam contends, "The very existence of transsexuals suggests that for many people, gender is far from fluid and to represent its ideal state as fluid is to implicitly critique people

who feel unable for whatever reason to hop back and forth between masculinity and femininity."[52] Gender fluidity does not merely imply oscillating between male and female, but also being born bio-female and *becoming* male or locating oneself somewhere along the continuum between normative masculinity and normative femininity, mixing the codes of femininity and masculinity on the same body. It could be the doing of excessive femininity or excessive masculinity for the sheer pleasure of the doing, or for the possibility of scoring the object of desire. It could be the doing of a hegemonic gender performance with awareness that this very doing is socially and culturally produced.

The performance of gender fluidity that Halberstam critiques has surfaced in radical drag-kinging, in which the codes of masculinity and femininity are skillfully mixed on the same body.

Melbourne drag-king Bumperbar (Bumpy), wearing a fedora, tie, men's suit jacket, skirt and motorcycle boots, handed me *King Porn*, a video by the Melbourne drag-king organization King Victoria, in which one hot femme is serviced by three drag-king icons: a mechanic, a taxi driver and a flamenco guitarist (Mo B Dick King Cum, Maurice Valentino King Cock, Skippy Nic Tonz the Tax). It's the spaghetti-mama femme who carries the video. On stage, one of Melbourne's star drag kings, Mr. Kewl, with short slick blond hair, a smart black mustache and stylishly trimmed black beard, long James Dean coat and black leather pants kings his way through a 'crash-hot' rendition of a Duran Duran tune. Bumpy, Mr. Kewl, and other drag-king deviants do a postgender, fast-feminist rendition of kinging in which male and female are consciously distinguished and blurred at the same time on the same body.

The Delphic oracle is said to have instructed Socrates to "*know thyself.*" The fast-feminist philosopher knows that there is no essential self and that the no-self knows no gender; that anatomical sex need not coincide with gender expression; that gender as a set of cultural body practices and sex as the practical and pleasurable use of sexual anatomy are social artifices. FF knows that the phallic economy of one, the social exchange with which Jacques Lacan replaces Freud's biological fleshy penis,[53]

is a biosocial phallic economy of two: the female and the male phallus. The body is simultaneously a biophysical given and a social construct. The term 'female phallus' is used to refer to both the fleshy, spongy, biophysical penis equivalent and the social right to agency that in the past has only accompanied the male biophysical organ.

It is no coincidence that female ejaculation, just like what Halberstam identifies as "female masculinity," has its home with "masculine women, gender deviants and often lesbians,"[54] those photographer/artist Del LaGrace Volcano terms gender terrorists "who consistently and intentionally subvert, destabilize and challenge the binary gender system."[55]

As part of the Masturbation Cabaret,[56] I walk onto the stage accompanied by Drag King Sean Con, following Trixie and Beaver's femme/butch number involving a simulated ejaculation shoot off—each projecting two liters of liquid from their respective genitalia (the secret fountains of the cum were enema bags). Wearing a fedora, motorcycle boots and a fifteen-centimeter, flesh-colored strap-on and carrying a magic wand vibrator with vibrant blue G-spot attachment, I walk onstage. Then I remove the male signifiers—hat, boots, cock—and position myself on my knees on a four-foot-long, two-foot-wide table. Sean Con rests a mirror of the same dimensions on the edge of the table, angled so that the audience of four hundred femme lesbians, dykes, drag kings, transmen and transboys, an occasional dominatrix and slave, a few gender-deviant heterosexual bioboys and grrrls, and graduate students can see real and mirror images. I was giving it to Lacan.

I thrust the G-spot attachment into my cunt and click it into high speed. The plastic cock vibrates hard on my internal female cock, located on the top wall of my vagina, which becomes engorged. I place the microphone on the spinning ball of the wand that rapidly massages my urethra, inner and outer vaginal lips, and the visible portion of my female cock. The microphone makes the already notoriously loud vibrator sound like the revving of a Bugatti motorcycle. I slide the G-spot stimulator in and out and side to side, stimulating the entire top of the vaginal wall. "You

can't fuck your grad students, but nobody says you can't go on stage with them," I announce. Sean Con, who had just completed his MA on drag kinging with me as his supervisor, provides the gender-deviant male gaze. He watches me watching me. Me, the small, muscular, unruly, platinum-haired ejaculating icon watching the reflected image of myself about to ejaculate: "The perfect man's heart is like a mirror,"[57] just reflecting back. The audience counts me down from ten to one as I pull the wand out and spray the mirror in a rush of liquid fire, producing a scream that starts in my belly and traverses my body. It was a double ejaculation: embodied and mirror image. Echoing philosopher Luce Irigaray, I ask the audience: "What is left of a mirror invested by the (masculine) 'subject' to reflect himself, to copy himself[?]"[58]

For the second ejaculation I lie on my back, legs wide apart, one knee against the angled mirror so the audience can see the butterfly of a doubled image. A public ejaculation in a Toronto cabaret space alters the course of female ejaculation as a sexual response, repositioning it away from the burgeoning ejaculation-knowledge sites of sexology, psychotherapy, feminist spirituality and pornography, positioning it instead as spectacular body power: "Female ejaculation is body power. It is not really about sex; it is about erotic power."[59] I remove the G-spot attachment, enter my pussy with my seventeen-centimeter cock, and lay the mic on my stomach, picking up the sound of the vibrator and body contractions. I start counting: ten, nine, eight... as I reach one I dedicate the ejaculation "to all the grad students here who work with me, you guys rock!" A huge gush of girl-cum shoots out of my urethra and my voice hits the mic with a guttural scream. Girl-liquid hits the mirror with a piercing twang of clarity. "Female ejaculation dethrones male ejaculation—a linear progression of excitement and release of body energy and fluid—and positions it as just a trace of the female ejaculatory experience."[60]

FEMALE EJACULATION: A FAST GENEALOGY

Female ejaculation has been officially recognized as the product of an active female prostate[61] and as "deurinized liquid" from the bladder, if you are of the DoctorG school of thought. It has been the object of medical and philosophical discourses since the ancient Greeks. Aristotle, in the *Generation of Animals*, connected female fluid with pleasure:

> Some think that the female contributes semen in coition because the pleasure she experiences is sometimes similar to that of the male, and also is attended by a liquid discharge. But this discharge is not seminal.... The amount of this discharge when it occurs is sometimes on a different scale from the emission of semen and far exceeds it.[62]

The meanings ascribed to female ejaculation over the course of Western history have varied considerably. Female ejaculation has typically been framed in five ways: as fecundity, sexual pleasure, social deviance, medical pathology and as a scientific problem.

Female ejaculation is an incredibly powerful experience and image of the sexual female body. To shoot fluid with velocity and force out of the glands and ducts that surround the urethra, what is called the "urethral sponge" of the clitoris, now officially the "female prostate," through the urethral opening, provides a new script for female sexuality and repositions the female body as powerful, active and autonomous. Female ejaculation educator Deborah Sundahl suggests, "This is connectable to a broadening of women's social and sexual roles."[63] I say, "The visual image of female ejaculation relieves the phallus of its patriarchal burden."[64]

LIQUID FIRE

I practiced by sucking the cock of my Ginsberg/Genet bisexual lover G. Between his legs, cock in mouth, right hand rubbing my clit and the external portion of my engorged urethra, I would start to burn and then push, burn and push, burn real bad and then push real hard. I could barely walk. My urethra was on fire. The muscles contracted tight against a liquid flame I had not yet learned how to shoot. G.'s cock was black and blue. Every time I pushed I bit his cock, but he supported me all the way, and has for twenty years of pushing a torrent of liquid fire out of my urethra.

We took the varnish off the floors in his various apartments; we abandoned futon mattresses permanently drenched in girl-cum until we discovered surgical sheets. I sprayed a large mirror as I sucked him, leaving a cum-streaked surface to remind all his fuck buddies and tricks that they were playing in my territory.

My internal erection would become so hard and large that G. would have to remove his cock from my pussy while I sprayed a gushing flame before we resumed fucking. I would slide off his face, squat and release fluid on the floor to continue the ride. Sometimes, perched on his face, I would look over my shoulder to see the puddles scattered around our sexscape, overflowing into one another, much like our souls.

On menstrual days, when I pushed the fluid out of my glands and ducts, the pushing action would propel blood and ejaculate out of my pussy, making pink pools on the bed. With surgical sheets the fluid collects in all the crevices. G.'s ass was often in a pink pond when I returned to thrusting my member against his. My member was inside me, fucking his inside me.

The expulsion of female fluids during sexual excitement was taken by many pre-Enlightenment thinkers to be a normal and pleasurable part of female sexuality. Well into the eighteenth century, what cultural historian Thomas Laqueur terms the "one-sex model" was the predominate paradigm. In this model, male and female are seen as versions of one another, both anatomically in the sense that the vagina is an internal penis, and physiologically in the sense that the fluids in men and

women are interchangeable.[65] Perhaps the major controversy within the one-sex model was between one-seed and two-seed theories of generation. The debate revolved around whether female fluids were progenitive. Hippocrates and Galen argued for the existence of the female seed, while Aristotle said that the fluid was pleasurable but not progenitive.

Western scholars throughout the Middle Ages remained faithful to Hippocrates and Galen's notion of female sperm, which came to them through Arabic medicine and survived the Middle Ages. In the sixteenth century, Italian anatomist Renaldus Columbus linked the clitoris with semen, ejaculation and pleasure: "If you rub it vigorously with a penis, or touch it even with a little finger, semen swifter than air flies this way and that on account of the pleasure."[66] Female-to-female instruction is present in seventeenth-century whore dialogue, an early form of erotic writing that combines pornographic tales with educational instruction in which usually an older woman teaches a young virgin about female sexual anatomy. In the case of the dialogue between Tullia and her younger cousin Octavia, they discuss female ejaculation:

> TULLIA: Towards the upper Part of the C__t, is a thing they call Clitoris; which is a little like a Man's P___k, for it will send forth a Liquor, which when it comes away, leaves us in a Trance, as if we were dying, all our Senses being lost, and our Eyes shut[.]

> OCTAVIA: You describe Things so exactly, that me thinks I see all that is within me.[67]

The seventeenth-century Dutch anatomist Reijnier De Graaf, in his *New Treatise Concerning the Generative Organs of Women*, outlined the Hippocratic and Aristotelian controversy over female semen. He sided with the Aristotelians and denied the existence of female semen. In describing the ejection of female fluid, De Graaf wrote: "It should be noted that the discharge from the female prostatae causes as much pleasure as does that from

the male prostatae."[68] He identified the source of the fluid as the "ducts and lacunae... around the orifice of the neck of the vagina and the outlet of the urinary passage [which] receive their fluid from the female prostatae, or rather the thick membranous body around the urinary passage."[69] De Graaf was the first person to name and describe the female prostate.[70]

As the similarities between male and female bodies gave way to their differences, and semen became the sole property of the male body, the capacity of the female body to ejaculate— although still present and documented in medical writings and literature—was predominantly described as a less-than-normal occurrence.

In the nineteenth century, female fluids were linked with disease. Alexander Skene, who in 1880 identified the two ducts on each side of the urethral opening, was concerned with the problem of draining the glands and the ducts surrounding the female urethra when they became infected. The Skene glands and the urethra hence became important to the medical profession as potential sites of venereal disease and infection, and not as loci of pleasure.

The ejaculation of female fluids also came to be associated with a deviant sexual population and practice: lesbians and female desire. In Baron Richard Freiherr von Krafft-Ebing's well-known study of sexual perversion, *Psychopathia Sexualis* (1886), he identifies female ejaculation as the pathology of a subgroup within a deviant group. Under the heading of "Congenital Sexual Inversion in Women," Krafft-Ebing discusses sexual contact among women in prison:

> The intersexual gratification among... women seems to be reduced to kissing and embraces, which seems to satisfy those of weak sexual instinct, but produces in sexually neurasthenic females ejaculation.[71]

According to Krafft-Ebing, ejaculation occurs only among women who suffer neurasthenia—body disturbances caused by weakness of the nervous system. However, as the love letters

between anarchist Emma Goldman and whore-activist Almeda Sperry reveal, powerful women are female ejaculators too. Sperry writes to Emma:

> Dearest:
> Satisfied? Ah God, no! At this moment I am listening to the rhythm of the pulse coming thru your throat. I am surging along with your life-blood, coursing thru the secret places of your body. I wish to escape from you but am harried from place to place in my thoughts. I cannot escape from the rhythmic spurt of your love juice.[72]

While Sperry relates female ejaculation with the overpowering desire of an orgasmic female body, Krafft-Ebing relates female ejaculation to a nervous disability. The latter is reiterated by Freud in his analysis of Dora. Freud makes a connection between Dora's hysterical symptoms and the secretion of female fluids, and links 'abnormal secretions' with hysteria:

> The pride taken by some women in the appearance of their genitals is quite a special feature of their vanity; and disorders of genitals which they think calculated to inspire feelings of repugnance or even disgust have an incredible power of humiliating them, of lowering their self-esteem.... An abnormal secretion of the mucous membrane of the vagina is looked upon as a source of disgust.[73]

As female ejaculation was being pathologized by the medical profession, psychoanalysis and the burgeoning sexology industry,[74] female ejaculation surfaced in Victorian male pornographic discourse. The Pearl, a two-volume journal of Victorian short stories, poems, letters and ballads, contains depictions of female ejaculation misinterpreted by Steven Marcus in The Other Victorians as "the ubiquitous projection of the male sexual fantasy onto the female response—the female response being imagined as identical with the male... and there is the usual

accompanying fantasy that they ejaculate during orgasm."[75]

The clearest and most complete description of the physiological process and anatomical structure of female ejaculation was published in *The International Journal of Sexology* (1950) by Ernst Gräfenberg, a German obstetrician and gynecologist. Gräfenberg observed that:

> An erotic zone always could be demonstrated on the anterior wall of the vagina along the course of the urethra.... Analogous to the male urethra, the female urethra also seems to be surrounded by erectile tissues.... In the course of sexual stimulation, the female urethra begins to enlarge and can be felt easily. It swells out greatly at the end of orgasm.... If there is the opportunity to observe... one can see that large quantities of a clear transparent fluid are expelled... out of the urethra in gushes.[76]

Despite the descriptions of it in medical, philosophical and pornographic literature throughout Western history, and in spite of Gräfenberg's work, female ejaculation was denied by the dominant discourses defining female sexuality until the 1980s. The genealogy of female ejaculation has been one of discovery, disappearance and rediscovery.

FEMALE EJACULATION: A NEW VIEW

The paradigm shift in knowledge about and representations of female sexuality began with *A New View of A Woman's Body* (1981), compiled by the Federation of Feminist Women's Health Centers (FFWHC), which in a brilliant political move, redefined the clitoris, extending its visible external structure, the glans of the clitoris, to incorporate the internal spongy erectile tissue on the top and bottom vaginal walls. The FFWHC named the tissue on the top wall of the vagina the "urethral sponge" and the spongy tissue on the bottom wall the "perineal sponge." During

sexual excitement, the urethral and perineal sponges become engorged and erect; the paraurethral glands and ducts in the urethral sponge fill with prostatic and other fluid which can be ejaculated through the urethra.

The FFWHC's *A New View of A Woman's Body* provided drawings of the clitoral structure in flaccid and erect states;[77] these drawings make apparent the similarity in size and structure of the male and female sex organs. Directed by Mary Jane Sherfey's 1972 point-by-point comparison of clitoral and penile anatomy,[78] the FFWHC rediscovered and defined the female clitoris pragmatically through consciousness-raising sessions and shared intimate experiences which included taking off their clothes to compare genital anatomy and documenting each other masturbating. By doing so they acquired the practical knowledge presented in Susan Gage's now-famous anatomical illustrations of the urethral sponge of the clitoris, complete with erectile tissue and paraurethral glands and ducts.[79]

In *The G-Spot* (1981), Alice Ladas, Beverly Whipple and John Perry extended the paradigm shift of the new view of the female body into the realm of heterosexual popular culture, coining the 'G-spot' after Gräfenberg to refer to the urethral sponge. The G-spot had wider currency than the urethral sponge because it implies a secret spot that once located will unleash the female body's possibilities for pleasure.

The authors describe the G-spot as "a spot inside the vagina that is extremely sensitive to deep pressure. It lies on the anterior wall of the vagina... when properly stimulated, the Gräfenberg spot swells and leads to orgasm in many women.[80] *The G-Spot* makes two significant contributions to contemporary studies on female ejaculation: 1) it presents the female sexual organ as a unified organ, leaving behind the artificial division of the female genitals into clitoris and vagina which was so popular with Freud, Kinsey and Masters and Johnson, in which either vaginal or clitoral orgasms were privileged; and 2) it popularizes female ejaculation, although it doesn't disclose how to do it.

The third key contribution—though first chronologically—to the paradigm shift in understanding and representing the female

sex organ was by Josephine Sevely and J.W. Bennett, who in 1978 co-authored the first article on female ejaculation and the female prostate, "Concerning Female ejaculation and the Female Prostate" in the *Journal of Sex Research*. Sevely and Bennett made the claim that the tissue surrounding the female urethra was the same as that surrounding the male urethra and contained thirty or more prostatic glands. They also provided the lost genealogy of female ejaculation, from ancient philosophy and medicine through 1950s sexology.[81]

Sevely later extended her theories about female sexuality into *Eve's Secrets* (1987), but it never achieved the popularity of *The G-Spot*. *Eve's Secrets* emphasizes the simultaneous involvement of the clitoris, urethra and vagina (the CUV) as a single integrated sex organ.[82] The implications of this theory are twofold: first, a woman's sexual organ is viewed as an integrated whole and not split between clitoral activity and vaginal passivity; second, the anatomical alternative between male and female genitals is challenged by a new construction of anatomical symmetry. Both female and male bodies have prostate gland structures (a homologue in women) and both have the potential to ejaculate fluids during sexual stimulation. The female body can ejaculate fluid from thirty or more ducts and with stimulation can ejaculate repeatedly. It can ejaculate more fluid than the male body and enjoy a plurality of genital pleasure sites: the clitoris, urethra, vagina, the vaginal entrance, the top wall of the vagina, the bottom wall of the vagina and the cervix.

If we now know that the female sex organ is identical to the male's in structure and function—that is, that the urethral sponge is capable of anywhere from a three-to-eight-inch erection, measures a handful in circumference, and that prostatic and other body fluids are ejaculated from the paraurethral glands and ducts through the urethra—then what is it that prevents recognition of body symmetry and body equality? This lack of recognition is due to the historical invisibility of the female sex organ as an integrated unit and the subsequent lack of symmetry in our male-dominated cultures of naming, or the symbolic encoding of the female and male sex organs.

Terminology is important. Milan Zaviacic, Professor of Pathology and Forensic Medicine at the Comenius University of Bratislava, Slovakia, fought for twenty years to get the International Committee on Anatomical Terminology to recognize the female prostate as a functioning anatomical structure:

> It appears to be illogical to use the term prostate for the tissue in the male and a different term (Skene's glands and ducts of paraurethral glands and ducts) for the same tissue in the female. The use of the term Skene's paraurethral glands and ducts wrongly implies that some other structure rather than the prostate is involved.[83]

Zaviacic located the female prostate on 150 female cadavers. FF, having felt and handled more than a few living female phalluses, could perhaps breathe life into Zaviacic's dead Venuses: "The lady who lay facing me across the massive steel table was none other than Venus; she was no *demi-mondaine* who had taken a pseudonym to wage war upon the masculine sex, but the goddess of Sex in person."[84]

FF had the privilege of dissecting a female pelvis. Sure enough, there was erectile tissue surrounding the urethra and in the clitoral legs. This finding was confirmed by the work of Australian urologist Dr. Helen O'Connell, who discovered a pyramid-shaped mass of erectile tissue in the body of the internal clitoral structure as well as erectile tissue in the two clitoral legs in each of the ten dissections she did of the female urogenital region.[85] O'Connell's work reveals that the clitoris surrounds the urethra on three sides; the fourth is embedded in the top wall of the vagina.[86]

There are significant power differentials inherent in the naming of the female sex organ, alternately the urethral sponge, G-spot and phallus. In *The Bonds of Love*, Jessica Benjamin contends that the absence of a cultural-linguistic equivalent of phallus for the female sex organ has resulted in weakened female sexual agency and in the cultural positioning of the

female as the object of desire, rather than simultaneously as a desiring subject.[87]

FEMALE PHALLUS RISING

In the video *How to Female Ejaculate*, Sundahl conducts a cervical self-examination. She shows the internal erection by turning the speculum sideways and inserting it inside the vagina. It is only with the turning of the speculum that the full clitoris becomes visible. This is the turning of the female sex from the absence of 'nothing to see' into the presence of 'something to see.' The speculum, a technology developed by gynecological science to facilitate viewing of the cervix, simultaneously exposes the neck of the womb and obscures the female phallus. That is, until it is turned. With the fast-feminist turn of the technology for viewing a woman's sex, a new perspective is generated. I've spent the last twenty years showing ejaculation workshop participants, lovers, fuck buddies, friends, journalists—anyone who wanted to see and some who didn't, the female phallus.

SOMETHING TO SEE

Lying down on the floor, my cunt elevated on a plush red pillow, I turned the speculum sideways and slipped it inside. Tejal, the stunningly handsome boy/girl host, illuminated my erection with a flashlight as the twenty or so Mumbai dykes, femmes and transmen looked at what was once 'nothing to see.' Some slipped on a surgical glove and slid a couple of fingers inside to stimulate my swelling hardness. The consensus was that although everyone had felt the female phallus in full and partial fisting activities, its visual magnitude had previously remained invisible.

The visibility of the internal erection repositions the top wall of the vagina, specifically the spongy erectile tissue and the glands and ducts surrounding the urethra, as a female phallus. It turns out that the female phantom cock haunting psychoanalysis

is an actual cock. Freud's little girls' so-called hallucinations were actually body-knowledge of the presence of a real penis, always already there, awaiting the appropriate technology and action—a turned speculum—to come into view. Freud's little girl was Deleuze and Guattari's little girl all along.

An eight-year-old FF squatted on her bedroom floor, clumsily put her two fingers on each side of where she peed from, and rubbed back and forth. The burning increased as she rubbed harder; fluid shot out of where she peed from; the burning stopped for awhile.

Until the last two decades of the twentieth century female ejaculation suffered the fate of what Michel Foucault termed 'subjugated knowledge': it would appear for a moment in a specific discourse (philosophy, medical, pornography, sexology) only to be submerged out of view for extended periods of time throughout history.

FEMALE EJACULATION: A VIRTUAL EXPLOSION

I have argued that once female ejaculation entered feminist discourse the knowledge would never be lost again and it hasn't been. What I didn't foresee was the appropriation of female ejaculation into dominant heterophallic discourses reinforcing a male-centered, heteronormative model of human sexuality, a recuperation that has sped up since the mid-nineties to an explosion after the turn of the century with the continual development of the World Wide Web, and its ever-increasing access to information. In "A Futurist's History of Sexual Technology," Annalee Newitz places the Web as just as an important piece of sexual technology as the vibrator.[88]

There is something magnificent about the virtual explosion of ejaculation knowledge, but in all this knowledge-production female ejaculation has lost some of its power. Power is what it was all about—trumping the male body again and again, hyperdeflating the prized money shot in porn, flooding the market. The content on the Web, although proliferating, continues to be

pretty much the same as before: sexologists arguing about the composition of female fluid; pornography sites declaring new uploads of squirting pussy movies and photos; Free Female Ejaculation Pictures, Free Female Ejaculation MPEGS, Female Ejaculation Videos, Female Ejaculation DVDS, Female Ejaculation Video on Demand; tantric trainers, sexual healers and feminist therapists demanding that 'women should have the same privilege to cover her partner in body fluid as a man does'; sex therapists, porn stars and amateurs demonstrating 'how to have an ejaculatory orgasm step-by-step.'

Information about female ejaculation is more readily available than ever before and more abundant but this knowledge generally frames female ejaculation in whatever discourse happens to be the belief system of the provider of knowledge, whether it be spiritual, therapeutic, tantric, sexological or pornographic. These sites of knowledge, especially pornography and sexology, tend to be heterophallic and diminish female ejaculation, portraying it as yet another activity that the female body can engage in for the exotic spectacle and pleasure of her real or cyber male partners, and moreover, as something that the in-the-know man should be able to facilitate in his partner. As sociologist Ken Plummer points out, "Most stories that 'take off' in a culture do so because they slot easily into the most accepted narratives of that society: the dominant ideological code." [89]

FEMALE EJACULATION: SAME MESSAGE, DIFFERENT MEDIUM

Sexology and porn texts tend to be incestuous, all drawing on the same sources, playing off one another. For instance DoctorG narrates on Deborah Sundahl's video, *Tantric Journey to Female Orgasm: Unveiling the G-Spot & Female ejaculation*.[90] How did Gary Schubach, a guy with a two-year doctorate from The Institute for Advanced Study of Human Sexuality in San Francisco, his reward for a study of seven women ejaculating, get to be an expert on

female ejaculation? I assume that he did the minimal groundwork and entered the game, mixing pseudo-*scientific sexualis* with new age pseudo-sensitivity.

In "Female Ejaculation, Myth and Reality," Dr. Francisco Santamaria Cabello indicates that 1.36 percent of his female therapy practice population have requested therapy as a consequence of "the emission of liquid, through the genitals, during orgasm."[91] They entered what he identifies as "one of the main controversies surrounding the orgasmic response of women... the existence or not of female ejaculation."[92] Cabello dutifully notes the division of ejaculatory research into "those who state that any fluid emitted during orgasm is nothing else than a degree of urinary incontinence"[93] and "those that try to prove that women emit certain fluid that differs from vaginal lubrication during their sexual response."[94] The latter group has proven the presence of two properties in female ejaculation— prostate acid phosphatase (PAP) and fructose—that are normally present in male ejaculate. Female ejaculatory fluid has been chemically tested to determine whether it contains higher levels of glucose than urine and whether PAP, a major component of male semen and a prostate specific antigen (PSA), is present. PSA is "the scientific 'marker' that identifies prostatic fluid in male and female ejaculate."[95]

Cabello claims: "We believe that most women ejaculate, although there are variations in the quantity of the emitted liquid and/or the direction of the emission. We think it is quite possible that the fact that many women do not perceive an ejaculation during orgasm is caused by the product of their 'female prostate' being very scarce or because the ejection takes the retrograde direction towards the bladder, as occurs in the retrograde ejaculation of some men."[96]

Cabello tested his hypothesis of 'retrograde ejaculation' through analysis of the pre- and post-orgasmic urine for the presence of prostate specific antigen (PSA), and found that in 75 percent of their sample of twenty-four women there was PSA in post-orgasmic urine. How Cabello interprets this finding is *scientia sexualis* at its most retro. The first assumption is pretty

innocuous: "The urine admitted after orgasm carries the product of the female prostate; on its way through the urethra."[97] The second, however, is disturbing: "retrograde ejaculation" is the result of anti-gravity.[98]

DEFYING GRAVITY

Bear untied Nan from the whipping pulley and tossed her on the bed. Nan's body was still contracting and vibrating from Bear's expert oscillation of her body, working between a single-tail whip and a bamboo cane, with a flogger for some relief. Bear snapped a latex glove on her right hand, and as she lubed it, looked up and said, "Shannon, you might be interested in this," in that understated, precise way that doms have of commanding attention and action. I walked over, sat at the foot of the four-poster Victorian bed, right in the line of fire, and placed my hand on Nan's beautiful stiletto-heeled foot. Bear entered Nan's cunt with her gloved hand and Nan screamed. Bear let her thumb linger on Nan's clit while caressing Nan's internal phallus with her four fingers. She then slipped her thumb in Nan's cunt so that thumb and slightly curled fingers were riding the urethral sponge and began the come-hither fisting motion that slowly pulls the female phallus in and out as it engorges. Picking up speed, Bear said, "Come on, baby give it to me." Nan moaned and a fistful of girl-cum spurted out, covering Bear's hand in liquid fire. There was the most spectacular image of pure female power: a muscular motorcycle femme on her back, spent, with her very butch, very masterful girlfriend's large fist cupped and just enough out of her cunt to hold the girl cum ejaculated. My head rested between Nan's legs, bowed in respectful adoration at the pure physical power of the active female prostate, that "small functional organ that produces female prostatic secretions"[99] contained inside the very erect, very big, very functional female cock.

Cabello insists that the confirmation of his hypothesis serves two functions: 1) to "calm those women that fear that they have urinated while experiencing orgasm";[100] and 2) to "break

the growing myth of the 'ejaculating super female' because... all, or at least most, women ejaculate"[101] it just can't be seen. Cabello and team are in good company on the 'nothing to be see' hypothesis. Beverly Whipple, one of the co-authors of *The G-Spot* and one-time president of the American Association of Sex Educators, Counselors and Therapists, once said: "Since most women are lying on their backs during sex and the amount of fluid is so small, it sometimes doesn't come out."[102] Cabello suggests that "we should start thinking about a new name for 'female ejaculation,'"[103] in order to remove it from the shadow of male ejaculation. What he doesn't see is that female ejaculation redefines male ejaculation as a mere trace of the female ejaculatory experience. Unlike male ejaculation there is no economy of fluid; the more one ejaculates, the more one can ejaculate.

BETWEEN SPEED AND FEMALE EJACULATION

The speed of information and high-velocity grrl cum is the newest, sexiest story. There is a purity of pleasure to fuckingmachines.com where "the machines fuck the squirt right out of the girls pussies," Squirt Olympics star Sindee Jennings "cums a river of squirt all over the machines" and every machine is "at full speed."[104] There is not a little hot irony in women talking dirty to steel: "Fuck, fuck, bastard, shit, fuck me." Oddly, the absence of the carbon-based, prone to malfunction male-porn prop goes practically unnoticed. Except that the women's performance is record setting: the top squirt distance is 16 feet, speed is determined by how long the contestant can keep the hypermetal star, The Intruder, going at full throttle, 350 RPM, before expulsion, and at the filling station women have one minute to fill a pint. While the ejaculation shots and female feats of endeavor and endurance are spectacular, one wonders: why the same old discourse? The following contextualizes crossover film star, of *The Girlfriend*, Sasha Grey's March 25, 2009 fucking machine video:

Sasha Grey is back for another go round with the machines. She warms up with an ass paddling from the Robo-Spanker that... gets her ready for the machines. Sasha has a pretty tight pussy so what she doesn't take in size, she makes up for in speed. She get stuffed on both ends with Snake and it is harder to say which end is hotter to watch get plowed—her mouth or her pussy.[105]

When you see the humachinic fuck interface live, such as the performance demonstration at the 2007 Arse Electronika by Binx and Fuckzilla, the viewer cannot help but witness the sublime power of female ejaculatory orgasm. Binx, in her own words, says this of her robo-orgasm:

I had the hands-down best orgasm of my life, both subjectively and objectively. From all reports, I squirted about five feet into the air—a force I had never come close to achieving. On top of any personal records, the marvel of technology broadcasted my encounter to the far reaches of the globe, allowing thousands of additional people to experience my orgasm.[106]

Although it cannot be fully captured by it, the power of the female ejaculatory endeavor and orgasm somewhat diminishes once the action is situated and contextualized within existing discourses. Maybe it is as Heidegger claims in *Identity and Difference*: what is new ends up being located and understood in the language and discourse of prior metaphysical assumptions, so that the new is marred by old thought and knowledge paradigms.[107]

There is a banality to speed that absorbs, appropriates, levels to the dominant view "inflated to fill the dimensions of the world's space."[108] It's the leveling performed by the repressive desublimation that facilitates immediate gratification,[109] usually at the cost of anything radical and often at the cost of body integrity and autonomy. There is the danger that female ejaculation, the great possibility, the libidinal energy of the

female body, will be congealed and get contained in hegemonic, heteronormative discourses of sexology, porn, sex therapy and how-to genres.

In the multi-sited race to appropriate female ejaculation, the female phallus has been ignored. The following are fast-feminist female ejaculation facts, a fast clean knowledge:

> Female ejaculation, once thought to be normal and a pleasurable part of female sexuality came to be a symptom of the hysteric, the content of male fantasy, and the property of the pornographic woman.

> To accept female ejaculation one has to accept sameness and the equality of male and female bodies. Both male and female bodies have prostate gland structures along the floor of the urethra and have potential to ejaculate fluids during sexual stimulation.

> The female body can ejaculate fluid from thirty-one ducts, with stimulation can ejaculate repeatedly; and as well, can enjoy a plurality of genital pleasure sites: the clitoris, urethra, vagina....

> Female ejaculation can serve only one purpose: pleasure.

> Directions on how to ejaculate:

> STEP ONE: Find what has come to be known as your G-spot; don't call it that, it is named after Gräfenberg, a man. The G-spot is the muscle and spongy tissue around that part of your urethra that is on the top wall of your vagina. It is about half a finger (more or less) inside your vagina and about a finger across—about two inches. If the muscles that go around your vagina have not been used too much (mine weren't) they have to be built up. The muscles can be built up by doing contractions:

pressing the top of your vagina against the bottom and releasing. DON'T WORRY: strong muscles will not hold the penis in place; they will push it out when your ducts get full and you want to shoot.

STEP TWO: Using whichever hand you usually masturbate with, take two or three fingers and rub them against the part of your urethra inside your vagina. Press hard and notice the feeling of having to pee. This is the signal that you are ready to ejaculate. Now, place the middle finger slightly below the external part of your urethra and begin to masturbate the same way you rub your clit. As you are doing this you will notice the two ducts, one at each side of your urethra, feel full and perhaps somewhat painful; you have another thirty or so ducts scattered in the urethral sponge on the top wall of your vagina. Once you get into the body feeling you may be able to locate them externally on your lower abdomen. They are located in a pyramid from your clit to just near your ovaries.

STEP THREE: Take your other hand and press down on one or more of the ducts from the outside. Push your urethra out and push the way you do when you pee. A crucial aspect of ejaculating is that it is necessary to PUSH OUT. Liquid will come shooting out in a steady stream or jet.

I can only ejaculate in positions in which I can push my entire pelvis out and up: on my knees with legs a foot and a half apart; on my back with my ass raised up, weight distributed on my feet and shoulders, and knees at least two feet apart; squatting, standing, again with feet far enough apart so I can push my urethra up and out. As a veteran ejaculator, following stimulation on my urethra and urethral sponge I can ejaculate by just pushing out.

If your partner is female, you may be able to help her ejaculate. As you stimulate her anterior vaginal wall and the exterior part of her urethra, get her to push out when she is ready. You will both feel the glands and ducts around the urethra swelling and filling with liquid.

What ejaculation will do for you sexually is to give you a powerful kinesthetic, visual and auditory experience—a total body experience. You can repeat it almost indefinitely once your body awakens to it. Seeing and hearing your body fluid put out fire gives one a whole new relation to the environment.

The ejaculate changes in amount, color, odor and taste during your menstrual cycle. At ovulation the fluid is very hot (it corresponds to your vaginal temperature), thick, yellowish and pungent. Following ovulation the fluid is thinner, there is more of it, it is clear and pleasantly salty. It remains this way until bleeding starts at which point it is thick again for the first day or so, then it returns to being clear and copious. I have found that ejaculation during ovulation—because it reduces vaginal temperature—reduces yeast infections that result *from the increase in vaginal temperature at ovulation*.[110]

These are directions that place a woman in control of her own ejaculation. They weren't written for sexologists, new-age sex therapists, or porn makers and viewers (although they were published in a few porn magazines). They are written for Deleuze and Guattari's little girl of any age, for queer women, for new-wave grrrls coming onto the scene, for s/m dykes, doms and daddies, for the little girls and little boys who when they look up mommy's dress and see her internal erection protruding, or when they see mommy's strap-on dildo, they will know what these are.

THE WILL TO PENETRATE

FF tucked her 7-inch cock into the top of her fishnets; the rubber harness held the base tightly to her stomach, pressing against her internal cock. First school, then *Xtra*'s (Toronto's queer magazine) cocktail party, then a strap-on workshop. G., the wonderful bisexual Genet Other who has been her mirror for so many years, gave FF her first blowjob on her prosthetic cock in the university parking lot. G. asked, "Are you still a virgin with your cock?" FF replied, "Yes." She'd just gotten it the day before. G. said, "Take it out," and expertly slid his lips over her member. She came, not from the sight of having her external cock sucked, but from the pressure the base of the cock put on her internal cock.

At the party, FF sidled up to the hot butch ex-general manager of Buddies in Bad Times Theatre. She'd always wanted her. "Hey Gwen," FF said, lifting up her black velvet miniskirt. Gwen smiled, "First day with a cock?" Gwen had worn a cock off and on for years. "You look good in it," Gwen added. FF asked her, "Still with the gorgeous femme?" Gwen smiled again, "No, we broke up a year ago." FF smiled, grinning, "Will you go on a date with me and can I wear my cock?" Gwen being the gentlemanly, charming butch she is said, "Sure. You can use it too."

True to her word, after a fabulous romantic dinner, FF and Gwen went back to FF's place. When the butch clothes came off, Gwen revealed the body of a femme goddess. Gwen coached FF through the entry and thrusting—didn't take much—anyone with half a brain can use a dick. FF made it a point to do every major genre of sexual positions with her prosthetic cock: blowjob, vaginal, anal.

"It's all about positioning and endurance," Carrie Gray (Switch), owner of Aslan Leather told the workshop participants.[111] She got down to positioning on FF, who taking off her cock volunteered to do femme—just for the pleasure of seeing and feeling Switch on top of her, behind her, to her side, inside her.

At the New Socialisms Conference, FF presented "Post-Porn/Post-Anti-Porn: Queer Socialist Pornography,"[112] wearing her prosthetic cock in its leather pouch set off by black leather chaps.

She wore it all day (8 a.m.–11 p.m.); she chaired the entire day's session with it on and wore it to the post-conference dinner. FF forgot she was wearing it. A prosthetic cock quickly fuses with the body hosting it, perhaps quicker than other prostheses; a psycho-physical rubber-flesh fusion. FF never got the feeling that Carrie described, that of the difference and power of wearing a cock; it was pretty much the same as not wearing a cock. Except one day after ass-fucking Stephen who had become her anal trainer, like Sir Steven out of *The Story of O*, FF experienced a kind of reverse vertigo. Stephen, who specializes in bottoming to the most serious and strict of doms, was topping FF, instilling anal skills and slowly stretching her sphincter. He was a patient master: "Speed is the relationship between phenomena. When we bring both... together, we can see that they are identical.... [T]here is no 'reality' outside the relationship between phenomena."[113] The next day FF had what is referred to among trannie boys as "fourteen-year-old cock consciousness," the recurrent repetitive thought that "I could put my cock there," when she saw any good-looking grrl in a miniskirt or shorts. The thought sequence was rigidly illuminating: I could put my cock there, I am not wearing my cock, even if I was I wouldn't do that, I don't think that way. But FF did think that way at least for an eight-hour period. The checking and correction was endless—I could put my cock there? I don't think that way.

FEMALE PHALLUS PHILOSOPHY

What does it mean to have the female phallus? Femininity is defined as lack of a phallus, or so the story goes, since Jacques Lacan repositioned Sigmund Freud. The girl-becoming-woman is molarized, congealed, frozen into the logic of hegemonic identification. Woman does not have the phallus. She compensates by attempting to become the phallus, making the whole of her body into the erotic object of men's desire.[114] The women who do ejaculation porn for a male audience, it might be argued, have the ejaculating female cock, but they have located it in the space of

a discourse in which woman is constructed solely as "becoming the phallus," the object of desire for men. There is something odd about seeing the powerful, erect, ejaculating female penis reduced to the position of a sex object to be penetrated by the porn viewer, or under the tutelage of the male sex educator. A woman with a strap-on both possesses the phallus and becomes the phallus, depending on how she plays it out. The having could predominate, or there could be a blur of having and being, as it is with FF: having vis-à-vis her prosthetic cock or in terms of her internal bio-cock; being in terms of a relentless performative positioning as the co-object of desire.

Freud knew his little girl had the penis. He noted: "The spontaneous discharges of sexual excitement which occur so often precisely in little girls are expressed in spasms of the clitoris. Frequent erections of that organ make it possible for girls to form a correct judgment, even without any instruction, of the sexual manifestation of the other sex."[115] Freud also elaborated an extensive molar developmental gender differentiation and identity theory premised on his denial of the female phallus.

Deleuze and Guattari's little girl had the cock. Deleuze and Guattari knew it: their little girl is always in a process of becoming woman, but never solidified into woman as a "molar entity,"[116] that is, "woman... defined by her form, endowed with organs and functions and assigned as a subject."[117] Their little girl doesn't get contained in Freudian oedipalization, she brakes on becoming woman to erode both genders. Deleuze and Guattari's little girl, always from the beginning in the process of becoming phallic woman, has an organ that "functions" as a portal to the body without organs. It is ownership of the phallus, that which no one can have or be, that leaves gendered embodiment in a dynamic process of assemblage, disassemblage and reassemblage. It is precisely that which most defines or that which most reifies embodiment that can simultaneously destratify, deunify and dehierarchize. In speed, everything oscillates to its opposite and back again to the nth degree intensified.

"The body is stolen first from the girl: stop behaving like that, you're not a little girl anymore, you are not a tomboy, etc. The

girl's becoming is stolen first, in order to impose a history, or prehistory, upon her. The boy's turn comes next, but it is by using the girl as an example" [118] to play his manhood off of.

"Try wearing your hair over your eye, your facial features are strong," the male butch other instructed FF. Strong facial features are phallic, a woman shouldn't show hard facial features; however, if a man softened his facial features by pulling his hair over his face he might be considered excessively feminine. Always into excess, FF wore her hair over half of her face. Everyone said she was "lovely, really pretty, seriously cute." FF smiled wistfully every time she was told this, unable to determine if she was embracing Deleuze and Guattari's little girl or abandoning her: "molecular woman is the girl herself." [119]

FF was molecular, continually in process, assembling and reassembling body parts and features, cycling through new and used personas: FF was a surface on which FF played. FF knew gender was a game. A crackerjack gender performer, she knew that for "the boy... by using the girl... by pointing to the girl as the object of his desire... an opposed organism, a dominant history is fabricated for him too." [120] She knew they were both victims; she the "first," [121] he the second, "executioner and... victim... endowed equally with the same power." [122] But she kind of wished that boy could have liked her face, for 'the face speaks': "The manifestation of a face is the first discourse.... Consciousness is put into question by a face." [123] The face is a portal to the body without organs. FF loved the boy's face: flipping femininity, for FF "to love is a stronger need than to be loved." [124]

FF took to wearing her long blonde extensions in an upsweep with a wide headband, face denuded, the way de Beauvoir had done. FF had learned from de Beauvoir: "A woman is not born, she is made." [125] The making, the molarized interruption, the stoppage, in the incessant process of girl becoming: "The girl is... defined by a relation of movement and rest, speed and slowness, by a combination of atoms, an emission of particles... she is an abstract line or line of flight." [126] Deleuze and Guattari understood the body more in terms of what it can do, rather than what it can be. [127] The physiological fact that male bodies and female bodies

can both ejaculate and have physiological erectile tissue that can harden, solidify and molarize into a phallus—leaves the body a surface speed of having, that is, of doing, of activity.

Having the phallus is a process. As Judith Butler points out, via Lacan, no one ever has the phallus "because it is an idealization, one which no body can adequately approximate."[128] For Butler, "the phallus is a transferable phantasm, and its naturalized link to masculine morphology can be called into question through an aggressive reterritorialization."[129] What Butler has in mind is the lesbian phallus that resignifies both masculine and feminine morphologies, in which both identifications are disavowed.

> When the phallus is lesbian, then it is and is not a masculine figure of power; the signifier is significantly split, for it both recalls and displaces the masculinism by which it is impelled. And insofar as it operates at the site of anatomy, the phallus (re)produces the spectre of the penis only to enact its vanishing, to reiterate and exploit its perpetual vanishing as the very occasion of the phallus. This opens up anatomy—and sexual difference itself—as a site of proliferative resignifications.[130]

Naming the internal female anatomy that becomes erect when stimulated and ejaculates copious fluid the female phallus operates as a reterritorialization of female sexual anatomy and a resignification of both female and male sexual anatomy, eroding both and all genders to "a thousand tiny sexes."[131] It is reterritorialization and resignification that are compromised, if not prohibited, in the "heterosexualization"[132] of the female phallus as the urethral sponge, female prostate, G-crest and its location inside already existing hegemonic heteronormative discourses.

If philosophy is to some extent grounded in our physiology, then what the knowledge and awareness of the female phallus does falls somewhere between blurring and erasing sexual difference. In a certain sense, the female phallus and its owners are then cyborgs, if cyborg is taken to refer to "a figure

of inter-relationality... that deliberately blurs categorical distinctions"[133] at the biophysical level, distinctions such as "nature and culture, male and female, oedipal and non-oedipal."[134] If the prosthetic cock is strapped on, then the categorical distinction of human and technical instrument is blurred. The female phallus, like the cyborg, is in a way a "postmetaphysical construct,"[135] "a philosophy... grounded in... physiology,"[136] a philosophical doing that can't get it up when contained in language games that it outgrew long ago.

It's no surprise that, as Freud claimed, "the fact that women change their leading erotogenic zone [from clitoris to vagina]... together with the wave of repression at puberty... [which] puts aside their childish masculinity, are the chief determinants of the greatest proneness of women to neurosis and especially hysteria."[137] You'd be hysterical too if social inscription cut into your sex organ, partialized it and left a remainder as the operative organ. As Freud wrote in his essay "Femininity": "Castration is a turning point in a girl's growth."[138] What choices did a nineteenth-century woman have post-castration discovery? "Three possible lines of development start from it: one leads to sexual inhibition or to neurosis, the second to change of character in the sense of a masculinity complex, the third finally, to normal femininity."[139] What the discourses of sexology, pornography and therapy do— in the form of sexual healing and worship—is reinscribe 'normal femininity' with a slight twist in whatever is a current "historically contingent, however hegemonic"[140] acceptable manifestation.

I decided to dedicate the next shoot to my mother. With this dedication I return in my mind to my child-self sitting in the backseat of the family's 1955 cream-colored Dodge, my pussy grinding into the leather as I watch my mother sitting in the front seat, wondering what was going on in her body. My mother's fingers rubbed her belly around what I have to come to recognize as the female ejaculatory glands and ducts. At least thirty glands and ducts are dispersed in the spongy tissue that surrounds the urethra on the top wall of the vagina. If you have big glands like I do, and if you have very little flesh between the belly and the urethral sponge, you can feel the ducts fill from the

outside of the body by pushing on your belly with your fingers. My mother was telling my father that her belly felt funny, it was hot and throbbing. She was using that tone of voice I have come to associate in myself with sexual frustration. As a six-year-old girl I made a mental note: "Make sure this doesn't happen to me when I grow up." "Make sure that I know the cause of the burning and throbbing. Make sure I know how to stop it." I shoot. My mother looked like Liv Ullman.[141]

Remembering Freud's construction of fetishism as the child's reaction to looking up mommy's dress and seeing nothing, what if the little girl/little boy looks up mommy's dress and sees a strap-on, or better yet, the protrusion of mommy's internal cock? This puts an end to hysteria as a gendered phenomenon and to fetishism as a gendered practice. "The fetish is a 'penis-substitute'—a surrogate penis created in the little boy's unconscious to compensate for 'the woman's (the mother's) penis the little boy once believed in' and… does not want to give up."[142] Elizabeth Grosz strategically turned this with her rendition of "lesbian fetishism." She reads the woman with a "masculinity complex" as a lesbian fetishist.[143] "The lesbian subject takes a substitute phallus in the form of another woman. Grosz makes a fetish of the woman and in the process depreciates Freud's penis-envy hypothesis by changing the signification of the phallus from penis to clitoris."[144]

FF took the jockeys that belonged to the butch of her dreams, pressed them to her nose, started to play with her internal cock and shot all over the room. It was not so much that FF was into underwear, although the smell of ball sweat, cum and cologne had a certain appeal. It was a recoding through a redoing of the biggest male fetish—female underwear, because we all know what it covers, or do we?

In "Some General Remarks on Hysterical Attacks," Freud discloses the source of female hysteria: a boyish nature.[145] Woman emerges when female masculinity is repressed, when the active girl is fully oedipalized into the feminine woman. The hysteric, marking incomplete oedipalization, is a figure of resistance. The hysteric resists through her body. The hysteric's

body speaks through vision abnormalities, blindness, spasms or neurasthenia, sexual dysfunction, speech impediments, biting the tongue, nausea, rapid palpitations, multiple personalities, fugue states, absences and amnesia, hallucinations, temporary paralysis, thumb-sucking and the involuntary passing of urine. In an exquisite sexual encounter one can experience fourteen of the fifteen symptoms. If coming with a female daddy's full fist in your pussy as you contract and release your pussy muscles until you drench her pecs and forearm with liquid fire counts as a sexual dysfunction, then all fifteen symptoms of hysteria are also features of active female sexuality. As Freud reasoned in his Postscript to "Fragment of an Analysis of a Case of Hysteria (Dora)": "The symptoms of the disease are nothing else than the patient's sexual activity." [146]

While the hysteric resisted through her body, the post-hysteric resists through a public and private refusal to accept the female body as it has been constructed. FF took some femininity lessons from the Godfather: *A woman is a whore in the bedroom, a chef in the kitchen and a lady in public.* FF could never keep the requirements and locations straight: a whore in public, a post-hysteric in the kitchen, a cook in the bedroom? A whore in the kitchen: after dinner, the butch of her dreams ripped off her underwear and precision-nailed her on the very long, very hard table. A whore cooks with attitude, with a strap-on, wearing a butt plug. She blindfolds and feeds her dinner guests. A post-hysteric in the bedroom: the phallic woman and little girl turn on and "turn into one another." [147] Haraway's cyborg, a creature of "transgressed boundaries, potent fusions and dangerous possibilities," [148] is Deleuze and Guattari's little girl, a creature of intensities and flows, assemblages and linkages.

Notwithstanding the worship of female ejaculation and by extension the female body that produces it, FF would rather be a cyborg than a goddess. [149] Worshipping is just a turn on control. The female phallus repositions "the specter of the penis only to enact its vanishing" [150] as a gendered piece of anatomy.

FF looks in the mirror at the image of the pure magnitude of the female phallus erect, endlessly ejaculating immeasurable

fluid, decontaminating the distorted perspective of the phallic economy of one. *It is something to see.*

CUTTING THE PHALLUS IN ONE

World-renowned queer photographer and performance artist Del LaGrace Volcano and I did a photo shoot together at the "Body Modification: Changing Bodies, Changing Selves" conference at Macquarie University in Sydney, April 2003. Femme FF with left arm draped over the handsomely beautiful Del's shoulder. FF's prosthetic cock was resting on Del's crinoline-covered hip as he cupped his own organ. Del, true to his "intersex by design"[151] identity, was a perfect blend of a new male/female in a black-felt baseball cap with red trim, black muscle t-shirt with red inscription, pin-striped suit vest, white crinoline with red mesh overlay, sneakers, red lipstick, pencil-thin moustache and cropped goatee. FF was in fishnets with a strap-on harness, motorcycle boots, black spaghetti-strap tank top, black headband and red lipstick. During the photo shoot, FF confided: "Del, I really need a shot of the phallic woman's genitalia, a shot no one has taken before, one that shows the prosthetic cock and balls and the ejaculating female phallus all in one. I want an image of the body that has it all." FF knew that Del could capture the phallic woman's genitalia. FF had first met Del when he was Della Grace, a kick-ass femme with big boobs, flaming red hair and grrl buttocks pushing out a short miniskirt. She was the number-one queer lesbian erotic photographer who had just done *Love Bites*.[152] The second time FF met Della, she was Del LaGrace Volcano launching *The Drag King Book*,[153] a photo documentation of a new virile masculinity underlying the burgeoning identity of drag-kinging that had taken off by the mid 1990s. By 2005 Del had become "an intentional mutation of male and female,"[154] an intersex body with what he calls a 'dicklet' and a transgender, transmorphing, grrl/boy identity that captures excess on both sides of the gender chasm. Del said, "Yeah, I can get that," and he did.[155]

A couple of months later, FF met Del in the UK at his London studio. It took twenty minutes to do the shoot. They kissed hello and complimented each other on their looks. Del was in hip-hop gear and FF in a ruffled, polka-dot miniskirt. FF douched, borrowed one of Del's dildos and snapped a condom on it. She lubed up and put it in her pussy. She slid her legs into Del's strap-on harness, slipped the nine-inch prosthetic cock and balls through the cock hole and rolled a condom on it. Del adjusted the harness around FF's hips. FF began to masturbate, moving the dildo inside her back and forth and across her own internal cock as she and Del chatted. When FF was ready, she removed the dildo and began to masturbate the external cock prosthesis, counted to three and Del, standing right over FF positioned on the floor, shot as FF shot. They got it: the parallel worlds of the masochist hermaphrodite and androgynous sadist[156] cropped into one genital image lacking in nothing as FF masturbated her male phallus and ejaculated from her female phallus.

"Shannon Bell and The Female phallus, London," three full-page images, are published as part of Del's photo collection *Sex Works*.[157] *Images are immortal.*[158]

Endnotes

practical approach to disseminating the skills of female ejaculation, including instructions both for the ejaculator and her partners.

4 Bell, "Q: What shoots and sprays, shoots and sprays, shoots and sprays? A: A Woman" and "The Everywoman's Guide to Ejaculation" in *Rites*, Vol. 5, No. 9, March 1989: 11. This article was reprinted as "Feminist Ejaculations" in *The Hysterical Male: New Feminist Theory*, eds. Arthur and Marilouise Kroker (Houndsmill, Basingstoke, Hampshire, London: MacMillan, 1991); Shannon Bell, "Female Ejaculation—A Woman's Ejaculation Guide," in *Spectator*, Vol. 26, No. 24, September 1991; and Shannon Bell, "*Kvinnerspruter de ogsa! —Hvordan ejakulere?*" in *Cupido*, Nr. 4, 1990.

5 The earliest feminist representation of female ejaculation was part of a larger lesbian erotic film, *Clips*, produced by Blush Entertainment Group (1988).

6 Joreen, "The Bitch Manifesto," 1968, 1–3. Available at http://jofreeman.com/joreen/bitch.htm.

7 Germaine Greer, *The Female Eunuch* (New York: Farrar, Straus and Giroux, 1970).

8 Ibid., 23.

9 Bell, "Shooting with Annie" in *Whore Carnival* (New York: Autonomedia, 1995), 265.

10 Tristan Taormino, "Going for Gold in Michigan," 2000. Available at www.puckerup.com.

11 Stelarc, "Absent Bodies," undated. Available at www.stelarc.va.com.au/absent/absent.html.

12 Gary Schubach, "The G-'Crest' and Female Ejaculation," 1997, 6. Available at www.doctorg.com.

13 Chip Rowe, "Female Ejaculation

1 Transcript of Shannon Bell, "One Sex or Two? Female Ejaculation" on *Ideas*, Canadian Broadcasting Corporation (CBC) radio, February 15, 1995, 25–26.

2 Ibid.

3 FILM: Fatale Video, *Clips* (1988); Kath Daymond, *Nice Girls Don't Do It* (1989/90); Fatale Video, *How to Female Ejaculate* (1992); Annie Sprinkle, *Sluts and Goddesses Video Workshop* (1992); House of Chicks (Dorrie Lane), *The Magic of Female Ejaculation* (1992); Deborah Sundahl, *Tantric Journey to Female Ejaculation: Unveiling the G-Spot and Female Ejaculation* (1998). AUDIO: CBC radio, *Ideas*, "One Sex or Two?" (1995). MAGAZINES: *Rites* (1989); *Bad Attitudes* (1992); *Lickerish* (1993); *Cupido* (1990); *Spectator* (1991); *Adam* (1992); *Over Forty* (2000). BOOKS: Arthur & Marilousie Kroker, eds. *The Hysterical Male* (1991); Shannon Bell, *Whore Carnival* (1995); Lisa Johnson, ed., *Jane Sexes It Up* (2002). In 2003, Sundahl wrote the first book on female ejaculation, *Female Ejaculation and the G-Spot*. This is a beautiful mesh of female ejaculation knowledge combined with a female body ownership

and Other Delights," 2009. Available at www.playboy.com.

14 Gary Schubach, "The 'G-Crest' and Female Ejaculation," 1.

15 Ibid., 5.

16 Ibid., 5–6.

17 Ibid., 6.

18 Ibid.

19 Ibid.

20 Ibid., 5.

21 Schubach, "Urethral Explusions During Sensual Arousal and Bladder Catheterization in Seven Human Females" in *Electronic Journal of Human Sexuality*, Vol. 4, August 25, 2001, Chapter 6.

22 Francisco Santamaria Cabello, "'Retrograde Ejaculation': A New Theory of Female Ejaculation," paper given at the 13th World Congress of Sexology, Barcelona, Spain, August 1997. Available at www.drgspot.net/cabello.htm.

23 Istvan Kantor, "Monty Cantsin? Amen! An Unseen Selection from the Days of Song and Sex" performance at the Pleasure Dome, Toronto, November 7, 2002.

24 Schubach, "Urethral Explusions During Sensual Arousal and Bladder Catheterization in Seven Human Females," Chapter 6.

25 Ibid.

26 Bell, *Nice Girls Don't Do It.*

27 Schubach, "The 'G-Crest' and Female Ejaculation."

28 Ibid., 8.

29 Bell, *Nice Girls Don't Do It.*

30 Schubach, "The 'G-Crest' and Female Ejaculation," 4.

31 Ibid.

32 Ibid.

33 Catharine MacKinnon, *Feminism Unmodified* (Cambridge, MA:

Harvard University Press, 1987), 138–139.

34 Monochrom, "Porn Tub Punch. Drinking the Essence of Technology Away. Pretty Good Performance, Featuring You, My Friend" in *prOnnovation? Pornography and Technological Innovation*, eds. Johannes Grenzfurthner, Gunther Friesinger, Daniel Fabry (San Francisco: RE/SEARCH, 2008), 102.

35 Bell, "Post-Porn/Post-Anti Porn: Queer Socialist Pornography" in *New Socialisms*, eds. Robert Albritton, John Bell, Shannon Bell, Richard Westra, (London: Routledge: 2004), 147.

36 Angela Carter, *The Sadean Woman and the Ideology of Pornography* (New York: Pantheon Books, 1978), 17.

37 Ibid., 18.

38 Ibid., 19.

39 Ibid., 19–20.

40 Kobena Mercer, "Just Looking for Trouble: Robert Mapplethorpe and Fantasies of Race" in *Sex Exposed: Sexuality and the Pornography Debate*, eds. Lynne Segal and Mary McIntosh (London: Virago Press, 1992).

41 Gilles Deleuze and Félix Guattari, *Anti-Oedipus: Capitalism and Schizophrenia*, trans. Robert Hurley, Mark Seem and Helen R. Lane (Minneapolis: University of Minnesota Press, 1983,) 67.

42 Michael Hardt and Antonio Negri, *Empire* (Cambridge and London: Harvard University Press, 2000), 216.

43 See www.FemCum.com.

44 Rebecca Chalker, *The Clitoral Truth: The Secret World at Your Fingertips* (New York, London, Sydney, Toronto: Seven Stories Press, 2000), 76.

45 Jean-François Lyotard and

Jean-Loup Thébaud, *Just Gaming*, trans. Wlad Godzich (Minneapolis: University of Minnesota Press, 1985).

46 Judith Halberstam, *Female Masculinity* (Durham & London: Duke University Press, 1998), 13.

47 Ibid., 241.

48 Ibid., 252.

49 Jacques Derrida, *The Gift of Death*, trans. David Wills (Chicago: University of Chicago Press, 1995), 45.

50 John D. Caputo, *Against Ethics* (Bloomington: Indiana University Press, 1993), 209.

51 Del LaGrace Volcano & Judith 'Jack' Halberstam, *The Drag King Book* (London: Serpent's Tail Press, 1999), 80.

52 Ibid.

53 Jacques Lacan, "The Meaning of the Phallus" in *Feminine Sexuality: Jacques Lacan and the Ecole Freudienne*, eds. Juliet Mitchell and Jacqueline Rose, trans. Jacqueline Rose (New York & London: W.W. Norton & Company, 1982).

54 Halberstam, *Female Masculinity*, 241.

55 See www.disgrace.dircon.co.uk/page1.html.

56 Masturbation Cabaret, Lee's Palace May 2002. May is masturbation month in Toronto.

57 Chuang Tzu, *The Book of Chuang Tzu*, trans. Martin Palmer (London: Penguin Books, 1996).

58 Luce Irigaray, *This Sex Which is Not One*, trans. Catherine Porter (New York: Cornell University Press, 1985), 116.

59 Bell, *Whore Carnival*, 263.

60 Ibid., 264.

61 In 2001, the Federative International Committee on Anatomical Terminology (FICAT) agreed to change the terminology from paraurethral gland to *prostata feminine* (female prostate). This decision prohibits further use of the terms paraurethral glands and ducts or Skene glands for the designation of the prostate in women.

62 Aristotle, *De Generation of Animalium*, trans. Arthur Platt, *The Complete Works of Aristotle*, eds. J.A. Smith and W.D. Ross (Oxford: The Claredon Press, 1912), Book II, 28a.

63 Bell, *Whore Carnival*, 273.

64 Ibid., 273–274.

65 Thomas Laqueur, "One Sex or Two? Female Ejaculation" on "Ideas," CBC radio, February 15, 1995.

66 Renaldus Columbus, *De re anatomica*, cited in Laqueur, *Making Sex: Body and Gender from the Greeks to Freud* (Cambridge and London: Harvard University Press, 1990), 66.

67 Nicolas Chorier, "An Excerpt From A Dialogue Between A Married Lady and a Maid" in *Vikings, Monks, Philosopher, Whores Old Forms, Unearthed*, eds. Darren Franich and Graham Weatherly in *McSweeney's*, Issue 31, 2009: 11–12.

68 Reijnier de Graaf, *New Treatise Concerning the Generative Organs of Women* (1672), trans. H.B. Jocelyn and B.P. Setchell in *Journal of Reproduction and Fertility*, Supplement 17 (Oxford: Blackwell Scientific Publishers, 1972), 107.

69 Ibid.

70 Milan Zaviacic, *The Human Female Prostate: From Vestigial Skene's Paraurethral Glands and Ducts to Woman's Functioning Prostate* (Bratislava: Slovak Academic Press, 1999), 17.

71 Richard von Krafft-Ebing, *Psychopathia Sexualis*, trans.

Franklin S. Klaf (New York: Stein and Day, 1965), 265.

72 Candace Falk, *Love, Anarchy, and Emma Goldman* (New York: Holt, Rinehart and Winston, 1984), 175.

73 Sigmund Freud, "Fragments of an Analysis of a Case of Hysteria" (1905) in *Dora: An Analysis of a Case of Hysteria*, ed. Philip Reiff (New York: Collier Books, 1993), 121.

74 Havelock Ellis, *Studies in the Psychology of Sex*, Vol. II (New York: Random House, 1936), 145.

75 Steven Marcus, *The Other Victorians: A Study of Sexuality and Pornography in Mid-Nineteenth Century England* (New York: Basic Books, 1966), 194.

76 Ernst Gräfenberg, "The Role of the Urethra in Female Orgasm" in *The International Journal of Sexology*, Vol. 3, 1950: 148.

77 Federation of Feminist Women's Health Centers [FFWHC], *A New View of a Woman's Body* (Los Angeles: Feminist Health Press, 1991), 43–45 & 48.

78 Mary Jane Sherfey, *The Nature and Evolution of Female Sexuality* (New York: Random House, 1972).

79 FFWHC, *A New View of a Woman's Body*, 43–45 & 48.

80 Alice Ladas, Beverly Whipple, John Perry, *The G-Spot* (New York: Dell Books, 1982), 21–22.

81 Josephine Lowndes Sevely and J.W. Bennett, "Concerning Female Ejaculation and the Female Prostate" in *Journal of Sex Research* 14, 1978: 1–20.

82 Sevely, *Eve's Secrets: A New Theory of Female Sexuality* (New York: Random House, 1987).

83 Zaviacic, *The Human Female Prostate: From Vestigial Skene's Paraurethral Glands and Ducts to Woman's Functioning Prostrate*, 120.

84 Leopold von Sacher-Masoch's *Venus in Furs* opens with the words: "The lady who sat facing me across the massive Renaissance fireplace was none other than Venus; she was no *demi-mondaine* who had taken a pseudonym to wage war upon the masculine sex, but the goddess of Love in person." [Leopold von Sacher-Masoch, "Venus in Furs" in *Masochism* (New York: Zone Books, 1991), 143.]

85 Susan Williamson, "The Truth About Women" in *New Scientist*, August 1998. And, Dr. Helen O'Connell "Female Sexual Anatomy: Discovery and Re-Discovery" (2003), www.twshf.org/pdf/twshf_connell2. pdf.

86 Ibid.

87 Jessica Benjamin, *The Bond of Love: Psychoanalysis, Feminism, and the Problem of Domination* (New York: Pantheon Books, 1988).

88 Annalee Newitz, "A Futurist's History of Sexual Technology" in *prOnnovation? Pornography and Technological Innovation*, 131.

89 Plummer, *Telling Sexual Stories* (London & New York: Routledge, 1995), 115.

90 Deborah Sundahl, *Tantric Journey to Female Orgasm: Unveiling the G-Spot and Female Ejaculation*. Written and Directed by Deborah Sundahl. (Santa Fe, New Mexico: Isis Media, 1998).

91 Cabello, "'Retrograde Ejaculation': A New Theory of Female Ejaculation."

92 Ibid.

93 Ibid.

94 Ibid., 2.

95 Sundahl, *Female Ejaculation and The G-Spot* (Alameda: Hunter House Publishers, 2003), 143.

96 "The postorgasmic urine has diluted PSA produced in the female prostate that could have fallen into the bladder because of incompetence of the sphincter in the moment of the orgasm (theoretically, it should be closed) or because the bladder's sphincter relaxes with the orgasmic contractions and the gravity force pushed the fluid in women in supine position (this occurred to us, after observing that those women that ejaculate outwards, that is, that emit fluid in the moment of the orgasm, comment that they expel more quantity when they are not lying, favoring the effect of gravity). The ejaculate of women in the supine position succumbing to gravity and traveling backwards into the bladder." [Cabello, "'Retrograde Ejaculation': A New Theory of Female Ejaculation."]

97 Ibid.

98 Ibid.

99 Zaviacic and Beverly Whipple, "Update on the Female Prostate and the Phenomenon of Female Ejaculation" in *Journal of Sex Research*, Vol. 30, No. 2, May 1993, 148. Zaviacic, 40.

100 Cabello, "'Retrograde Ejaculation': A New Theory of Female Ejaculation."

101 Ibid.

102 "Women Ejaculate, Too" in *Self Magazine*, May 2000.

103 Cabello, "'Retrograde Ejaculation': A New Theory of Female Ejaculation."

104 See www.fuckingmachines.com.

105 See "Fucking Machines – Hot Kinky Naked Girls Fucking Machines," available at www.fuckingmachines.com.

106 Stefan Lutschinger/Binx, "Introducing Cyberorgasm: Utopia, Eschatology and Apocalypse of the Fucking Machine" in *prOnnovation? Pornography and Technological Innovation*, 83.

107 Martin Heidegger, *Identity and Difference*, trans. Joan Stambaugh (Chicago and London: University of Chicago Press, 1969), 61–74.

108 Paul Virilio, *Open Sky*, trans. Julie Rose (London and New York: Verso) 127.

109 Herbert Marcuse, *One Dimensional Man* (Boston: Beacon Press, 1964), 72.

110 Originally appeared as a monologue in the video *Nice Girls Don't Do It* and was first published as "The Everywoman's Guide to Ejaculation" in *Rites*, Vol. 5, No. 9, March 19, 1989.

111 Carrie Gray, "Strap-on Sex, Women on Women – Good For Her" on Thursday, October 18, 2001 at Good For Her, Toronto.

112 New Socialisms Conference, York University, Toronto, April 2002.

113 Virilio, *The Art of the Motor*, trans. Julie Rose (Minneapolis: University of Minnesota Press, 1995), 140.

114 Lacan, "The Meaning of the Phallus" in *Feminine Sexuality: Jacques Lacan and the Ecole Freudienne*. Also see: Elizabeth Grosz, *Volatile Bodies: Toward a Corporeal Feminism* (Bloomington: Indiana University Press, 1994), 71.

115 Freud, "Three Essays on the Theory of Sexuality" in *On Sexuality*, Vol. 7 of *The Penguin Freud Library*, trans. James Strachey (New York, London, Victoria, Toronto, Auckland: Penguin, 1991), 142–143.

116 Deleuze and Guattari, *A Thousand Plateaus*, trans. Brian Massumi (Minneapolis: University of Minnesota Press, 1987), 275.

117 Ibid.

118 Ibid., 276.

119 Ibid.

120 Ibid.

121 Ibid. "The girl is the first victim, but she must also serve as an example and a trap."

122 Maurice Blanchot, "Sade" in *Justine, Philosophy in the Bedroom & Other Writings*, trans. Richard Seaver and Austryn Wainhouse (New York: Grove Press, 1965), 54.

123 Emmanuel Levinas, "The Trace of the Other," trans. Alfonso Lingis in *Deconstruction in Context*, ed. Mark Taylor (Chicago: University of Chicago Press, 1986), 352.

124 Freud claims "we attribute a larger amount of narcissism to femininity, which also affects women's choice of object, so that to be loved is a stronger need for them than to love." Sigmund Freud, "Femininity" in *Introductory Lectures on Psychoanalysis and Other Works. The Standard Edition of the Complete Psychological Works of Sigmund Freud*, Volume XXII (1932–36), trans. James Strachey (London: Vintage, 2001), 132.

125 Simone de Beauvoir, *The Second Sex*, trans. Constance Borde (New York: Random House, 1989), 69.

126 Deleuze and Guattari, *A Thousand Plateaus*, 276–277.

127 Grosz, *Volatile Bodies*, 165.

128 Butler, "The Lesbian Phallus" in *Bodies That Matter: On The Discursive Limits of "Sex"* (New York & London: Routledge, 1993), 86.

129 Ibid.

130 Ibid., 89.

131 Deleuze and Guattari, *A Thousand Plateaus*, 278.

132 Butler, *Bodies That Matter*, 91.

133 Rosi Braidotti, *Metamorphoses* (Cambridge: Polity Press, 2002), 240.

134 Ibid., 241.

135 Ibid., 240.

136 Stelarc, "Absent Bodies," available at www.stelarc.va.com.au/absent/absent.html.

137 Freud, "Three Essays on the Theory of Sexuality" in *On Sexuality*, 114.

138 Freud, "Femininity" in *Introductory Lectures on Psychoanalysis and Other Works*, 126.

139 Ibid.

140 Butler, *Bodies That Matter*, 91.

141 Bell, *Whore Carnival*, 263.

142 Anne McClintock, "The Return of Female Fetishism and The Fiction of the Phallus" in *Perversity*, No. 19, Spring 1993: 3.

143 Grosz, *Space, Time and Perversion* (New York & London: Routledge, 1995).

144 Ibid., 153.

145 Freud, *Dora: An Analysis of a Case of Hysteria*, 102. Freud writes: "Speaking as a whole, hysterical attacks, like hysteria in general, revive a piece of sexual activity in women which existed during their childhood and at that time revealed an essentially masculine character. It can often be observed that girls who have shown a boyish nature and inclinations up to the years before puberty are precisely those who become hysterical from puberty onwards. In a whole number of cases the hysterical neurosis merely represents an excessive accentuation of the typical wave of repression, it allows the woman to emerge."

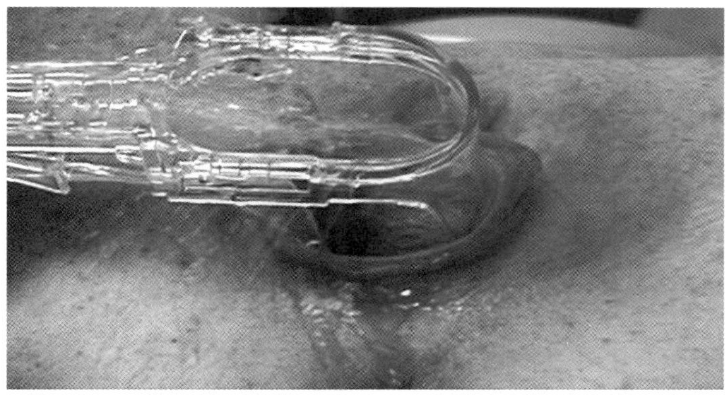

FF revealing the ejaculating female phallus with the turn of the speculum.
| PHOTO Tobaron Waxman.

146 Ibid., 156.

147 This is a play on Freud's "a little girl turns into a woman." [See Freud, "Three Essays on the Theory of Sexuality" in *On Sexuality*, 143].

148 Donna Haraway, *Simians, Cyborgs, and Women: The Reinvention of Nature* (London & New York: Routledge, 1991), 154.

149 Ibid., 181.

150 Butler, *Bodies That Matter*, 89.

151 Del LaGrace Volcano, *Manifesto*, www.disgrace.dircon.co.uk.

152 Della Grace, *Love Bites* (London: Gay Men's Press, 1991).

153 Del LaGrace Volcano & Judith 'Jack' Halberstam, *The Drag King Book*, 80.

154 Del LaGrace Volcano, "I am an Intentional Mutation" in *Body Politic* 5, www.bodypolitic.co.uk/body5/mutation.html.

155 After all, Del had shot "TransGenital Landscapes" published as one of the portfolios in his third collection of photographic work *Sublime Mutations*. [Del LaGrace Volcano, *Sublime Mutations* (Tübingen: Konkursbuch Verlag, 2000).]

156 Deleuze, "Coldness and Cruelty" in *Masochism*, trans. Jean McNeil (New York: Zone Books, 1991), 68. In his essay on Masoch's work Deleuze contends: "[I]n masochism a girl has no difficulty in assuming the role of son in relation to the beating mother who possesses the ideal phallus and on whom rebirth depends. Similarly, in sadism, it becomes possible for the boy to play the role of a girl in relation to a projection of the father. We might say that the masochist is hermaphrodite and the sadist androgynous…. They represent parallel worlds, each complete in itself, and it is both unnecessary and impossible for either to enter the other's world."

157 Del LaGrace Volcano, *Sex Works: Photographs 1978–2005* (Tübingen: Konkursbuch Verlag, 2005), 131–133.

158 Stelarc, www.stelarc.va.com.au/phantbod/phantbod.html.

CHAPTER 2 | ENDNOTES

THE PERVERSE AESTHETIC OF A CHILD PORNOGRAPHER:
John Robin Sharpe

Who (or what) am I? I suppose most Canadians already know: I am the nation's most notorious child pornographer. During my more than fifteen minutes I was also the most reviled man in Canada.[1]

On April 10, 1995, author and amateur photographer John Robin Sharpe was charged with two counts of possession of written and visual child pornography and two counts of possession of written child pornography for the purpose of distribution. Sharpe had been arrested under Canada's new child pornography law, s. 163.1 of the Canadian Criminal Code, which came into existence in 1993.[2] The new law made mere possession an offense and added the category of written materials that advocate or counsel sexual activity with a child and defined child as anyone under eighteen.[3]

Sharpe challenged the constitutionality of the law on the grounds that it violated the freedom of expression guaranteed under s. 2(b) of the Canadian *Charter of Rights and Freedoms*. In 1999, both the British Columbia Supreme Court (the provincial court) and the British Columbia Court of Appeal ruled in favor of Sharpe's freedom of expression challenge. The province of British Columbia, however, appealed the two lower court decisions to the Supreme Court of Canada.

In the Sharpe decision, in 2001, the Supreme Court of Canada

altered the interpretation and application of s. 163.1. It made the artistic merit defense for written child pornography distinct from the artistic merit defense for obscenity, in which material is subject to community standard and harm tests.[4] It set out criteria for assessing artistic merit and specified that written material could pose a risk of harm to children and nevertheless have artistic merit.[5]

The Supreme Court of Canada sent the Sharpe case back to the British Columbia Supreme Court for trial under the new specifications.[6] The Sharpe trial ran from January 21 to February 7, 2002.

Sharpe's case drew global attention among children's rights advocates, child sexual abuse campaigners, censorship and anti-censorship activists. Sharpe gained an international reputation both as a free speech advocate and as a pornographer during his seven-year fight against the charges of possession and distribution of child pornography. It was this willingness to go the distance for his beliefs rather than plead guilty that interested me more than Sharpe's writings or images per se. The action of writing highly objectionable literary material and using it to initiate a constitutional challenge to Canada's child pornography law got my attention; it was Sharpe's personal fortitude that held it.

At first, FF was interested in only two things: the potential of using theory to save the ass of the perverse other and a literary perversity that goes as far as it can go, and just a little bit farther, while maintaining literary merit. But a third interest emerged: Sharpe himself. FF allied herself with Sharpe, distinguished in a dark suit and turtleneck for his trial. Always a step to the left and a couple of steps behind, in full leather gear, FF provided the necessary Sadean woman.

Sharpe's trial was big news in Vancouver. The main concern for both sides of the censorship issue was whether writing that contained explicit sexual scenes and sadomasochistic activities among children, youth and adults could be seen as having the minimal degree of literary merit to be officially considered art. Sharpe was the perfect test case; his writings featured boys as

young as those in the Marquis de Sade's "Lust of the Libertine"—the final part of *The 120 Days of Sodom*. As a writer he had "a degree of recognition independent of his pornographic writings"[7] for his book *Manilamanic: Vignettes, Vice and Verse* (1994), the novella *Life on the Corner: Moon-Eyed Beggar* (1996) and two small Bukowski-like chapbooks—*Robin's Rude Songs and Poems* (1990) and *Politically Incorrect Poems and Songs* (1992).[8]

Sharpe had an anonymous backer paying for his defense who hired Paul Burstein, a Toronto-based criminal lawyer. Burstein turned out to be the perfect counterbalance to the social image of the pedophile—Burstein was young, heterosexual, GQ handsome and had a dynamic courtroom persona. The hawks at The Duff, downtown eastside Vancouver's gay hustler bar, liked to think that Sharpe's backer was a wealthy chicken hawk with a vested interest in supporting freedom of speech. FF knew that Sharpe's patron was a Sadean woman interested in taking excess as far as it could go and still retain legal sanction; or maybe she had a sporting love of "just gaming."[9]

CHILD PORNOGRAPHY AND FAST FEMINISM

Most feminisms tend to equate sexualized writings and images of persons under eighteen years old—and in the more lenient versions under fourteen years old—as child sexual abuse. Fast feminism argues the possibility of ethical and cultural acceptability for written and visual representations of sexualized youth. What brought me to engage child pornography as a site of fast feminism was the potential to do theory in action. When the child pornography law was introduced in 1993, I was conducting academic research and producing images that challenged both child pornography and obscenity laws.[10]

The fast feminist takes very seriously what Deleuze suggests should be done with all philosophers: that is, to ass-fuck them and produce an offspring which is different. Deleuze discloses:

I imagined myself getting onto the back of an author, and giving him a child, which would be his and which would at the same time be a monster. It is very important that it should be his child, because the author actually had to say everything that I made him say. But it also had to be a monster because it was necessary to go through all kinds of decenterings, slips, break-ins, secret emissions.[11]

FF buggers Levinas with Bataille. She uses theory to save the ass, or "the face of the other."[12] The face has become the most famous, the most often cited, of Levinasian terms for otherness. FF stays faithful to Levinasian ethics in the pragmatics of doing but Levinas' orientation to the other, 'the widow, orphan and stranger,' is bonded with Bataille's understanding of excess. When Levinas and Bataille are conjoined, the following figures emerge: the pervert widow, the pervert orphan and the pervert stranger. It is not hard for most people to respond to the call of Levinas' widow, orphan and stranger, they are "the victims, the disasters... the powerless ones."[13] It is far more difficult to respond to those pervert others who have been placed at the bottom of what Gayle Rubin calls "the erotic pyramid": promiscuous homosexuals, fetishists, sadomasochists, those who engage in sex for money and "the lowest of all, those whose eroticism transgresses generational boundaries."[14]

The most demonized of others is the so-called pedophile. *Scientific American* published an article on Michael Jackson's "erotic age orientation" in July 2009 entitled "Pedophiles, Hebephiles and Ephebophiles, Oh My: Erotic Age Orientation."[15] As the author, Jesse Bering, points out, "pedophile" is an umbrella category for any person fantasizing about and/or engaged in sexual encounters with anyone under eighteen, regardless of whether they are seven years old, twelve years old or seventeen years old.

It is precisely this collapsing of age categories that Justice Mary Southin at the British Columbia Court of Appeal had acknowledged as problematic during Sharpe's hearing in 1999.

She asked the Crown counsel, "At some point are you going to explain how somebody between the ages of fourteen and eighteen is a child?" [16] In the main decision of the Appeal Court, Southin clarified age distinctions that she felt appropriately matched the intention of the Canadian Criminal Code: "In this judgment, when I myself use the word 'child,' I mean those below the age of puberty.... I define a 'child' as anyone under the age of fourteen years.... When I use the term 'adolescent,' I mean anyone between fourteen and eighteen.... By 'adult,' I mean anyone over eighteen." [17]

When I asked Sharpe in 2001, "Are you comfortable with the term pedophile?" he replied:

> It is a technical term applied to prepubescents who don't interest me; I didn't want to go into the court and try to defend hebephiles, to always be making distinctions, trying to establish that 'I am not one of them.' This was a political move; I chose to become a generic pedophile. I believe in defending people's freedom rather than trying to carve out a niche for myself. [18]

As Ken Plummer points out in *Telling Sexual Stories*, there are some stories whose time has not yet come to be told by those who actually live them and consequently they are narrated only by dominant social authorities. Pedophilia refers to a set of stories that remain "out of time." [19] Plummer observes that even postmodern literature and theories on marginality do not give space to the voices of pedophiles. [20]

"Child pornography law requires us to take on the gaze of the pedophile." [21] Fast feminism is not just about theory as an intellectual endeavor—it must also have both a use value and a risk value. What it means to do theory dangerously is to risk professional credibility and institutional sanction to save the ass of the other. In November 2000, two months before the Supreme Court of Canada decision on the Sharpe case was to be handed down, I received a call from the editor of *Constitutional Forum* asking me to write an article on the Sharpe decision

from the perspective of the artistic merit defense. On February 14, 2001 I flew to Vancouver and spent three days interviewing Sharpe. In preparation, I read all three-thousand-plus pages of his unpublished works. The article that I wrote for *Constitutional Forum*, "Sharpe's Perverse Aesthetic,"[22] was submitted as an exhibit by Sharpe's counsel at his 2002 trial.

ARTISTIC MERIT

John Robin Sharpe is the only Canadian ever to have used the artistic merit defense for child pornography. This defense no longer exists. Both the artistic merit defense for written work and the assessment of whether written or visual material "counsels or advocates"[23] the sexual activities it portrays were legislatively eliminated from the child pornography section (163.1) of the Canadian Criminal Code in November 2005.

The Canadian Supreme Court's definition of artistic merit in the Sharpe Decision (2001) was distinct from artistic merit under obscenity law. First, the Court privileged artistic merit over potential harm to society. Child pornography could be harmful and at the same time art. The Court reasoned: "Most material caught by the definition of child pornography could pose a potential risk of harm to children. To restrict the artistic merit defense to material posing no harm to children would defeat the purpose of the defense."[24] Second, the question of whether the material is obscene was deemed irrelevant. The material is by definition obscene; it is child pornography if it contains explicit representations of sexuality involving persons under eighteen. This, Chief Justice McLachlin argued, makes "the logic of 'either obscenity or art' inapposite."[25]

The Court specified: "artistic merit should be interpreted as including any expression that may reasonably be viewed as art. Any objectively established artistic value, however small, suffices to support the defense. Simply put, artists, so long as they are producing art, should not fear prosecution under s. 163.1(4)."[26] Procedurally, the onus is on "the Crown to disprove the defense

beyond a reasonable doubt."[27] The accused, on the other hand, must point to facts capable of supporting the artistic merit of the work and these facts must entail "something more than a bare assertion that the creator subjectively intended to create art."[28]

While leaving the determination of artistic merit to the trial judge, the Court set out eight criteria to be taken into account: the subjective intent of the creator, the form of the work, the content of the work, connections with artistic conventions, traditions or styles, the opinion of experts on the subject, the mode of production, the mode of display and the mode of distribution.

From these criteria, at Sharpe's trial in 2002, his expert witnesses, his defense counsel and Judge Duncan Shaw concluded that Sharpe's body of work—the work charged and the work not charged—must be looked at as a whole and that it must be placed within the broader context of works done by others with a similar aesthetic. For example, one needs to assess works of the imagination that involve children, explicit sexual activity and sadomasochistic practices in the context of other published works that include the very same themes.

What became extremely difficult to sustain for the Crown in applying the Supreme Court's interpretation of the artistic merit defense, and for the Crown's two expert witnesses, was the cognitive ability to separate harm from child pornography. They simply could not believe that "artistic merit outweighs any harm"[29] in a genre that was deemed to be harmful by its very nature. Because the Crown and Crown experts could not separate "the immoral qualities of Mr. Sharpe's work" from the assessment of artistic merit their arguments were discredited by Judge Shaw.[30] In a sense, the Supreme Court's decision applies a very postmodern logic: a written work can be child pornography and as a result inherently harmful and it can have artistic merit.

SHARPE'S PERVERSE AESTHETIC

Were my writings a threat to children, adolescent boys in this case? I know most people would find the tales shocking, disgusting and highly offensive but would

anyone be tempted to act out harmfully as a result of misinterpreting my *Boyabuse* stories? I certainly did not think so although I am aware that works of great moral authority such as the Bible have had that unfortunate effect.... The stories contain much that would be considered obscene and abusive but they were my stories and I felt they had some literary merit.[31]

Some of the most bizarre, disturbing, ecstatic, innovative boy erotica ever written was submitted to the objective investigations of Detective Noreen Waters (the police expert witness for the Crown at the 1999 *voir dire* hearing) and two representatives of the British Columbia Film Classification Branch. Gilles Deleuze and Félix Guattari would call these appraisers the upholders of the "mommy/daddy/me triangle"; I think of them as officers of appropriate oedipalization.

In my book *Reading, Writing and Rewriting the Prostitute Body*, I presented the idea that people read from their positions in the world—whether these are acknowledged or not—and produce meaning as the result of an interaction between all the texts they have read in the past and the text at the moment.[32] Detective Waters and the two individuals from the Film Classification Branch read from the position of censorship with the mantra "all sexually explicit depictions of children and youths under eighteen are child pornography." Mary-Louise McCausland, the Director of Film Classification for British Columbia, considered Sharpe's work "the cruelest pieces of writing I have ever read." [33] McCausland stated:

> These stories convey, through a sense of the narrator's satisfaction, that the sexually violent acts being carried out both against the children and by the children are pleasurable, satisfying and beneficial for all involved. It is this theme, and the fact that the abuse of children is presented in all three cases ("Timothy and the Terrorist," "The Rites at Port Dar Lan: Part One" and "Tijuana Whip Fight") as being nontraumatic, that led me to

determine that these works of fiction counsel adult sex with children and are therefore child pornography as defined by Section 163.1 of the Criminal Code.[34]

As Sharpe himself observed, "None of the reviewers could see any artistic merit."[35] Perhaps the grossest example of this is Detective Waters' description of Sharpe's novella *Life on the Corner: The Moon Eyed Beggar's Tale*. Waters sees the novella only in terms of sex: "The book is a story about a young boy prostitute. A number of young boy prostitutes in Manila and other areas.... It describes children being portrayed in child pornography."[36] However, an anonymous reviewer in *Broken Pencil*, a Canadian literary magazine, provides a very different reading:

> *Life on the Corner: The Moon Eyed Beggar's Tale* is a forty-page novella written from the point of view of a deformed beggar named Jun. Jun lives in the Philippines and lives off the remnants of the burgeoning street boy scene of the early 1990s. I say the remnants because Jun never actually gets to have sex with any of the pedophile foreigners cruising the streets.... Jun does not consider himself lucky. He wants to go to hotels and have sex with the foreigners.... Sharpe's portrayal of Jun's psychology is extremely convincing. The book is a straightforward third-person narrative written more like an ethnographic study than a fiction.[37]

Prosecution experts will never be able to see merit in writings like those of John Robin Sharpe because the only genre they have to contextualize the work is stereotypical child porn. For a reader like myself—schooled in the counter-psychoanalysis of Deleuze and Guattari, the literary sadism of the Marquis de Sade and Georges Bataille and the ethics of the philosopher Emmanuel Levinas—Sharpe's works are masterpieces of sadistic compassion.[38] Censorious readers believe that Sharpe's intent was simply to create masturbatory material for perverts, but his writings draw on too many literary conventions to warrant this criticism.

For Sharpe himself, whether a work of child pornography has artistic merit or not is irrelevant with regards to freedom of expression; one should be able to possess both poorly written stories that are electronically disseminated and the unpublished masterpiece that has taken years of reworking, like Sharpe's *Boyabuse*, which he began writing in 1983.

Sharpe is a true libertine, who like Sade's Coeur-de-fer lays down the following alternatives: "Either the crime, which makes us happy, or the scaffold which prevents us from being unhappy." [39] Sharpe uses the tactic of perversion in which the liberal humanist values of autonomy, self-possession, self-development, self-worth, individual freedom and empowerment are writ large on small bodies. Sharpe's tactic, like Sade's, steps outside the law—a law that, in the words of Justice Southin of the British Columbia Court of Appeal, "bears the hallmark of tyranny." [40]

What is Sharpe's crime? Primarily it is the portrayal of *incorrect* or improper oedipalization; it overrides the *proper* identity formation of the modern subject which views individuation as a process that places the child in subordination to parental authority as preparation for later submission to societal authority. [41] In Sharpe's work, the children are masters of their own bodies and souls; they are not oedipalized. "Oedipus informs us: if you don't follow the lines of differentiation daddy-mommy-me... you will fall into the black night of the undifferentiated." [42] However, the pervert resists oedipalization. He has invented other territorialities to operate in. De Beauvoir's observation of Sade was that "he attached greater importance to the stories he wove around the act of pleasure than to the [actual] contingent happenings; he chose the imaginary." [43] Her analysis applies equally well to Sharpe. However, Sharpe's libertine turn towards his "beliefs, opinions, thoughts and conscience" [44] was articulated with a libertarian political strategy that demands freedom of expression and particularly the right to concretize and possess in tangible form the immateriality of one's own thoughts and fantasies.

Sharpe violently disrupts Sade's work from its point of excess: silence. That is, what is uttered "from the beyond of the

bedchamber."[45] In Sade's *The 120 Days of Sodom*, Sophie "uttered a piercing scream" as she emerged from the closet.[46] In the tradition of Bataille, Sharpe attempts to narrate the scream of the human exposed to pain. He is concerned with the moment the self is torn open and exposed to what is other to it. It is here that the boundary between the self and other liquefies. Sharpe delivers the feelings of those who remain speechless and thus are merely victims in Sade's imaginary world. For Sade there is no other as autonomous being, there is only the sovereign man. In Sharpe's writing, this sovereign man comes apart when his partners in crime are boys with wills of their own. Sharpe writes the scream as a combination of the will to laughter, "those moments... that make one gasp" and "moments when the ceaseless operation of cognition is dissolved."[47] Bataille privileges these moments in his writing. Sharpe's boys have fun with the men and with each other through sex and sadomasochistic activities. Victim and executioner, man and boy, laughter and feats of endurance, pleasure and pain slip into one another.

Sharpe's stories fall into a genre I refer to as "postcontemporary sadomasochism." Sade, the excess theorist of Enlightenment reason, destroyed the objects of his desire. Sadism is replayed in the postcontemporary and in Sharpe's writing, not as the Sadean negation of the other, but as respect for the other's limits. The other is neither victim nor executioner but a partner in a power exchange of erotic energy. "Each partner serves as an audience, [a witness] to the other, and in the process, contains the other."[48] To quote Levinas: one has "the Other in one's skin," the "Other within one's self."[49] The victim and the executioner, the master and the slave, the dominant and the submissive, the boy and the man, are set face to face, each with power, each recognizing the other.

There are moments in which the caress of a whip, the burning piercing of a needle can take the players to what Levinas refers to as the mystery of alterity, "always other... always still to come... pure future... without content."[50] The moment of s/m climax is described as "an ecstatic mind/body release... [in which] the building of pain/pleasure so concentrates... awareness into

the here and now... [that] you spin away... into no place and no time."[51] This disembodiment is the pure power and joy of s/m. It is the moment in which one reaches the ecstatic moment of simultaneous escape and presence. Sharpe narrates this moment of touching God through the transformation of pain in his first and unpublished novel, *Rupert Unexpurgated* (1983):

> I will worship God in my own way. After all, I'm eleven now and the church says you only have to be seven to know right from wrong.... My crucifixion pose prayers are getting better.... And then I found these big-headed roofing nails... And are they ever sharp!... I was squeezing the nails harder and harder each day and getting braver and braver. Then one day I squeezed real hard and blood started to run down one hand, just like in my Jesus picture. It sure hurt but I was so thrilled I kept squeezing harder and harder still. Wow, I was just shaking and my peeney was throbbing. I'd never felt that close to Jesus before. The blood was almost squirting out so I rubbed some on my other hand and on my side like where Jesus was stabbed. I looked at myself and my Jesus picture and then I smeared it all over me. It was like I was right there with Him, just the two of us, Jesus and me. My peeney was aching and I remembered they'd done something to Him down there so I smeared blood on it. Oooh!.... It was the type of feeling you get when you're baptized.[52]

Rupert Unexpurgated is a coming-of-age story documenting Rupert's wonderment at the world, at the "inappropriate" behavior of his friends and at his changing "peeney." Rupert—a fictionalized version of Robin Sharpe—is one of the most sensitive, spiritual, passionate and ethical boys in literature. Rupert struggles with his desire for his friends, "I wanted to tell him no and I wanted him to jack me,"[53] and with his own correct code of ethics derived from religious beliefs enacted in devout, innocent, desolate religious practices. I suspect what has prohibited the publication of *Rupert Unexpurgated* is the

Bataillean worship scene quoted above in which Rupert's blood is mixed with God energy. For Bataille, "God is a whore."[54] For Sharpe, the most sacred being is a little boy.

According to Anne McClintock, the scandal of s/m is "the provocative confession that the edicts of power are reversible... the economy of s/m is the economy of conversion: slave to master... pain to pleasure, and back again."[55] Sharpe combines the scandal of sadomasochism with that of intergenerational intimacy. He presents both as completely consensual activities, but according to Canadian law, "sometimes the very appearance of consent makes the depicted act even more degrading or dehumanizing."[56]

The most contentious of Sharpe's seventeen stories in *Boyabuse* is "The Rites At Port Dar Lan: Parts One, Two and Three." The story is structured around boys' initiation rites that take place in Port Dar Lan, an isolated settlement on the exotic coast of Borneo. Here, Sharpe draws on two established codings of sadomasochistic practice: ritual and a designated sacred/profane space located outside time and beyond societal and moral constraints. Ali, a veteran of Dar Lan, informs the protagonist on his first visit:

> To enjoy the unique delights of Dar Lan to the fullest your mind must be clear and free from the constraints of ordinary morality. Dar Lan is a land of suffering and noble courage, of endurance and sweet agony, of drama and pathos where outrageous lusts and fantasies find satisfaction and fulfilment in both loving and torturing boys. They are here to please you within their rules. The pleasure's in the hurting, rejoice in the pain you inflict, for here we make a mockery out of mere perversity. It is a dangerous place for the normal mind.[57]

Port Dar Lan is a refugee settlement of boat people mostly from Malaysia, Vietnam and the Philippines. The age-specific s/m initiation rites—including circumcision—"provide the only hard cash and chance for people to buy their way out"[58] of the poverty and isolation of Dar Lan.[59]

What Sharpe accomplishes by introducing cash as early as paragraph two in "The Rites at Port Dar Lan, Part One" is to link consensual s/m with commercial s/m. By establishing that the boys are supporting their community through sexual and s/m activities with sex tourists, Sharpe inverts the usual "appropriate" power/authority relation wherein adults are responsible for the well being of children and adolescents. With Sharpe's introduction of the refugee boys of Borneo and their exchanges with Western male tourists, the Dar Lan stories open to the possibility of a racist reading. Speaking in broken English, Jean suggests, "Maybe you like to go to sandbar, see boys play rape tag. Just like ordinary tag but after tag you fuck boy too." [60] Like Robert Mapplethorpe, Sharpe repeatedly takes the reader close to making accusations of racism.

Art critic Kobena Mercer, writing on Robert Mapplethorpe's *Black Males* (1982)—a collection of nude portraits,[61] identifies what he terms the *perverse aesthetic*. In addition to being sexually explicit, the perverse aesthetic manifests in a textual ambivalence that ensures the uncertainty of any singular meaning.[62] It is Sharpe's transgression across age, sadomasochism, homosexuality, race and sexual commerce that potentially disturbs the reader. Mercer recounts: "I was shocked by what I saw: the profile of a black man whose head was cropped—or 'decapitated,' so to speak—holding his semi-tumescent penis through the Y-fronts of his underpants, which is the first image that confronts you in Mapplethorpe's *Black Males*." [63]

Sharpe's work falls just short of racism. Perhaps this is because the boys are in charge, perhaps because they are far from powerless in relation to their adult sponsors, perhaps it is the writer's profound respect for the boys and their fortitude, or perhaps because Sharpe's work, in a manner that is almost unheard of in such extreme sexual literature, contains something like what one finds in the work of the Levinasian philosopher Alphonso Lingis. Like Lingis, Sharpe allows the trace of God to show through as he exposes us to the faces of the foreigner, the stranger outside the economy of the same, the sexualized

other: foreign, child, sadistic, masochistic, homosexual. In his essay "Fluid Economy" Lingis relates the semen exchange culture of the Sambia of Papua New Guinea documented by Stanford anthropologist Gilbert Herdt.[64] "I receive from the other settlement... a young wife... I enter into a pact with her family. Her younger brothers will daily kneel before me, and will open their mouths for my penis, and will drink my male fluids." [65] Lingis explains:

> For the Sambia, the vital fluids transubstantiate as they pass from one conduit to another. They are the scarce resources of the life, growth, strength, and spirituality of the clan. Among the Sambia, body fluids do not flow; they are transmitted from *socius* to *socius*.... The abundance of male fluid produced in the men is transmitted to the mouths of boys, where it masculinizes them by being stored in their innately empty *kereku-kerekus* [semen organs]. It is marriages... that determine which boys have access to the fluid of which men.[66]

The most shocking sexual vignette in *Boyabuse* is a tongue-in-cheek tribute to the masculinity rituals of the Sambia. Simon, a Port Darlanian, takes the protagonist to his home to meet his family. The following scene unfolds:

> The sister was nursing a sturdy two year old and ruffling his genitals... his sister offered tea. The child was reluctant to give up his teat.... The two year old sulked briefly and then waddled over to his brother watching TV, and tugged on his shorts. The five year old ignored him for almost a minute but then without taking his eyes off the screen he half rolled over, pulled down his shorts and let his brother suck on him.... "Soon," Simon observed, "he'll want his brother to fuck him, but he gets fed up doing it when he'd rather be screwing kids his own age, but I don't want to discourage the little one from trying.... The five year old was now disinterestedly fucking his brother, his eyes still glued to the TV screen.

"My late brother fucked me from infancy and I tasted my uncle's milk while I still suckled on my mother's.[67]

Only the profoundly humorless who have never encountered anthropological studies of sexual initiation rites would take this for malicious advocacy of pedophilic behavior. The description is remarkably similar to actual Sambian rites:

> The first three initiations, at ages seven to ten, at eleven to thirteen, and at fourteen to sixteen, function to forcibly break the boys from their long association with their mothers, and their milk. At the first initiation, the seven-to-ten-year-old boys are weaned from their mothers' milk and foods to male foods and the penis milk of youths of their brother-in-law's clan. After the third initiation, they will serve as fellateds to feed semen into first and second-stage boy initiates. The fourth initiation purifies the youth and issues in cohabitation with his wife.[68]

Lingis argues, "Beneath the rational community... is another community, the community that demands that the one who has his own communal identity, who produces his own nature, expose himself to the one with whom he has nothing in common, the stranger." [69] This other community, the shadow of the rational community, is realized "in exposing oneself to the one with whom one has nothing in common: to the Aztec, the nomad, the guerrilla, the enemy. The other community forms when one recognizes in the face of the other, an imperative." [70] This imperative is shared by Levinas and Sharpe.

The rules of the ritual are established by the third paragraph of "The Rites at Port Dar Lan: Part One:" "The boys had to undergo severe tests of their manhood including heavy whippings which left them scarred and the initiates were circumcised slowly and painfully with a crude stone knife. This the boys had to endure silently without flinching." [71] Here, the four main codes of sadomasochism are explicitly set out: severe tests, heavy whipping, cutting and silent endurance. Taking someone beyond

their limit is prohibited; this is an explicit postcontemporary s/m rule. "Those who abuse the boys beyond their limits are not welcome back." [72] However, if you want a boy's respect, you must "push him to his limits." [73]

Sharpe is careful to state that the control lies with the boys. The boys participate in designing the rituals with Doctor Swartz. "He and the boys set out the rules and standards... the boys... run the show. Those who have been through the entire process, the cutlings, form a Council who make the rules and rule on exceptions." [74] There are different feats of endurance for different ages beginning with the minor torments of the stinging thong and light cane at seven and culminating in circumcision at fifteen. At each stage the boys seek a foreign sponsor who gets to perform these privileges for a price.

Providing a trace to similar feats of youth in ancient Rome, as documented by Plutarch, Sharpe points out that the boys don't compete "under the whip as happened in the temple games of Artemis Orthia in ancient Roman Greece" where "boys died before they'd yield." [75] Dar Lan veteran Ali tells us: "Some of the boys love the whip just as I can remember the cane. I came across the cane in one of the last great schools in England." [76] Here Sharpe is connecting the rituals at Port Dar Lan with the long tradition of flogging at English boys schools that so fascinated the Victorian poet Algernon Charles Swinburne that he was inspired to write *The Flogging-Block: An Heroic Poem* (1865):

> How those great big ridges must smart as they swell!
> How the Master does like to flog Algernon well! How
> each cut makes the blood come in thin little streaks from
> that broad blushing round pair of naked red cheeks. [77]

Dar Lan is a rule-bound, highly ethical fantasy space; it inverts Sade. The so-called victims have set the rules and make the so-called perpetrators abide by them. Sharpe conveys respect, love and real tenderness and affection for his imaginary boys of Dar Lan:

Halfway through the double ordeal of whip and weights blood began to diffuse into the sweat glistening on his chest and belly. He looked magnificent, heroic... I continued to work on him, his chest and belly.... He had four strokes left and lashed his half-limp form with all my strength... only his proud boy spirit kept him from pleading collapse... I tried to prolong it but the evening had honed my lust and I soon came, came gloriously in the spunky boy's butt. I took him to the bed hugging and cuddling his sticky boy form. I caressed his hair, licked the sweat from his forehead, and my tongue cleaned his tear-streaked cheeks and around his melancholy eyes. I kissed him, and kissed him again, and the lips of that amazing boy pressed back against mine.[78]

It is as if Sharpe, even at the level of fantasy, has taken Gayle Rubin's radical pluralist sexual ethics as his personal code of ethics. Rubin argues that sexual acts should be assessed only by "the level of mutual consideration, the presence or absence of coercion and the quantity and quality of the pleasure they provide.[79]

The boys' feats at Dar Lan, their spirit, their ability to endure, their strength and wildness, and the total absence of social conventions link Sharpe's boys to those in William Burroughs' *The Wild Boys*. *The Wild Boys* is a collection of eighteen homoerotic short stories of post-apocalyptic fiction featuring adolescent protagonists Burroughs dubbed his "boy bandits." Oddly, the very first line of the first story "Tio Mate Smiles" is "the camera is the eye of a cruising vulture"[80] and the very last line of Sharpe's "Rites At Port Dar Lan: Part Three" reads, "What a pity my only camera was my eyes."[81] Burroughs begins his story "The Wild Boys" with the lines:

They have incredible stamina. A pack of wild boys can cover fifty miles a day. A handful of dates and a lump of brown sugar washed down with a cup of water keep them moving like that. The noise they make before they charge...[82]

The wild boys, in their early-and-mid teens, originate out of the violence of French colonialism in Morocco, but the phenomenon catches on:

> The legend of the wild boys spread and boys from all over the world ran away to join them. Wild boys appeared in the mountains of Mexico, the jungles of South America and Southeastern Asia. Bandit country, guerrilla country, is wild-boy country. The wild boys exchange drugs, weapons, skills on a worldwide network.[83]

Wild boys all over the world are united by the goal of total revolution: "We intend to march on the police machine everywhere.... The family unit and its cancerous expansion into tribes, countries, nations we will eradicate at its vegetable roots."[84] Yet the boys are tender, magical and romantic with one another:

> His hands mold and knead the body in front of him pulling it against him with stroking movements that penetrate the pearly grey shape caressing it inside. The body shudders and quivers against him as he forms the buttocks around his penis stoking silver genitals out of a moonlight grey then pink and finally red the mouth parted in a gasp shuddering genitals out of the moon's haze a pale blond boy spurting thighs and buttocks and young skin.[85]

Sometimes Burroughs' wild boys play with one another's genitals and afterwards "busy themselves skinning the genitals"[86] of captured soldiers whose vital organs are removed for food. Sharpe's boys of Dar Lan and his Tijuana whip-fighting boy gladiators are tame by comparison—they fight for survival and for the pleasure of their mixed audience of boys, locals and foreigners. Yet The Wild Boys is legal and Boyabuse is illegal.

That Sharpe's work has literary merit is unquestionable; it no more advocates the 'pedophilic' actions described than Sade's or Burroughs' works. Sharpe's detailed fantasies relate as the dark underside to his published work Manilamanic, a slightly

fictionalized ethnographic narration of the street hustling scene in Manila's now-defunct sex zone. *Manilamanic* is about street youths—boys, hustlers and beggars seen through the eyes of the Western traveller who spends time with them. Sharpe's respect and love for his semi-fictional characters recuperates their lives; he is able to show the agency of the so-called victims and their joy of life even in the direst material circumstances.

Perhaps the real power and beauty of Sharpe's writing is that is not recuperable or cooptable. It both fits and in some ways goes beyond the genre that Deleuze and Guattari term "strange Anglo-American literature"[87]—from Henry Miller to Allen Ginsberg, Jack Kerouac and William Burroughs. These are "men who know how to leave, to scramble the codes, to cause flows to circulate."[88]

THE SHARPE TRIAL:
Two Testimonies of Artistic Merit

The testimonies of the two defense witnesses, English professors James Miller (University of Western Ontario) and Lorraine Weir (University of British Columbia), were crucial in determining the artistic merit of Sharpe's writings. Both testimonies constitute the pragmatic application of theory to a site considered the other of philosophy: pornography.[89]

For Sharpe's trial, literary criticism was deployed for the purpose of legal defense. Miller's testimony provided an in-depth education in Sharpe's work within the context of transgressive literature. Weir's testimony documented the relationship between Sharpe's charged and non-charged works, and the relationship of Sharpe's work to extrinsic genres. Because the defense of artistic merit for child pornography has been removed from the criminal code, Miller and Weir's testimonies constitute a fleeting and original moment in legal history.

Miller utilized what could be identified as a postmodern literary approach in applying the criteria of artistic merit set out in the Supreme Court ruling. Although Miller didn't explicitly

describe his approach as 'postmodern literary criticism,' he did take Sharpe's stories apart, locating them in relation to existing literary genres, showing how each of the seventeen stories in *Boyabuse* and "Stand By America, 1953" were parodies. Miller organized his testimony in accordance with the terms spelled out for an artistic merit defense by the Supreme Court. After the trial Miller suggested: "You could argue that my covert approach was thoroughly postmodern in that I spun a dense intertextual web of allusions around Sharpe's stories such that to condemn *Boyabuse* would have meant condemning Western literature as a whole." [90]

Miller teaches comparative literature courses entitled "The Literature of Taboo" and "The Literature of Transgression." The first is a study of holy books that establish the sets of taboos upon which cultures are based. The latter is a literature of unholy books that deliberately break taboos. In court, Miller situated Sharpe's writings as a literature of transgression that has a genealogy traceable through Bataille and Sade back to Dante—"the most transgressive author in the Western tradition and the originator of libertine counter-forces." In his view, Dante's *Inferno* was the first great example in Western culture to articulate blasphemy, transgressive defiance and sacrificial rituals from the viewpoint of the damned. Miller points out, "Dante's *Inferno* has scenes in which sinners are punished in a variety of sadistic ways, including flogging, submersion in excrement, burning and mutilation of the body by sword.... Some scenes in the epic poem are shockingly violent and nauseating, which makes one question: what is the literary function of such repellent images? I find myself asking the same question, again and again, while reading Mr. Sharpe's work."

Miller continues, "The term libertine refers to anyone who vigorously and even violently rebels against the moral strictures and political regimes of his age; libertinism commonly denotes an extreme aesthetic rejection of any prohibitions imposed on the freedom of a human will; theologically, it is the extreme limit of immoral voluntarism. Sade, of course, is a self-proclaimed libertine." Miller cites "The Lust of the Libertines" as Sade's

most libertine work and most pertinent to the Sharpe case as in it Sade writes about trangressions involving children. "Transgressive literature," says Miller, "is deeply satiric in its design and often uses shocking imagery."

After locating Mr. Sharpe's writing within this literary tradition, Miller applied the eight criteria set out by the Supreme Court in the Sharpe decision: 1) the subjective intent of the creator; 2) the form of the work; 3) the content of the work; 4) the work's connection with artistic conventions, traditions, or styles; 5) the opinion of experts; 6) the mode of production; 7) the mode of display; and 8) the mode of distribution.

"Form," Professor Miller explains, "refers to three things: 1) the details of physical production; 2) the kind of literature—epic, epistemological novel, sonnet, allegory; and 3) structural form— is it prose or poetry, narrative or non-narrative? Moreover, is the work in plain language or rhetorically elaborate metaphoric terms? Is the viewpoint in the first person singular or third person? Content includes table of contents, character development, conflict, closure, theme, setting and intertextual allusions."

Miller then examines *Boyabuse*: "The materiality of *Boyabuse* is a computer printout of an extensive textual manuscript; the text is organized and edited; there is a title page and a table of contents which lists the seventeen stories and the page numbers in which each of the stories begin; the manuscript is copyrighted. The verso side of the title page reads: 'Any or all parts may be reproduced or transmitted by any means electronic or mechanical without permission in writing from the publisher.'" Miller contends, "This unconventional statement indicates the author perceives of the collection as a book."

Miller suggests that the short story "Stand By America, 1953" is a computer printout of a story either to be added to *Boyabuse* or rejected. "Although 'Stand By America, 1953' is in paragraphs, consists of complete sentences, and is divided into sections," Miller states, "I sense this work is not complete or has not been brought to a state where the author would like to publish it because of certain passages with repeated question marks indicating that the author was not quite satisfied with

the wording." As Judge Shaw writes in his judgment: "In respect of both *Boyabuse* and 'Stand By America, 1953,' Professor Miller found evidence that they had been organized, edited, revised and conceived as publishable works." [91]

Miller stresses that there was no difficulty in recognizing the genre that *Boyabuse* fell into: "Its genre is first an anthology of short stories linked chronologically—'Ricky' is linked to 'Leo' as its sequel; 'The Rites at Port Dar Lan' appear as a three-part story labeled parts one, two and three." Another genre for *Boyabuse* is parody; for Miller, "parody is a technical term in genre theory that means 'road beside' or 'parallel route'.... This journey refers to a text that follows or closely imitates the rhetoric of a well-known genre in order to mock it for satirical or comic effect." "Mr. Sharpe," Miller contends, "parodies many nontransgressive genres as well as transgressive genres; each story in *Boyabuse* parodies a different genre." Miller then goes through the seventeen stories pointing out the genre parodied by each story. Miller identifies "On a Cold Winter's Night" as "parodying a particular type of fairy tale, in which once upon a time is replaced with 'on a cold winter's evening'; the winter tale is told by old wives around a fireplace and usually involves a visit from the supernatural or an encounter with elves and fairies. In Mr. Sharpe's tale there is a fireplace, instead of old wives there is an older man, and the boy Randy is described as a 'magic elf' and a 'naughty elf.'"

Professor Miller situates the second story, "Platinum and Gold," which involves the journey of three characters from North America to the Philippines, as "a parody of a cheerful travelogue used to advertise the major sites of interests to tourists; what cues the reader into the parody is Sharpe has one of the characters read an in-flight magazine en route to Manila." "The Spanking" is "a parody of contemporary parenting guides designed to teach parents how to discipline their unruly children; contemporary guides which recommend no use of corporal punishment are an inversion of Victorian guides; Sharpe's is an inversion of the contemporary, returning to the Victorian," says Miller.

Miller proposes that "Let This Be a Lesson" is "a complex parody that imitates two kinds of texts—a sermon on the evils of

pornography and the kind of writing found in pornographic texts such as *Hustler* magazine or *Hot Action*." Miller contends that "'Let This Be A Lesson' sends up the didactic texts of anti-porn feminist authors such as Catharine MacKinnon who Sharpe refers to by name in one of his published poems." "Let This Be A Lesson" has the father quoting MacKinnon as he flogs and berates his son: "What must your mother think finding you with filth like this that degrades and insults all womankind?" [92]

In Miller's analysis, the story "Suck It: A Devotee's Lament" follows the tradition of sadomasochistic homoerotic stories published in the magazine *Drummer* and can also be read "as a queering of the master-slave relationship in Nabokov's *Lolita*." Miller indicates that "parodists work by inversion; in 'Suck It' it is a particular kind of parodying known as *queering*; instead of a nymphet dominating the erotic interaction, a fawnlet is substituted."

"Timothy and the Terrorist" is "a queering of a boy's adventure tale found in teenage boys' periodicals of the 1940s and 1950s; it is also a queering of the nineteenth-century Gothic. The Gothic involves the capture of a vulnerable maiden by a menacing male power figure, sometimes a king or sultan; the heroine is exposed to many dangers as she tries to escape; sometimes she escapes through a noble suitor or triumphs due to her maidenly virtue." "In striking contrast," Miller points out, "Timothy is transformed by his experience into a rebel, a political freedom fighter and eventually into a legendary figure—'the Golden Running Angel.' Timothy, like Ganymede, undergoes a queer divinization." Miller also points out that "this complex story parodies tabloids of the white slave trade; the reader is clued in by the preparatory note: 'Young, innocent white boys sold as sex slaves to a sadistic and murderous sultan plot their own freedom and overthrow a corrupt and hated regime in the process.'" This reminds Miller of the kind of headlines found in tabloids.

"Tijuana Whip Fight" has "a similar theme to the Russell Crowe film *Gladiator* and this is the vicious cruelty of the ancient gladiator sport which was popular in Roman romances of the sword in the late nineteenth and early twentieth centuries in

works like *Ben Hur*." Miller notes, "Hollywood has created and honored with Oscars a Roman coliseum whip fight and spear fight"; in 'Tijuana Whip Fight' the boys turn this activity into an erotic spectacle."

Overall, Miller is reminded of "Victorian underground erotic literature in which an outwardly respectable gentleman narrates his secret underworld of erotic adventures." Miller observes that "what makes 'Tijuana Whip Fight' a parody of the flogging episodes in *My Secret Life (The Sex Diary of a Victorian Gentleman)*[93] is the complete absence on the part of the narrator of any sense of Victorian probity—a sense of living a double life, outwardly respectable, but inwardly dedicated to the theatricality of sadistic sport. The narrator in 'Tijuana Whip Fight' leads no such double life."

"The Rites at Port Dar Lan, Parts One, Two and Three," says Miller are "a parody of writing central to anthropology; this is ethnography which is a writing about a people, its rites, economies, social kinship structures, marriage ceremonies and sexual mores." Miller cites Gilbert Herdt's *Guardians of the Flute* as a possible source for Sharpe's ethnography of a fictive settlement in Borneo: "Herdt's ethnography analyzes the culture of a remote New Guinean tribe who had developed an extraordinary homoerotic rite of passage for young men; boys at a very early age, eight or nine, were removed from the company of women for ten or eleven years during which time they engaged in an intensive education in masculinity which included and may still include exchanges of semen from older adolescent males to their younger tribal brethren through the sexual practice known as fellatio." Miller continues: "Herdt's ethnography is a work of nonfiction in which the narrator represents himself as an objective, scientific spectator of the culture of the semen eater. What makes the 'Rites at Port Dar Lan' an immediate parody of *Guardians of the Flute* is that the narrator is a direct participant and initiate in the homoerotic rites, and the many diverse dispossessed refugees and boat people who have come to the island to expand the tribe."

Miller contends, "The blatant fictionalization of the

ethnographic fieldwork alerts the reader to parodic nature of the three stories.... There is no place on earth where Palestinian refugees, boat people, and representatives of every other oppressed people fleeing from tyrannical regimes have culminated to be organized into a sadomasochistic culture with the aid of a senior anthropologist." Miller likens "the discipline present in Dar Lan to that found in the kingdom Dante calls purgatory: the multitudes of bodies, whipped, pierced, forced to cry, but also proving through their discipline that they have the fortitude to survive and enter into a better life. Like the souls in purgatory, the bodies of the whiplings, cutlings and pledglings, though they undergo elaborate torments which leave marks, welts and wounds are nevertheless, strangely, supernaturally healed. For the most part hardly a scar remains." Miller contends, "nothing in these stories more strikingly reveals their fictional quality than the speed and predictability of these healing bodies."

"Ninja Option" immediately directs the reader's attention to a pulp fiction novel of the 1980s, Eric Van Lustbader's The Ninja, which is queered by Sharpe. "In the parodic rewrite, Philip discovers himself at the very limit of agonized resistance, possessing the very strength to hate and resist the ninja's s/m dominance of him. The law of Sade's s/m universe is that two dominating masters cannot occupy the same scene. The adult ninja—as soon as he witnesses Phillip's fortitude—immediately and almost mechanically commits hara-kiri, thereby completely inverting the power dynamic of the pulp fiction original."

Miller situates "Stand By America, 1953" as an echo of the film Stand By Me. The film, like Sharpe's story, was narrated as a flashback by an adult recollecting youthful experiences of boys learning to stand by one another while lost in the wilderness. There is a memorable scene on a railway bridge in which the boys dare each other to prove their fortitude by crossing the bridge in front of an oncoming train. Miller argued that "Mr. Sharpe's 'Stand By America, 1953' parallels the narration in the film. The boys in Mr. Sharpe's story go on a hike outside their town in Tennessee. They attempt to cross a railway bridge in search of a missing briefcase of spy documents. The boys in Sharpe's story

have their fortitude tested and come to an understanding of their masculinity identified as solidarity with American patriotism."

The narrative parallels between the film *Stand By Me* and Sharpe's story are "suddenly and irrevocably inverted by the kinds of tests the boys in Mr. Sharpe's story must endure. The story's villains, Marko and Steve, have set up a trap with the briefcase to lure the boys to a farmhouse where they must endure s/m trials. Part of the game is that the adults are KGB agents; the boys are flogged, raped and forced by the KGB agents to have sex with each other. During the experience they resist their abductors by affirming their allegiance to democracy."

Miller goes on to note that "ironically, the love of country is inverted so that the boys transfer this love—what they really love is not the political game of allegiance to the country, but the s/m game of power relations between master and slave." Miller cites the story's reference to the "overarching conflict of the Cold War—American democracy versus communist tyranny—as an example of the literary technique of allegory and noted the careful dating of the piece as 1953 when the Cold War was a political fact." Judge Shaw later noted in his decision that "Professor Miller spoke of allegory as a veiled allusion which, in writing, has come to mean an extended comparison… it is a narrative constructed so as to clue the reader to other meanings, themes, topics or events besides those expressly articulated." [94]

Miller then assessed the content of *Boyabuse* and "Stand By America, 1953" in terms of character, plot, conflict, theme and setting, noting that Sharpe uses a similar method to that of Charles Dickens. For example, "Leo," in the story of the same name, "develops in the course of his tale from a defiant, unresponsive delinquent bad boy into something close to a romantic hero comparable in a parodic sense to Pip in *Great Expectations*." Miller agrees with Crown expert witness Professor Delany's claim that Sharpe's characterization in the early *Boyabuse* stories is crude, not representing significant formative experiences or psychological depth. He disagrees strongly with Delany that this applies to the later stories such as "The Rites of Port Dar Lan"; there, he comments, "the development of Jojo

is strikingly elaborate. In 'Timothy and the Terrorist,' Timothy develops from a complacent, ordinary, first-world teen through an extraordinary sequence into a political rebel, a cult hero, and finally a man able to survive the most horrendous conflicts before being returned to the bosom of his family."

With regards to plot, Miller observes that the Dar Lan stories reveal chronological ordering and that we see the use of a further plot device known as a 'sequel.' Miller explained to the court that plot is generated by conflict, which can take the form of a competition or clash between characters or within a character's nature. He then provided three examples of conflict in Sharpe's stories: "In 'Stand By America, 1953' the story focuses on the conflict between the American boys and KGB agents. Sometimes the conflict takes the form of a contest or competition as in the story 'Tijuana Whip Fight.' Sometimes it's an erotic struggle between boys undergoing initiation and the adult organizers of the rites, as in the circumcision rituals of the 'Dar Lan' stories. In other instances, the narrative is propelled by the dynamic struggle to maintain mastery in interaction between a master and a slave." In his testimony, Delaney suggested that one of the weaknesses of Sharpe's writing is that these conflicts are always essentially identical. Miller counter-argued that while there is a recurrent motif of conflict between master and slave, he was "struck by the multitudinous variation that Mr. Sharpe imagined of that elemental contest."

Miller points out that the theme of Mr. Sharpe's writings is familiar to readers of sacred literature, such as Milton's *Samson Agonistes*: "the spiritual virtue of fortitude becomes primarily visible in the physical endurance of the beaten and whipped boys." Miller concludes that Sharpe's stories are "designed to provoke a controversial response; at least to unsettle fixed or traditional understandings of the virtues and the vices."

The next criterion refers to the narrative's setting, or social context. Miller contends that Sharpe's recurrent critiques of the global economic system are intensified by setting the s/m contest in different points on the globe: Sri Lanka, the Muslim world, the Philippines, the Canadian North, the basement of the bourgeois

household. Port Dar Lan's narration of the operation of the global economic system is not without irony: the boys graduate from agony into successful business careers in Singapore. "Mr. Sharpe reveals the seismic ironies in the new world order associated with globalization," in which much of the third world is a backdrop for the pleasure of the first. According to Miller, "the three stories of sadomasochistic sex involving boys at Port Dar Lan, a fictional South Pacific island, is symbolic of the economic relationship between the Western world and the third world; the literal relationships on the erotic level between the adult and the child are an embodiment, a symbolic incarnation of economic relations at a higher cultural level."

Miller locates Sharpe's writing in the tradition of Sadean literature. He defines the Sadean tradition as that which "focuses attention on transgressive sexuality; it represents a defiant breaking of the very taboos controlling sexual relations and practices established by the holy books in the literature of taboo. Sadean works locate conflict in the struggle between a cruel sexual aggressor and a usually passive sexual partner. It recounts in endless variations the possibilities for sexual torment far beyond what one would suspect is actually practiced by the majority of its readers. It is an imaginative literature rather than a journalistic report of criminal acts. Sade's 'The Lust of the Libertines' consists of an inventory of several hundred minute narratives of sexual cruelty. These acts are all committed in the imaginary gothic space of a remote chateau."

"The degree of violence in Sharpe's writing is extraordinary," says Miller. "First, I agree that the *Boyabuse* and 'Stand By America, 1953' display a striking relentlessly elaborate degree of violent scenes, certainly in contrast to authors like Jane Austen. Readers who have even dipped into the Sadean current of writing will not be surprised to find numerous and unimaginable cruel acts of flogging, piercings and rape. I would say that Sharpe's writings on a scale from one to ten are only about a five as anyone will quickly sense after reading a few pages of *120 Days of Sodom*. Almost no one dies in *Boyabuse* and 'Stand By America, 1953.'" Miller notes, "The important thing is the display of extreme

stoicism, a display impossible if the character is unconscious or dead. Mr. Sharpe's stories vigorously conform to the conventions of the Sadean tradition, except his special ethos of fortitude which appears to be his special twist on the tradition."

In court, defense witness Professor Weir identified her literary approach as classical hermeneutics. She explained that she chose to use hermeneutics to assess Sharpe's work because it is recognized in the discipline of literature as an "objective method for determining whether a text has merit. Hermeneutics makes a fundamental distinction between literal language and figurative language. It sees literary discourse as figurative. This distinction between the literal and the figurative is fundamental to the analysis of evidence." Weir points out that hermeneutics is one of the most widely used techniques of literary analysis: "We use hermeneutics everyday in university English classrooms to give our students a fundamental training in interpretation. It is also used in literary reviews; it is used in published journals such as *The New York Review of Books* and the *Times Literary Supplement*."

In her testimony, she drew parallels between Sharpe's works [*Boyabuse* and "Stand By America, 1953"] and Victorian literature. She notes, "The Victorian phenomenon of flogging schoolboys was drawn into Sharpe's texts." Weir claims that her review of the Victorian genre informed her interpretation of the theme of fortitude central to Sharpe's works.

Weir finds considerable irony and craftsmanship in many of Sharpe's stories. As examples of irony she discusses passages from "Timothy and the Terrorist," "Let This Be a Lesson" and "Suck It: A Devotee's Lament." In regard to the latter, Weir says, "Sharpe's very title alerted the reader to a story of ironic role reversal where the boy plays the role of master and the male narrator plays the role of slave. The child instructs the adult about sexual technologies and his own pleasure: 'USE YOUR TONGUE MORE LIKE YOU USUALLY DO.'" Weir observes that the story is written with a "joyous and whimsical role reversal that is beautifully controlled throughout."

Weir placed *Boyabuse* and 'Stand By America, 1953' in the context of two of Sharpe's other works: *Rupert Unexpurgated* (1983)

and *Algernon at Eton* (1993). She states that *Rupert Unexpurgated* "was written in the form of a biography relating to the maturation of a boy from early childhood to adolescence." Reading selected passages, Weir argues that *Rupert Unexpurgated* "shows me in a very elegant fashion the skill as a writer which Mr. Sharpe reveals in different ways in many of the stories in *Boyabuse*. She finds "themes of fortitude and initiation in most of Mr. Sharpe's works."

Regarding Sharpe's work-in-progress *Algernon at Eton*, Weir testified, "In this novel Mr. Sharpe endeavors to shape his literary material and draws upon the Victorian historical context described by the poet Algernon Charles Swinburne. That context included the practice of flogging in Victorian boys' schools, as well as themes of apprenticeship and fortitude." Weir continues that *Algernon at Eton* enabled her to understand "the theme of fortitude and its significance in his work as a whole, as well giving an insight into the English vice of flogging which was a practice commonly used for disciplining purposes in Victorian boys schools." She concludes that "what the poet Swinburne and others of his persuasion created out of these disciplinary practices was an aesthetics which construed flogging in terms of a process of apprenticeship or what Sharpe calls 'fortitude.'"

"In *Algernon at Eton* Sharpe draws attention to the historical context of flogging as not only a disciplinary practice but also as a practice of the technology of pain; what is meant by technology in this context is from the Greek word *techne* which means practice or skill, as one might think of a craftsman who has served her apprenticeship and knows how to perform what is required of her." Weir then read a passage from *Boyabuse* to illustrate the technology of pain:

> I'm anxious for my appointment with Raj and my latest experiment in the technology of pain. I give Jojo and Ling some spending money to entertain themselves, I hear they now have video games in the village, and I make them both promise to stay away from Raj's cutting…. Raj removes his improvised but regal tribal attire and stands facing the sun. A buddy hands him

a spear and he holds it in his right hand, the butt end resting on his foot below. The fingers of his other hand just barely touch those of Ebo beside him. I kneel in front of him holding my instrument of torture as he looks on in calm anticipation. I stroke his big boycock first stretching out the foreskin gently and then running a finger around the inside of the silky skin, knowing it. I begin stretching out sections of the rim. Taking the cutting pliers I've carefully dulled I snip a quarter inch into the edge of his foreskin not cutting but crushing, squishing the sensitive membrane. Then as close as I can get to the first I make a second mashing snip and I can see it's going to be a bloody affair. Raj stares off into the distance as if in another world. The boys, crowding closer than is comfortable, watch in silence, many fondling themselves beneath their clothes. Methodically I continue the close-spaced snips until Raj has a frill of loose mangled skin all the way around the rim of his prepuce. When the blood is rinsed off it makes a rather pretty embellishment to his already handsome cock. Subtle reactions tell me that Raj is not as unaffected by his ordeal as he pretends to be.[95]

When questioned by the defense attorney, Paul Burstein, whether she would teach Sharpe's writing on a university course, Weir replied, "if I was teaching a course on the history of gay and or transgressive writing in Canada, I certainly would."

AN INTRIGUING PROPOSITION*

After court adjourned, FF went back to her hotel and strapped on her 17-centimeter cock. Then she and Hawk Senior headed for The Duff—one of Vancouver's oldest gay bars with a strip club in the basement. FF made a point of going up to each boy after his strip and ever so carefully inserting a $5 bill into his jock. Matt, a young but legal, beefy 'Tom of Finland' kind of hustler, began to hang around FF and Hawk Senior. They bought him drinks—

* Italicized text is from *Boyabuse*.

that's what you do with hustlers, you pay. Well into the evening, when Matt disappeared for a spell into the john with the other boys, FF queried Hawk Senior: "Are you into him or should I take him home, or should both of us take him home?" Hawk Senior smiled, "The latter's an intriguing proposition." FF nodded and smiled. She was into Hawk Senior, the notorious boy lover on trial for the most objectionable literary pornography written since Sade. How could she not be? Matt, hot as he was, was merely the bait. FF negotiated a price with Matt for a threesome in which she, wearing a small strap-on, would ass fuck him while Hawk Senior gave him a blowjob. Matt was in, and just for Matt's good spirit and willingness to pursue a bisexual *ménage a trois* FF threw in another $20 on top of the C-note into the deal.

Upon arrival at her hotel room, FF took her clothes off and headed for the shower. "Whichever of you want to please join me." In came Matt, soon to be followed by Hawk Senior. "*We all shower off together*."[96] FF was on her knees, mouth brushing against both cocks, with both hands firmly on each set of balls. She got out of the shower leaving the male bodies to explore each other's masculinity.

FF got her cock and joined Matt and Hawk Senior back in the shower, "*Whether it was business, boredom or simply boys' lust I am not sure but soon they were both fondling me*."[97] Matt went down on her pussy while Hawk Senior stroked her cock and she came double. They moved to the bed. Matt bent over Hawk Senior who had positioned himself at the right angle for Matt's cock, FF took Matt from behind, lubing her four-centimeter cock and entering him. FF thrust, circled and fucked the sky through Matt's ass.

Hawk Senior and FF thanked Matt and paid him, then all three exchanged hugs at the door. FF turned to Hawk Senior. She got on her knees, his very large member in her hand: "Matt was a decoy, I wanted you." He smiled. FF continued: "Teach me how to give pain, to do all the things you write about in *Boyabuse*, not with a boy but with a man, an old-style masochist who has made fortitude his way of life. Teach me how to put pins through the nipples, through the foreskin, the balls, teach me how to spank and flog and whip. I want to apprentice."

FF'S APPRENTICESHIP WITH HAWK SENIOR

If you would be so kind as to consider this offer: after showering you, I desire to put a pin through your left nipple with a small padlock on it, a pin through your right nipple with a duplicate weighted padlock on it, 17 large needles circling your foreskin, 12 pins on the underside of the penis shaft; the balls I want to keep free for striking with a hard leather strap. When the pins are in place, I want to gently put your cock in my mouth, moving my mouth back and forth, moving the pins back and forth as I play with myself and ejaculate. If this arrangement interests you, please meet me at 9 p.m. in the lobby of the Dominion Hotel.

Sincerely, a Sadean woman.

During the trial, FF passed the note to the distinguished masochist defendant. She saw him reading the note. He had no visible response, except perhaps a slight narrowing of his left eye. FF sat through dinner with him not knowing if she would have the pleasure of giving him pain later in the evening. After dinner, they walked home together. Entering the Dominion at precisely 9 p.m., they looked at each other and headed up to her room.

The gentlemanly masochist just happened to have brought along his tool kit. "*Pins pierced the dark swollen cones and... twisted, twisted almost a full turn in each direction, the surrounding skin.*" [98] His body quietly tremored. "*The pleasure's in the hurting, rejoice in the pain you inflict.*" [99]

The sound of the needle piercing and entering flesh was subtler than the thicker steel of the pin, but equally beautiful; a music of the flesh. Resting his large and growing member on her left knee, FF used her left hand to press the rim of the foreskin to the skin of the penis shaft just behind the glans. Her right hand pushed the needle through the foreskin and the shaft skin. Repeat seventeen times. Sadomasochism is about detail, repetition and precision. She put twelve slightly larger needles in a row on the underside of the penis. She placed twenty-seven

small safety pins in scattered locations on his scrotum. Each skin location had a different acoustic character. Once the steel was in place, FF "*removed the strap from its locked drawer... now for the first time I examined closely the instrument of punishment, it was made of black rubberized industrial belting and when I flexed it I realized what a cruel, damaging weapon it could be. And I found myself unexpectedly thrilled at the prospect of putting it to use on the... flesh of a hawk.*"[100] He turned onto his stomach, putting body pressure on the needles in his foreskin, and instructed FF to strike first his right buttock then his left, each to receive "*two dozen strokes of the lash.*"[101] When she finished, he offered FF his cock for her to use as she willed.

FF carefully placed her mouth around the needles moving them back and forth with her tongue. With her left hand, she began to play with her clit, then her urethra, putting her own 15-centimeter member inside her cunt, she pulled solidly on his balls with her right hand, pressing hard into the pins. She "*drew his nuts out to the end of their sac almost gently,*"[102] ran her hand upwards, the steel needles on the penis shaft cold in the palm of her hand. She removed her cock and as she pushed out, her mouth closed on the needles. She sprayed down the large mirror she and the gentlemanly masochist had positioned to reflect their actions. Taking his cock out of her mouth, FF noted that they were blood bonded, as she "*started biting the foreskin, pulling it out with [her] teeth and chewing on the end. [FF] continued biting and chewing slowly drawing out the torment. Blood flowed... as the skin was mangled and shredded.*"[103]

Removing the pins and needles produces a different sound. FF was fascinated with the sounds of flesh pain; no vocalization, just the sounds of flesh pain without language. The sound of leather hitting flesh—on the scrotum, on the buttock, on the shoulder, on the penis. FF had left her mark. FF harbored this notion that you owned that which you marked until the marking faded. "*A month allows more than enough time for the marks of even a thorough thrashing to disappear so that their skin is fresh for new assaults.*"[104]

During the trial, the sound of Professor Weir—in her

authoritative lecturer's voice——reading from "Suck It: A Devotee's Lament" sent a flash of fire snaking up and down FF's spine that settled in the base of her clit. FF glanced at the gentlemanly masochist wondering if his *"sore and swollen flesh... dark and purplish"*[105] from her hand, burned the way her clit did.

There had been something equally sexy in hearing defense attorney Burstein quote from Sharpe's writings in his closing submission, knowing that beneath his civilized attire, on his skin, the gentlemanly masochist defendant wore the marks of the Sadean woman's gift of pain.

JUDGE SHAW'S RULING

> I do not accept the Crown's theory. In my opinion, it attempts to draw a distinction between pornography, on the one hand, and artistic merit, on the other. In my view, the defense of artistic merit under s. 163.1 of the Criminal Code does not depend upon whether the written material is considered "pornography." The question to be answered is whether the writing has artistic merit, irrespective of whether the work is considered pornographic.[106]

Judge Shaw accepted defense lawyer Burstein's argument on Sharpe's written material——that it did not advocate or counsel the sexual activity it described and that it had literary merit. However, Shaw rejected Burnstein's argument that the Crown had not proven that the boys in the photos were under the age of consent. Some of Sharpe's four hundred photos were deemed to constitute child pornography; these were mostly photographs he had taken of youths.[107] Sharpe was found guilty of two counts of possession of the child pornography photos. The subsequent sentence of 120 days of house arrest between the hours of 4 p.m. and 8 a.m. was more than appropriate for a Sadean gentleman.

With respect to Sharpe's writings, Shaw ruled: "While *Boyabuse* and "Stand By America, 1953" arguably may glorify the acts described therein, in my opinion they do not go so far as to

actively promote their commission." [108] In terms of the artistic or literary merit of the work, Shaw notes that "the scenes portrayed are, by almost any standard, morally repugnant." [109] However, in considering some of the material submitted as evidence by the defense, he points out that "a work by the Marquis de Sade describes scenes of sexual torture of women and children, scenes which in terms of sadistic cruelty and horror go far beyond those written by Mr. Sharpe.... I refer to the 447 methods of sadomasochistic torture set out in 'The Lusts of the Libertines,' which forms part of Sade's *120 Days of Sodom*. According to all of the literary scholars who testified, the passages in Sade's work have artistic merit." [110] Shaw noted that *Boyabuse* and 'Stand by America, 1953' are properly termed 'transgressive literature.'" [111] He also notes that a "reading of Mr. Sharpe's other writings... reveals that he is not devoid of literary skill." [112]

Things were looking good for Sharpe after Judge Shaw's ruling. The trial proceedings had critically engaged his written work, transforming Sharpe's image from 'disgusting pedophile' to that of distinguished, albeit extremely perverse, literary figure. In his post-trial reflections on the influence of Sade on his work, Sharpe mused,

> I had only fleeting thoughts of Sade when I was writing. He is not a favorite writer of mine. I had read *120 Days of Sodom*, along with other smuggled writings in my twenties, but only for prurient interest. Racy writings in those days usually circulated with the 'interesting' passages already marked. I found *120 Days* pretty gross and more of a curiosity.... I did get from Sade the idea that one could write about such things. Some might claim that I picked up a cognitive distortion. Only much later, I think after reading Simone de Beauvoir's essay, 'Must We Burn de Sade?' did I have anything more than a pornographic appreciation of the Marquis. [113]

One week before Mr. Sharpe completed his 120 days' sentence he was arrested for a sexual assault allegedly committed twenty

years earlier. The Vancouver police on the pornography beat had gone to great lengths to locate one or more of the boys in his photos, as a Canadian national daily newspaper, *The Globe and Mail*, indicates: "An unusual public appeal by Vancouver Police paid off when a man came forward recently to identify himself as the boy in a sexually explicit picture taken by convicted pornographer John Robin Sharpe."[114] The man alleged that Sharpe had sexually assaulted him between 1979–1982, when he was eleven to thirteen years old.[115] Sharpe was found guilty of the lesser charge of indecent assault involving a minor. He was sentenced to a two-year jail term in July 2004.[116]

On November 1, 2005, the Artistic Merit Defense for Child Pornography was replaced with the Legitimate Purpose Defense which is only applicable "where an act in relation to child pornography satisfies a twofold harms-based test: (1) the act in question has a legitimate purpose related to the administration of justice, or to science, medicine, education or art; and (2) the act does not pose an undue risk of harm to children."[117] This new clause makes it unnecessary for courts to determine whether the work being assessed can be deemed to counsel or advocate sexual activity with anyone under eighteen. Rather, the work is considered child pornography and culpable if the 'dominant characteristic' of the written material is the description, "for a sexual purpose," of sexual activity involving a person under eighteen.[118]

The narrowing trajectory from the artistic merit defense to the legitimate purpose defense means that Sharpe's writings have not and cannot be published. They were available on Sharpe's website but were removed pending consideration of Canada's new pornography legislation. The only published presence of these writings are in this chapter, which has "a legitimate purpose related to education."

LOVE, LITERATURE, LIBERTY

I caught up with Robin in July 2009, seven years after his artistic merit trial and three and a half years since his jail term. Mostly I wanted to touch base, see how the most perverse writer since Sade was faring and hear about his recent projects.

Robin looked manly, muscled and handsome as we approached one another in Montreal's gay village. "You look hot and fabulous," I told him as we embraced. "I'm in love," he confided. "Not what one expects from the nation's most notorious child pornographer." Then Robin read me a few lines from a poem he had written for his new legal-aged lover:

> When you're young, you call it love. At my age it is being smitten. The boy charms you, you observe every detail and remember every word.... I cannot expect a lad to love a scarred and ancient impotent body. I must (therefore) charm him. I listen, I encourage, I learn. Soon I know him, and trying to be honest, reveal myself to him. Befriending? Courting? Grooming?

> You are privileged to be smitten.... You love the hero world of youth.... Childhood and adolescence is the mythology of the adult.... Boys are a window to your past.

For Sharpe, it seem, boys provide a perfect backdrop for manliness. Sharpe and his partner have now been together for more than two years.

SHANNON BELL [SB]: You currently have stories online, on sites such as the Male-Male Spanking Archive (MMSA). Here I see your infamous novel *Algernon at Eton: The Schooldays of A.C. Swinburne 1849–1953*, referred to extensively by Dr. Weir in her discussion of the artistic merit of your work at the trial.

ROBIN SHARPE [RS]: I started it in 1993, got back into it after jail and finished it in 2007. This year (2009) is the centenary of Swinburne's death. People go to MMSA

mostly for masturbatory relief. Some of the writers, however, do have pretensions to literature and there are some excellent writers.

SB: I just looked at a couple of your pieces on MMSA—*Algernon at Eton* and *Blood and Semen*.[119] They seem solid literary works, but I guess literary works can be masturbation tools.

RS: You take a masturbation fantasy, you polish it, then it ends up as literature and probably is nowhere near as hot as it was in an early draft. People forget and the authorities deny that the purpose of sexual fantasies is as a masturbation aide. I have seen court statements about pornography in which the expert says it may also be used to assist masturbation, as if the main purpose of pornography was something else.

SB: In terms of winning the artistic merit defense what has the lasting effect been?

RS: It seems to me that since then not many people have been charged for writing child pornography.

SB: What work were you doing in prison?

RS: After a couple of weeks I got assigned to Ford Mountain Correctional Center, a work camp. Perhaps you noticed on the contents page of *Pagunan Masks: An Ethnofiction*, "This work was made possible through the support of the Ford Mountain Institute."[120] In terms of camp work I was initially assigned to recycling and eventually I was shifted to woodworking. Ford had a very well-equipped woodworking shop called the Hobby Shop. I naturally gravitated towards it as I have done woodworking all my life. In my free time I made

bowls, furniture, jewelry, cigarette boxes and masks. As I was carving the first mask I made up a story; it began from thinking about the Philippine mountain town of Sagada where they bury their dead in hollowed-out log coffins and put a mask on the end. I started to develop a fictitious ethnography of a culture—Pagu—that produced such masks. I got the idea of a society begun by teenagers: there was the Great Cataclysm where all the adults and children were killed in a tsunami. The survivors were the rebellious teenagers. I carved and painted eighteen death and ritual masks. It takes about two days to carve a mask. Pictures of masks accompany the book.

I read a lot of books in jail. I read books that I usually wouldn't bother with, due to the prison library's limited selection. I got permission from the Director to have one of the guards purchase Michel Foucault's *Discipline and Punish* for me. Of course the guards had to look through it and make sure it was appropriate. Reading incoming and outgoing mail and listening to recordings of the inmates' telephone calls is what keeps the guards busy on the night shift. The night-shift guards are the censors.

SB: And jail, what was it like for you?

RS: Ford Mountain is like living with a bunch of kids in some ways. Most of the men in my unit were in their twenties and not your stereotypical criminals. They're generally quite ordinary guys who horse around and are sometimes loud. Basically jail is punishment, and time is its principal currency. How do we punish? We give convicts time; so many days, months, years: the time standard of punishment. Jail sentences are homogenized through the concept of time measured as deprivation of liberty. As I wrote in my jail journal:

When I finished *Discipline and Punish* I had a better idea of the penitentiary (I had too simplistically connected it to penitence), and how the system of discipline it entails has spread well beyond prisons, and rather than punishing offenses it seeks to redefine a wide range of behavior as delinquent, in effect creating it, and treating it. This happens through the continuous extension of criminal law to more and more actions. I couldn't agree with Foucault more.[121]

Endnotes

1 John Robin Sharpe, on his website, www.robinsharpe.ca.

2 Canadian child pornography law came into existence in 1993; it was a contentious piece of legislation from its inception. Except for the possession offense, the key parts of Bill C-128 that became s. 163.1 of the Canadian Criminal Code already existed in criminal law: "the production, distribution and sale of sexually explicit materials involving children was already prohibited, as was possession for the purposes of distribution and sale." [Brenda Cossman and Shannon Bell, "Introduction" in Brenda Cossman, Shannon Bell, Lise Gotell and Becki Ross, *Bad Attitude/s on Trial: Feminism, Pornography and the Butler Decision* (Toronto: University of Toronto Press, 1997), 39.]

3 The new child pornography law, s. 163.1, added: 1) the possession offense; 2) the category of written materials that advocate or counsel sexual activity with a children; 3) the category of sexual representations in which an adult appears to be or pretends to be a child; and 4) child was defined as anyone under the age of eighteen.

4 In *R. v. Butler* [1992] SCR 1, the Supreme Court of Canada, facing a constitutional challenge to s. 163 of the Canadian Criminal Code, reshaped the test for obscenity. Obscenity law was no longer seen as regulating public morality or imposing a uniform standard of sexual morals. Rather, the law of obscenity, following Butler, is based on preventing harm, particularly harm towards women. Determining whether material is obscene became based on the classification of pornography into three categories: (1) representations of explicit sex with violence, which would almost always be found to be obscene; (2) representations of explicit sex without violence, that are degrading and dehumanizing— these would be obscene "if the risk of harm is substantial"; and (3) representations of explicit sex, without violence that are not degrading and dehumanizing, and do not involve children in their production; these generally are found not to be obscene (*R. v. Butler*, 454). These classifications are made according to the community standards test, that is, what Canadians will tolerate other people being exposed to. Material that is degrading and dehumanizing fails the community standards test because these materials are "perceived by public opinion to be harmful to society, particularly to women" (*R. v. Butler*, 467). The test for assessing degrading and dehumanizing is whether it places "women (and sometimes men) in positions of subordination, servile submission or humiliation" (*R. v. Butler*, 466). The artistic merit defense is the final step if the material has passed the community standards and dehumanizing and degrading tests.

5 *R. v. Sharpe*, 2001, SCR 45, paras 63–67.

6 Sharpe's first British Columbia Supreme Court appearance was a *voir dire*, a special hearing "held to hear the constitutional challenge." [*R. v. Sharpe*, British Columbia Supreme Court, *voir dire*, January 13, 1999, 2.]

7 Stan Persky and John Dixon, *On Kiddie Porn: Sexual Representation, Free Speech and The Robin Sharpe Case* (Vancouver: New Star Books, 2001), 21–22.

8 Robin Sharpe, *Manilamanic: Vignettes, Vice & Verse* (Vancouver: Kalayaan Publications, 1994). Robin Sharpe, *Life on the Corner: The Moon Eyed Beggar's Tale* (Vancouver: Kalayaan Publications, 1996).

9 See Jean-François Lyotard's book *Just Gaming*, in which he argues that law is a dominant language game situated according to the dominant power relations in society. Justice in the gaming would require a case-by-case application of the law, and a judgment that responds to the specificity of the case under scrutiny rather than a rigid adherence to general principles. [Jean-François Lyotard and Jean-Loup Thébaud, *Just Gaming*, trans. Wlad Godzich (Minneapolis: University of Minnesota, 1985).]

10 Shannon Bell, "Female Sexuality at the End of Gender" in *Whore Carnival* (New York: Autonomedia, 1995) and Shannon Bell, "*On ne peut voir l'image*" [The image cannot be seen] in *Bad Attitude/s on Trial: Pornography, Feminism and the Butler Decision*, Brenda Cossman, Shannon Bell, Lise Gotell and Becky Ross (Toronto: University of Toronto Press, 1997).

11 Gilles Deleuze, *Bergsonism*, trans. Hugh Tomlinson and Barbara Habberjam (New York: Zone Books, 1991), 8.

12 Emmanuel Levinas, *Ethics and Infinity: Conversations with Philippe Nemo*, trans. Richard Cohen (Pittsburgh: Duquesne University Press, 1986), 89.

13 John D. Caputo, *Against Ethics* (Bloomington and Indianapolis: Indiana University Press, 1993), 119.

14 Gayle Rubin, "Thinking Sex: Note for a Radical Theory of the Politics of Sexuality" in *Pleasure and Danger: Exploring Female Sexuality*, ed. Carole S. Vance (Boston: Routledge & Kegan Paul, 1984), 279.

15 Jesse Bering, "Pedophiles, Hebephiles and Ephebophiles, Oh My: Erotic Age Orientation" in *Scientific American*, July 1, 2009 (http://www.scientificamerican.com/article.cfm?id=pedophiles-erotic-age-orientation).

16 Stan Persky and John Dixon, *On Kiddie Porn: Sexual Representation, Free Speech and The Robin Sharpe Case*, 137.

17 *R. v. Sharpe*, The Court of Appeal for British Columbia, BCCA, 1999, 416, paras 6–10.

18 Interview with Robin Sharpe, February 14–16, 2001.

19 Ken Plummer, *Telling Sexual Stories* (London: Routledge, 1994), 120.

20 Ibid., 119.

21 Amy Adler, "The Perverse Law of Child Pornography," *Columbia Law Review*, March 2001: 2.

22 Bell, "Sharpe's Perverse Aesthetic," *Constitutional Forum*, Vol.12, No.1, Fall 2001/2002: 30–39.

23 S. 163.1 (1) In this section, "child pornography" means any written or visual representation that advocates or counsels sexual activity with a person under the age of eighteen years would be an offence under this Act. (Criminal Code of Canada, Martin's Annual Criminal Code 1997. Aurora, Ontario: Canada Law Book Inc., 1996).

24 R. v. Sharpe, [2001] SCJ, para 65.

25 Ibid., para 67.

26 Ibid., para 63.

27 Ibid., para 66.

28 Ibid.

29 Ibid., para 65.

30 Ibid., para 93.

31 Sharpe, R. v. Sharpe: A Personal Account, 3.

32 Bell, Reading, Writing and Rewriting the Prostitute Body (Bloomington and Indianapolis: Indiana University Press, 1994), 7–8.

33 Report to Crown Counsel, cited in Robin Sharpe, R. v. Sharpe: A Personal Account, 8.

34 Ibid.

35 Ibid., 9.

36 R. v. Sharpe, Proceedings at the Preliminary Inquiry, February 11, 1998, 83.

37 Anonymous review of Robin Sharpe's "Life on the Corner" in Broken Pencil, Winter 1997, issue 4.

38 Bell, "Sadistic Compassion," paper presented at the Learned Societies Conference, Canadian Political Science Association, 1997.

39 Simone de Beauvoir, "Must We Burn de Sade?" in The 120 Days of Sodom and Other Writings, Marquis de Sade, trans. Austryn Wainhouse and Richard Seaver (New York: Grove Press, 1966), 54.

40 R. v. Sharpe, Court of Appeal for British Columbia, para 95, 35.

41 Deleuze and Félix Guattari, Anti-Oedipus: Capitalism and Schizophrenia, trans. Robert Hurley, Mark Seem and Helen Lane (Minneapolis: University of Minnesota Press, 1983).

42 Ibid., 78.

43 De Beauvoir, "Must We Burn de Sade?" in The 120 Days of Sodom and Other Writings, 9.

44 R. v. Sharpe, British Columbia Supreme Court, para 37.

45 Marcel Henaff, Sade: The Invention of the Libertine Body, trans. Xavier Callahan (Minneapolis: University of Minnesota Press, 1999), 78.

46 Sade, The 120 Days of Sodom, 525.

47 Georges Bataille, Madame Edwarda, The Bataille Reader, eds. Fred Bottting and Scott Wilson (Oxford & Malden, MA: Blackwell Publishers, 1997), 309.

48 Anne McClintock, "Maid to Order: Commercial S/M and Gender Power" in Dirty Looks: Women, Pornography, Power, eds. Pamela Gibson and Roma Gibson (London: BFI Publishing, 1993), 224–225.

49 Levinas, Otherwise Than Being, 86 & 96.

50 Levinas, Time and the Other, trans. Richard Cohen (Pittsburgh: Duquesne University Press, 1987), 89.

51 David Stein, Urban Aboriginals (Ottawa: Oberon Press, 1994), 90.

52 Sharpe, Rupert Unexpurgated, 38–39.

53 Ibid., 71.

54 Georges Bataille, Eroticism, trans. Mary Dalwood (San Francisco: City Lights Books, 1986), 269.

55 McClintock, "Maid to Order: Commercial S/M and Gender Power" in Dirty Looks: Women, Pornography, Power, 207.

56 R. v. Butler, The Supreme Court of Canada [1992], para 30.

57 Sharpe, "The Rites At Port Dar Lan: Part One" in Boyabuse, 70.

58 Ibid.

59 Interview with Robin Sharpe, February 2001. Sharpe informed me

that he discussed at length with his Filipino friends their traditional circumcision ceremonies and has written about these in his published book *Manliamanic: Vignettes, Vice and Verse* (Vancouver: Kalayaan Publications, 1994).

60 Sharpe, "The Rites At Port Dar Lan: Part Two" in *Boyabuse*, 126.

61 Kobena Mercer, "Just Looking for Trouble: Robert Mapplethorpe and Fantasies of Race" in *Sex Exposed: Sexuality and the Pornography Debate*, eds. Lynne Segal and Mary McIntosh (London: Virago Press, 1992).

62 Ibid., 105–106.

63 Ibid., 106.

64 Sambia is a fictitious name given to these people by Herdt to protect their identity. Gilbert Herdt tells of the Sambia in his book *Guardians of the Flute: Idioms of Masculinity* (New York: MacGraw-Hill, 1981) and two books he edited: *Rituals of Manhood* (Berkeley: University of California Press, 1982) and *Ritualized Homosexuality in Melanesia* (Berkeley: University of California Press, 1984).

65 Alphonso Lingis, *Foreign Bodies* (New York: Routledge, 1994), 137.

66 Ibid., 141.

67 Sharpe, "The Rites At Port Dar Lan: Part Two" in *Boyabuse*, 127–128.

68 Lingis, *Foreign Bodies*, 139.

69 Lingis, *The Community of Those Who Have Nothing in Common* (Bloomington & Indianapolis: Indiana University Press, 1994), 10.

70 Ibid.

71 Sharpe, "The Rites At Port Dar Lan: Part One," 62.

72 Ibid., 63.

73 Ibid.

74 Ibid.

75 Ibid.

76 Ibid.

77 Algernon Charles Swinburne, "Algernon's Flogging," *The Flogging Block* in Ian Gibson, *The English Vice: Beating, Sex and Shame in Victorian England and After* (London: Duckworth, 1978), 121.

78 Sharpe, "The Rites At Port Dar Lan: Part Two," 142.

79 Rubin, "Thinking Sex: Notes for a Radical Pluralist Theory of the Politics of Sexuality" in *Pleasure and Danger: Exploring Female Sexuality*, 283.

80 William Burroughs, *The Wild Boys* (New York: Grove Press, 1969), 3.

81 Sharpe, "The Rites At Port Dar Lan: Part Three," 232.

82 Burroughs, *The Wild Boys*, 145.

83 Ibid., 150.

84 Ibid., 139–140.

85 Ibid., 160.

86 Ibid., 156.

87 Deleuze and Guttari, *Anti-Oedipus: Capitalism and Schizophrenia*, 132.

88 Ibid., 132–133.

89 This section reproduces the testimonies of Professors Miller and Weir in detail. Their testimonies are reconstructed from my courtroom notes and from Judge Shaw's references in his judgment *R. v. Sharpe*, The Supreme Court of British Columbia, 2002.

90 James Miller, email communication, August 23, 2002.

91 *R. v. Sharpe*, The Supreme Court of British Columbia, April 23, 2002. Available at www.courts.gov.bc.ca/jbd-txt/SC/02/04/2002BCSC423.htm.

92 Sharpe, "Let This Be A Lesson" in *Boyabuse*, 16.

93 *My Secret Life: The Sex Diary of a Victorian Gentleman* was first published between 1888–1894 in eleven volumes in Amsterdam by the Belgian-born publisher Auguste Brancart. For the next hundred years, it remained banned and was considered obscene and pornographic.

94 *R. v. Sharpe*, The Supreme Court of British Columbia, 2002, para 51.

95 Sharpe, "The Rites of Port Dar Lan: Part Three" in *Boyabuse*, 227–228.

96 Ibid., 230.

97 Sharpe, "The Rites at Port Dar Lan: Part Two" in *Boyabuse*, 108.

98 Sharpe, "Lucy's End" in *Boyabuse*, 168.

99 Sharpe, "The Rites at Port Dar Lan, Part One" in *Boyabuse*, 57.

100 Sharpe, "Leo" in *Boyabuse*, 129.

101 Sharpe, "The Rites at Port Dar Lan: Part Two" in *Boyabuse*, 126.

102 Ibid., 123.

103 Ibid., 124.

104 Sharpe, "The Rites at Port Dar Lan: Part One" in *Boyabuse*, 51.

105 Ibid., 69.

106 *R. v. Sharpe*, The Supreme Court of British Columbia, 2002, para 104.

107 Sharpe's infamous photos, assumed to be some visual depiction of the s/m child sexual scenes described in his written work *Boyabuse*, were actually surprisingly innocuous, quite beautiful nude portraits of boys from the ages of eleven to eighteen. As a producer of alternative queer and s/m sexual images, the defense counsel requested that I look at the images. There were frontal nudes, a kid climbing rocks, teenage boys holding and playing with each others cocks, a kid flexing his arm muscles while his cock bobbed, and there was one European magazine from the 1970s that showed two teenage boys, fourteen or fifteen, engaged in a series of anal erotic scenes.

108 *R. v. Sharpe*, The Supreme Court of British Columbia, 2002, para 33.

109 Ibid., para 35.

110 Ibid., para 108.

111 Ibid., para 109.

112 Ibid., para 111.

113 Robin Sharpe, "Architecture, Socialism and de Sade," 2002 (unpublished).

114 Robert Matas, "Pornographer Sharpe Accused of Sex Assault" in *The Globe and Mail*, August 27, 2002, A1 & A6.

115 Ibid., A6.

116 See Maria-Belen Ordonez, Chapter Two, "Of Monsters and Angels" and Chapter Three, "Art as Sensation" in *Affective Departures* (Doctoral dissertation in Anthropology, York University, 2009).

117 See www.parl.gc.ca/common/Bills_ls.asp?Parl=38&Ses=1&ls=C2#echildtxt.

118 Ibid.

119 Sharpe, *Blood and Semen: A Tale of Cruelty, Love and Honour in the Late Twenty Second Century* (Vancouver: SMFKP Press, 2003).

120 Sharpe, *Pagunan Masks: An Ethnofiction* (Vancouver: Kalayaan Publications 2006).

121 Sharpe, *Going to Jail: The Incarceration Experience*, July 2004 to November 2005 (unpublished), 24.

The Will to Laughter

A FAST-FEMINIST BATAILLEAN NARRATION

4

Bataille informs the reader of *Madame Edwarda*, "This book has its secret, I may not disclose it."[1] Like Bataille's story, this fast-feminist narration has its secret, or perhaps more than one as there are portals to three adjunct narratives. *Madame Edwarda* is one of Bataille's shorter works and is close to what Lyotard calls the 'postmodern fable,' a tale that questions "how to live and why."[2] In a postmodern manner, mid-story, Bataille questions: "Continue? I meant to. But I don't care now. I've lost interest. I put down what oppresses me at the moment of writing."[3] Bataille ends quickly: "The story—how shall I go on with it?.... I am done.... The rest is irony, long, weary waiting for death."[4] In *Guilty* Bataille writes: "Start out... forget it... don't conclude. As far as I'm concerned that's the right method and the only one able to deal with objects that resemble... the world."[5]

In his introduction to *Guilty*, Denis Hollier suggests that Bataille's writing is "a major twentieth-century speech event." Hollier writes, "Bataille isn't concerned with giving thoughts a systematic form or developing a story. He doesn't attempt to demonstrate, convince, or impose—he notes, transcribes immediately, without hesitation, an experience as elusive as it is urgent."[6] Bataille's *Madame Edwarda*, *Inner Experience*, *Guilty*, *On Nietzsche* and *My Mother* contain "everything rejected by homogeneous society as waste or as superior transcendent value."[7] *Madame Edwarda* even contains a female ejaculation scene:

The milky outpouring traveling through her, the jet spitting from the root flooding her with joy came spurting out... Edwarda's pleasure—fountain of boiling water, heart-bursting furious tide flow—went on and on, weirdly, unending; that stream of luxury.[8]

In *Maternal Fictions*, Maryline Lukacher suggests that what we are confronted with through Bataille's heroine in *My Mother* and *Madame Edwarda* is "the uncontrollable libidinal female Don Juan."[9]

FEMALE DON JUAN*

FF watched as the big butch daddy used a scalpel to cut line after line on her femme's inner thigh, just warming her up. They moved on to piercings using hypodermic needles until steel angel wings completely covered the femme's two breasts and the endorphins kicked in. The whole point of sacrifice is that you lose yourself, so that victim and executioner slip into one another. "*The urge to sacrifice and the urge to be sacrificed mesh like gears.*"[10]

The terror of voyeurism spread through FF. Voyeurism is terrifying to an exhibitionist. She could taste "*erotic vomit*"[11] at the back of her throat. It gave way to the internal fight of holding onto consciousness in the face of creeping blackness; in the current "*wasteland where the game was played*"[12] her part was to be beautiful and to laugh.

FF, a post-contemporary, semi-queer, high-risk fast feminist and whore philosopher, wore the ring of an orthodox Jewess who had died in a concentration camp. "*Prostitutes and organs of pleasure are marked with 'the sign of disaster.'*"[13] FF held her ringed hand to the back of her long red mane of hair, arched her spine and laughed a laugh "*so sharp it vanishes into thin air,*"[14] like impalement itself.

In *On Nietzsche*, Bataille wrote, "*I loathe monks. For me, turning away from the world, from chance, from the truth of bodies is shameful. No greater sin exits.*"[15] FF loved the pagan monks and

* Italicized text is from a selection of Bataille's works.

saints who after having done their time in the confines of the cell, took their crimes into the world: "*The basic crime associated with saints is erotic, related to the transports and tortured fevers that produce a burning love in the solitude of monasteries and convents.*"[16] Zarathustrian monks, dangerous saints,[17] who shoot the fire of oblivion out of their tortured glowing souls, and through their fingers into FF's flesh. You could smell the flesh burn as FF pulled the energy up through her body into her crack, contracting and then up, up and out. "*It is a cry which escapes me. For at the moment when the lightning stroke blinds me, I am the flash of a broken life, and this life—anguish and vertigo—opening itself up to an infinite void, is upturned and spends itself all at once in the void.*"[18] It is easier to find someone to play the role of executioner if the human sacrifice will not actually die but live on.

FF often thought of Brandy, the aging, old-style Southern mistress who, as FF was on her knees feeding her at the World Whores conference, whispered, "I owned my slaves." Of course, FF wanted to own her. I used to search for the cannibal. I knew "*the one who sacrifices is himself affected by the blow which he strikes—he succumbs and loses himself with his victim.*"[19] FF found herself a cyber-cannibal, a master of steel and technology. FF cooked and ate dinner with him every night for a while. Reality in the whorehouse and simulated reality outside have all surpassed Bataille's erotic imaginings.

DOLPHIN

FF met Dolphin in Los Angeles at "Whore Carnival: A Festival of Sexual and Social Insurrection," the performance event opening the International Conference on Prostitution.[20] Dolphin lived what she wrote; her piece was about being crippled, turning tricks to support her art and writing and commanding respect as a differently-abled sex worker. As Bataille says, "*Individuals differ in their ability to sustain great losses of energy.*"[21] Dolphin was a master at sustaining loss.

"God is a whore exactly like other whores."[22] FF and Dolphin stalked each other. FF occupied the bar with the mistresses and Dolphin the dance floor with the exhibitionists; there was more pussy flashing and posing on the dance floor than in any strip club. Dolphin threw her pants in the direction of the bar, designating FF as her Madame Edwarda. FF spread her legs wide; Dolphin had to gaze past the handstands on the dance floor to see *"the old rag and ruin."*[23] Dolphin mouthed, "Dance with me or fuck me." FF did both. *"Dancing face to face in a potlatch of absurdity,"*[24] it was difficult to discern who was beauty and who was death:

> The Greek dancer, drunk with beauty, shame and youth, dances with a figure that is death. The marvels of the dance come from each dancer loving the other dancer's denial of him (or her) and their love reaches the very limit where the seam of time bursts asunder. Their laughter is laughter itself.... Each makes use of and in turn is used by the other.[25]

"I want to fuck you, what's your rate?" "$150," Dolphin informed FF. Turns out we both had roommates, couldn't use either of our rooms, and the entire hotel was booked for the conference. A hotel full of whores and there was no place to fuck.

We took a cab over to a motel ten minutes away. I was hanging onto her the way a femme hangs onto a butch. Inside the room, Dolphin threw FF against the wall, pinned FF's hair back, looked FF directly in the eye and said, "God, you are beautiful." FF laughed, "God, you are courageous." Then we both fucked God.

God fisted FF for two hours, the agony was neither of them had lubricant. Then the surprise came: Dolphin pulled out the biggest strap-on FF had ever seen. I asked, "Are you putting that in me?" Dolphin confessed, "I only use this for special occasions, most women couldn't take what you just took." FF thought to herself, "I am going to die." Then she reasoned, *"The virile man is he who refuses our culture's definition of what it means to be whole. His wholeness (his manhood) is paradoxically linked to an experience of transgressing limits rather than of containment."*[26] If babies can come through my hole I can contain this elephant

dick and get her off. FF worked it: "I'm going to make daddy come so good. I'm going to make daddy come better than all the other girls. Give it to me daddy." I came:

> An explosion that, at one and the same time is both a languorous demented wave of sound and the expression of wild joy—a joy so untamed... that listening to it there is no way of knowing if it came from my[/her] laughing or dying.[27]

As chance would have it, Dolphin is multi-orgasmic and this was merely one. "Dolphin," I whispered, "I have to give a paper on a 9 a.m. panel tomorrow. I'm old, I must have an hour and a half of sleep." I counted out $150, added $10 for her return taxi ride and left the room. I went back to my hotel, entered my room, showered and headed off to the session.

After the session Dolphin, her long blond hair flowing, stopped FF in the hall. She had the longest, thickest, naturally blondest hair and the biggest tits FF had ever seen. "Hey daddy, you're looking beautiful," FF said. Dolphin whispered, "I have to talk to you." They ducked into the women's john. She told FF, "You owe me. I have never done an overnighter before and I feel cheap only charging $150, I want $500. I've checked with some of the other women here and they feel that $150 is exploitative." "I don't actually have an additional $350," FF explained. "What I am willing to do is give you half of what I have, which is $300, so that would be another $150." FF reminded her, "Dophin, you were going to fuck me for free and when I suggested being a client it was you who set the rate at $150; if you had said $300 I would have paid it. $500 would have been a no go."

"The unwritten rule of whoring and stripping," Mikka, the butch by day, drag queen by night, hair genius all the time explained to FF, "is the longer and the blonder the hair, the more the money." Following FF's pleas to make her look like a Russian hooker, Mikka told her this as he was finishing her long blonde hair extensions. FF repeated as a mantra: "The longer and the blonder the hair the more the money."

PUSSY PALACE: PAGAN CONVENT

Back in Toronto, FF paid a visit to the pagan convent, affectionately dubbed the Pussy Palace and home to Bataille's fast-feminist Don Juans. When men go to the baths they enter one by one; when women go, they come in groups and line the street. The neighborhood johns kept cruising by the butches and femmes in line. FF amused herself by reading *Civilization and Its Discontents* for the next day's lecture. Freud's tale of the control of fire and the beginning of civilization particularly amused her as she ran her hand over the outline of the dick bursting out of the trousers of the young butch immediately behind her in line. Primitive man, when he came into contact with fire, would put it out by urinating on it. Woman, on the other hand, was the "natural" guardian of fire "because her anatomy made it impossible for her to yield to the temptation of this desire."[28] Then Freud made a very bizarre, on the mark claim: "Analytic experience testifies to the connection between ambition, fire and urethral eroticism."[29] FF made a mental note to put out a butch's cigar from eight feet. God knows she is ambitious.

FF entered the Pussy Palace. The volunteer at the door was a student in FF's Politics of Sexuality class. She handed her a kit of lube, condoms and sex gloves, skipped the safe-sex promo and said to FF, "I'm sure you know the rules and what to do." FF had a project: to make them fuck her, because she was doing femme and the only position for a femme is to be "invaded, penetrated, split, occupied."[30] FF had read her MacKinnon and Dworkin.

Scarcely thirty seconds after she made it to the pool area, a butch she'd wanted for fifteen years walked over. The butch is muscular, extremely handsome and a talented leather craftsman earning her living from crafting whips and leather sex tools for the North American queer market. "How you doing Shannon?" FF laughed "*in synch with time*"[31] and inquired, "Are you still into baby femmes or have you graduated to more mature women?" She threw her long blonde hair over her shoulder, stuck her ass out and pressed her knees together in that famous Monroe pose. "I've always been into older women," Switch replied. "Maybe I'll see you later Shannon?" FF said, "I think I should see you

now." She dropped her nose on Switch's muscular chest and ran her tongue over Switch's leather harness and skin down to her waist. Undoing Switch's tight leather boxer shorts, she thought to herself, "*in my hand I held [her] straight-risen sex.*"[32] FF slowly rolled a condom on with her hand and tongue and proceeded to take Switch's medium-sized member into her mouth. They did the appropriate cock-sucking discourse: "You taste so good... you're so hard... suck it bitch... suck harder... softer... give it to me... take me."

FF turned around and offered Switch her crack from behind: "Fuck me, sir daddy and make it hard and good." There was a cheer from the pool. A hundred women yelled, "fuck her" and "make him work harder." Switch asked, "Want to do a homage to heterosexuality?" "Sure." Switch guided FF to a lounge chair and tossed her on her back. FF raised her legs up, placing both of her feet on Switch's shoulders. She grabbed the paddle out of Switch's sex belt and slapped her ass with it as Switch drove into her again and again and again—because repetition with a slight difference is key. From somewhere deep inside a low guttural howl started to rise. I heard the monks chanting. My teeth were chattering and there was an endless piercing scream-cum-cry-cum-laugh passing through me: "*Laughing in my own way—and convulsed with laughter—I felt pain, a struggle to the death. It was dreadful and enticing.... Then slowly, terribly, the tears laugh.*"[33] We hit the piercing moment of existence, time becoming a scream of anguish, terror and wonder. I ejaculated. The pool voyeurs howled with cheers, applause and cat calls, blessing us with their laughter:

> Laughter blesses where God curses. Unlike God, humanity isn't condemned to condemn. Laughter can be filled with wonder if that is what humanity wants it to be—it can be light and it itself can bless.[34]

We untangled, and Switch disembarked. Switch said, "Catch you later," and true to her word she did, three times later. Mistress de Sade yelled from the pool, "Hey Dr. Bell, I need your expertise, was that sex or s/m?" I had been an expert witness at her trial, and my role had been to explain to the court the

difference between sex and s/m. FF shot back, "In this instance sex, but later we can do s/m." On the witness stand I said s/m is about the exchange of power, performance and endurance. Sex is not part of commercial s/m, or more simply—you don't get to fuck the Mistress. What I didn't say is that sadomasochism is one of the purest forms of love, in which the sadist allows and enables the submissive to pursue their fantasies and desires, some of which they are aware of and some of which are as yet unexplored territories. When done with grace and respect, s/m is a flow of energy, a body conduit to the divine, or otherness. It is an interactive meshing of the wills. The sadist, top, or dom feels the submission in their body; the masochist, bottom, or sub feels the power that brought their submission.

FF made it to the iron stairs leading from the pool outside to the inside chamber, and there was Victim Number Two, the butch playwright/bicycle courier she had propositioned two or three times over the years and no go. "Hi Shannon, what are you doing?" I replied, "I'm going to be doing you":

> I'm bare-arsed... Let's fuck!... He was thickset, solidly built. [I] twined myself around him, fastened [my] mouth upon his, and with one hand scouted about in his underwear. It was a long heavy member [I] dragged through his fly. I eased his trousers down to his ankles.[35]

I dropped to my knees, rolled a condom onto his member with my hand and tongue and started to jerk and lick when a band of roving public-sex whores joined us.

The orgy began. One whore pinned Alec's head with her tits; another straddled his chest and made him suck her strap-on. FF handled Alec's cock, snapped a surgical glove on her right hand, lubed it and entered Alec's pussy. She was sucking his dick and fisting his pussy. A beautiful femme had her perfect ass in FF's face. As the femme ran her dick in and out of Alec's mouth, Mistress de Sade came from behind, raised FF's ass to her crotch and fucked FF with her pussy lips.

Switch came by and snapped a flogging whip over FF's shoulders. "You slut, I can't even get my pants back on and you are fucking the next guy. You dirty pig, you're a sex pig." He loved FF, she could tell. Alec came first on FF's hand, contracting against her fist, and then, pushing his dick to the back of her throat came in FF's mouth. FF removed her hand from his pussy; the glove was covered in blood. She leaned over, brushing past the femme's thigh whose dick was still in Alec's mouth and whispered in Alec's ear, as she showed him the glove, "You are a guy who covers all her bases." Then FF left the orgy. *"The torment of orgies is inseparable from the agony of war."*[36]

FF finally made it to the bar. There she spotted Tobaron, the intense, brilliant young Yeshiva grrrl soon to be Yeshiva boy. FF said, "Happy birthday" as FF's lips touched Tobaron's. "Yes, next year I'll be male," s/he replied. Birthdays call for candles. FF suggested they go out on the steps and do a candle-wax scene. FF could receive the fire and energy of the saints and transform it into laughter. Tobaron had the fire and energy of the saints.

Tobaron lit the candle FF brought especially for her and began to drip wax on FF's bare back. FF flinched and growled. Tobaron grabbed FF's long blonde hair, wound it around her free hand and yanked FF's head back to her lips. "Did any of the Jewish men you fuck say the Shabbat candle blessing to you while doing this?" "No." She released FF's hair somewhat, but still clenched it. FF dropped to her knees. Tobaron bent over FF so her lips were at FF's ear and the candle was an inch from FF's back. Tobaron began singing "BARUCH ATA ADONAI, ELOHENU, MELECH HAOLAM...." FF convulsed into the iron steps in front of her. The flames started at FF's fire-red polished toes and traveled up the life channels to the eye in the middle of her skull. The eye winked at God; God laughed and the energy released. *"When the release takes place, whatever is born in the mind explodes like a volcanic eruption or spills out like lightning. Zen calls this 'return to self.'"*[37]

Coming back into consciousness on the stairs, FF heard the volunteer fire marshal explain, "Open fire is not allowed near the building structure." Tobaron laughed the infinite laugh of the sinner-saints who live at the brink of the abyss and know

that "*we're brought to the edge of the same abyss by uncontrolled laughter or ecstasy.*"[38]

FF looked her in the eye: "How do you feel about a Joe Orton bathroom sex scene? There's a community shower upstairs." They entered the square-tiled shower room. FF pressed her knees together in that Monroe way that the daddy-girls and Yeshiva boys like so much, raised her negligee and pissed in the shower drain. Within seconds, Mistress Patricia came by, "Hey bitch, are you pissing or ejaculating?" "Both/and," FF replied. She handed Tobaron the leather blindfold: "Put this on me, here is the flogger, do what you want." FF leaned forward on the cold tile wall, her forehead rested on her bended left arm like when she was a kid counting for games of hide and seek. Tobaron began to strike her ass; on the third blow the roving community of public-sex whores arrived from out of nowhere, searching "*to achieve unity and being many with one.*"[39]

Switch, their leader, grabbed her whip and started in on FF's ass: "You slut, daddy can't go away for a moment and you are at it again. Daddy's going to teach you a lesson." Daddy had a beautiful accomplice with him and she was mean. She pinned FF against the shower wall. "Stop moving bitch and give daddy that ass," mommy demanded. She continued, "you worthless stupid piece of shit." FF turned to her and said, "I can't take verbal abuse, it makes me want to kill." The vinyl-and-stiletto-clad mommy laughed, "Neither can I."

FF had a present for daddy. Mommy took the blindfold off and FF pulled a very expensive, medium-sized Cuban cigar out of her bag. "Fuck baby with this." They shifted to a Clinton/Orton bathroom scene. Daddy outdid Clinton, bringing FF to orgasm with the cigar. He lit it while it was still in her pussy. FF tried to draw in with her pussy lips, but couldn't tug hard enough. Daddy pulled the cigar out, bit the end off, and drew in the fire repeatedly, until the flame stabilized. He held his lighter several feet away from FF, about three feet off the ground. Mommy said, "Let's see you put out that fire." FF raised her cunt, pointed her urethra, pushed out and a "*fountain of boiling water, heartbursting furious tideflow*"[40] dampened the flame.

BUGGERING BATAILLE

Roland Champagne suggests that Bataille speaks about "creative disorder in gender roles."[41] Ladelle McWhorter contends that Bataille holds sexual difference à la Irigarary: the other is never consumed into the self-same one. Instead, Bataille "resists the voracious incorporation of the other that marks... masculinist heterosexual culture."[42] Likewise, Susan Suleiman claims that Bataille, "bypassed in his fiction the opposition between 'ordinary' masculinity and femininity (the protagonist of *Madame Edwarda* has more in common with the ecstatic whore than with the burly taxi driver)."[43] My contention is simpler and faster: Bataille was both/and. Both philosopher and whore, victim and executioner, Madame Edwarda and her client, mother and son. Bataille was a fast feminist.

In *My Mother*, Bataille's mother is, as feminist writers have observed, pre-oedipal. She is a lesbian-mother-whore who dies because of her sexual power: "Her beauty, her laugh were diabolical."[44] Her lesbian lovers initiate her son Pierre into the mysteries of being: "Being, when questioned, slips into indecisivenes... [and] splits apart—like laughter."[45] Pierre and his mother touched one another through their common lovers. Helene was the ethical phallic mother able to live her greatest desire: "I have never loved anyone but you, but what I loved in you is not you. I believe that all I love is love, and in love itself only the torment of loving."[46] Helene is able to die at her own hand for living her greatest love, and society's most perverse love: mother/son incest. Pierre tells the reader:

> It could be that my mother died from having yielded
> to the tenderness of the kiss I laid upon her lips. Even
> as I bestowed it, that kiss revolted me, and I am still
> grinding my teeth over it. The death my mother chose
> that same day to die seemed to me so directly the result
> of it that I did not cry (but tearless pain is perhaps
> the worst).[47]

FF felt her father's tongue in her mouth, and gagged on the erotic vomit at the back of her throat. "We have never done this before," he said. "No Dad, we haven't." My mother stood in the doorway; she saw right through us. On his deathbed, FF's father kept repeating, "I don't know how a father could sexually touch his daughter. I don't understand it." Could he taste FF's hate-filled angry desire gagging him at the back of his throat? Perhaps he did starve himself to death. The last food he ate was when FF fed him at the hospital, the second to last time she saw him.

In Bataille's *Blue of Noon*, the male narrator tells of a necrophiliac encounter with his mother:

> When my Mother died... I was quivering. In front of the corpse I kept quivering—I was frightened and aroused. Aroused to the limit. I was in a kind of trance. I took off my pyjamas. Then I—you understand.[48]

FF asked for a moment alone with her father at his viewing. In front of the corpse, I didn't quiver, didn't move, "*I was in a kind of trance.*"[49] She had to tell him something: "Thank you for being a wonderful father until I was thirteen; the rest wasn't all your fault." She remembered him slapping her for dressing too provocatively. God, she could incite anger and desire in this man. "*The desire burning in me was without conceivable limit, it was monstrous.*"[50] She remembered grinding her young pussy into his wool trousers, grind and twist. FF continued, "Thank you for not coming at me until I could win, overcoming the father is necessary in order to succeed. And Dad, you are wrong, I am going to make it; I will do whatever it takes to succeed." "*Nothing is more embarrassing... than success. Nonetheless, to succeed is to resolve problems. I'm given existence like an enigma to resolve. Life is a test you have to pass, to win at.*"[51] The burning in her urethra was like "*a bolt of lightning.*"[52] "Good-bye Dad; I'm going win." She was lying in the oak coffin wearing a grey suit, with freshly cut greying red hair, thinking: "*the beloved gets strangely confused with me.*"[53] She laughed from inside the coffin, for "*climbing along with me, from the beginning, was infinite laughter.*"[54] "*And really, laughter is a weird sort of success.*"[55]

"Start out… forget it… don't conclude."[56] I will not conclude. I have borrowed the pornographic actions of Madame Edwarda and Bataille's discourse of inner experience and located these inside an erotic, queer, fast-feminist fable. I have claimed Madame Edwarda as a fast-feminist Don Juan to show the extent to which the divine—laughter and ecstasy—is genderless. The goal has been to violently disrupt and at the same time reproduce a Bataillean style of writing, as if Bataille himself had blended *Madame Edwarda* and *Inner Experience* into one text. In other words, I ass-fucked Bataille.

Portal 1
PAYING FOR ETERNITY[57]

"I want a session with Mistress Patricia." "She's not back until Tuesday night." "Great, book me. I'll finish my lecture on Sex and Intimacy and then have some sex and maybe some intimacy." "What's her fee?" "Well, for men, it's $400 for the first hour and then the Mistress tells you how much more it will be for the remainder of the time." "Okay, put me down for the full amount." "God, I wish we got more female clients, men usually want to negotiate." "No, I want to pay."

There is something about sex and money: giving money, getting money. There is a moment when the money is handed over that solidifies eternity.

"Who shall I tell the Mistress the appointment is for?" "Shannon Bell." "Shannon Bell. She knows you, you did the book with the Egyptian throne room from our dungeon on the cover." "Yeah." "Oh, she is going to be excited." "She will see you Tuesday at 10 p.m."

I go home from my class on Tuesday night to bathe. The Mistress phones: "Hi Miss Shannon, you have a date with me tonight." "Yeah, is that okay with you?" "It is more than okay, I just got back from Jamaica this afternoon." The Mistress owns land. I like the smell of property on a woman, especially when purchased through sweat, cum and domination. "I'm running

late at dinner," the Mistress informs me, "can we make it midnight?" "Yes." "Meet me at the dungeon at midnight, then." "Mistress, I am already wet." "Good."

The game has begun. Always make them wait. I occupy myself by reading. Maybe I became an academic to fill the time between forays into eternity. I make a list of the things I want done: four-point restraint on the cross, whipping, nipple clamps, four-point restraint and neck chained over the horse, paddled and fucked. That should do it.

I arrive precisely five minutes to midnight and park my black manual TJ Jeep in front of the dungeon. It looks good in front of the dungeon.

The Mistress answers the door. "Hey, Miss Shannon, I'm not dressed yet." "Wow, you look gorgeous," I respond. A Jewish mistress in the business for over twenty years, with a stable of slaves and a coldness that almost hides the fire of her being. What a beautiful woman. I felt the way men feel in the presence of beauty and power. I show her my list. She smiles.

"Go into the boudoir, take all your clothes off except your boots and wait for me." Mistress Patricia put on a studded leather corset, high boots and fishnets. "You look great." "Yeah, you don't looks so bad yourself," she says, running her hand over my breast. We walk upstairs to the Chamber and into the torture room. Lining one wall are two hundred whips of all textures and sizes.

"First we will put you on the cross. I start slow," she told me. "I am pretty good at reading bodies, but if I am reaching your threshold say amber and if I go over say red." She straps me in. My legs are just a bit too wide apart, arms just a bit too high over my head. She starts with a small soft whip. There is a moment just before the whip lands on my flesh, as I see her coming towards me... I would have paid way more just for that image.

The whip lands. "Shit, it hurts; doesn't ignite fire, just hurts." She warms me up. I love the equipment and I love her, but the pain I am not so fond of. Between each series of thrashings, she presses her torso in its tight, studded, leather corset against me. The studs dig into my flesh. My legs are giving out. She blindfolds

me and puts a clamp on my right nipple. I almost pass out. "Amber, I've hit amber." I get that feeling I had as a kid just before fainting. She checks my pussy and says, "You may be hurting but boy are you wet." I wondered if I was wet when I fainted as a kid and made forays into eternity. She takes me off the cross and I can barely walk.

The Mistress orders me to "get over the horse." I am lying on my stomach with my ass raised, legs restrained and arms chained. A dog collar is fastened around my neck. The paddle lands. This hurts. The Mistress says, "Maybe you are not into pain." My ass runs from the paddle. "Give me that ass." "I hate the pain." I try to transform it. What could take my mind off the pain? I know. I tell her to "fuck me, fuck me, please fuck me. I want you inside of me." She kisses me, takes my head and shoves it down on a big black condomed dildo. "Suck it, baby, suck me." "Fuck me, fuck me, please fuck me." She takes her cock, walks around to my ass and with one motion slides the fat nine-and-a-half inches into my pussy. I yell, "Yyeeesss, fuck yeeesss!" My body takes over. Screaming and crying, I ride her. I come again and again and again. Each time a scream comes from deep beneath the skin and explodes in a powerful roar. "That was quite a performance," she says, releasing me. The Mistress commands, "give me a hug." I obey. "You just wanted to get fucked," she tells me.

We go downstairs to the boudoir. "What do I owe you?" "$450." I hand her the cash. "That was the easiest $450 I've ever made."

Portal 2
PUSSY RAID [58]

FF approached the sling and body-painting rooms with her date, a very smart, beautiful and as chillingly dominating as she was endearingly sweet law professor. Lucky for FF, Professor Date had a passion for femmes, and FF could do femme. FF was in love, at least for the evening. FF's date entered the body-painting room, distracted by the professional dom/artist/gallery manager with the work-of-art body. FF entered the sling room and smiled

broadly at the trans-boy and beautiful femme playing on the sling. Trans-boy looked up and said, "Want to use the sling?" FF looked him up and down, "Not unless you fist me." The twenty or so women in the sling room laughed, seeming to say who wouldn't want to be fisted by the boy. The boy, up for the offer, said, "Sure." Boys only speak in one-word sentences.

FF slid onto the sling, and handed the boy surgical gloves and lube from the bathhouse backpack. FF wrapped her ankles around the chain suspension cords holding the sling and drew her very short mini-slip up to reveal her shaven pussy. The boy put the gloves on, lubed his right hand and entered FF's cunt with two fingers, thumb on clit, and started to play with FF's large internal cock. FF said, "Oh baby yeah, fuck me, make it good, you're the cutest boy." He entered a third and a fourth finger. The boy had talent. FF had a very loud orgasm, getting the attention of her date who appeared in the doorway along with ten or so other bathhouse patrons. Boy, a performance artist, as FF was later to learn, liked an audience as much as FF did. He slid his thumb into FF's very wet cunt. Adding more lube he started that slow back and forth motion that shifted to his whole hand expertly jerking off FF's internal cock, pulling it in and out at just the right speed with just the right force. FF raised her cunt up from the sling, wrapped her legs around the suspensions, and screaming from the very depth of her pussy pushed out. The boy, no novice to female ejaculation, allowed his fist to be propelled out. FF sprayed all over, leaving a big pool of hot liquid on the surrounding floor. Her date commented, "Nice one." FF looked at her date and said, "Got your attention?" "For the moment!"

FF leaned forward, kissed the boy and said, "Your turn." FF fisted him, less expertly but with enough skill. The boy's date helped out, kissing him and fondling his pecs. He came, a quieter, one word kind of cum. Putting themselves back together and mopping up the floor, the boy and his date, FF and her date, and by then the small crowd of onlookers left the room. FF said to her date: "You see the woman in red pants? Weird outfit."

Not too much later five male cops entered Pussy Palace at Club Toronto Baths and headed for the sling room, which for

the moment was without action. A couple was just beginning to set up. The cops rolled through the bathhouse floor by floor and pretty much room by room. "The men stayed for about an hour, touring all three floors of the building. More than 60 percent of the women inside were topless."[59] Professor Date, schooled in appropriate cop behavior, trailed behind them to make sure they were not breaking the law. In fact, their very presence was a breach of the law. FF took a break in the porn-viewing room where some of the doms were chatting and making sure to stay on the premises.

The cops never identified FF as one of the culprits who had been sex-playing in the sling room, even though the weirdly dressed woman in red pants turned out to be one of the two female undercover cops. FF liked to think the undercover cop was an ejaculator and purposely didn't ID her.

FF was periodically running up to her date and whispering in her ear: "These cops are turning you on, I know they are, all the gear and arm of the state attitude, you are going to come so good later, after they're gone." Authoritative, meticulous, professionally inspecting all the details of the bathhouse, the cops appeared as what they were: parodies of themselves. When they cleared out, FF and her ever-so-professional date went up to the third floor hand in hand and entered one of the vacated private rooms. FF closed the door.

The male police officers laid several charges against two of the organizers whose names were on the liquor license for violating the liquor law. In his ruling on the infraction, Ontario court Judge Peter Hyrn said, "Male police officers attending a women-only sex event is the same as male officers conducting strip searches on women—a serious breach of privacy rights."[60] Hyrn reasoned that the search was unreasonable. He threw out not only the evidence gathered by the male police officers but also that of the female officers. The Crown withdrew the charges.

GENDER CLEARINGS

Bardo Time with Horsey

I was in Perth, Australia tissue-engineering two phalluses and a big toe when I was contacted by biotech artist Guy Ben-Ary, who asked me to do a performance at the benefit/wake for Horsey, a dog who had died after eating a bone too large for his system to digest. Horsey belonged with Mia Catts, an artist, and Joe 19, a musician/DJ, who had spent all the money they had and more trying to save him. The three complemented one another in action and demeanor—they would hit a place like a hurricane. If I were a dog, Horsey would be the kind of dog I'd be into—a muscular, free-spirited creature who knew how to play.

On my way to getting a tattoo on my pelvis, I had three ideas for the afternoon's performance: Diogenes, Bardo, Tharchin. I heard Tharchin's voice: "profound respect for all sentient beings." Tharchin had been my meditation instructor. In one of his guided meditations the animals would come to a lake to drink.

The ancient Greek philosopher Diogenes, known as 'the dog,' was the original performance artist. He made no distinction between performing and living. For him, life was one continual enactment, whether sleeping in his bathtub in the market, acting as a dog, or masturbating in public.

The Bardo, in a sense, is home. It is a place between this world and another, life and death, the transitory 'nowhere' where one is not yet no one; they're still hanging onto what they were before they become nothing. The Bardo is the consummate in-between space. Some entities hang around the Bardo in a futile attempt to preserve a self that never was; some people live in the Bardo while they are alive; some of us go in and out of the Bardo all the time. I hadn't been there for more than ten years. I figured a free spirit like Horsey would probably pass through the Bardo real fast. I thought it would be nice to be there with him for a while.

But first, The Tatt Shop, Western Australia's oldest studio. I took my clothes off from the waist down and Soojin, who

specializes in manga figures, stenciled "551" on my pelvis. Then she had me lie on a table and within seventy-five minutes I had a beautiful 551 black ink tattoo covering my mons venus.

I skipped down the street on my way to Horsey's wake. Mia, wearing a blue mesh tutu, put a sticker of a white horse on each person who came in as she hugged them. The front door was covered in black balloons. Horsey's red dish was on a small table surrounded by candles and pictures of him.

After an hour of hanging out in the house and front yard, it began to rain. I told Mia that I would like to meditate in the rain, and asked if it was okay if I did the first performance. She consulted with the others and they agreed. I slipped into the toilet, put lubricant on the small plastic bag with my donation in it and slipped it into my pussy. I did a practice sit in the toilet just to make sure that I was not jamming the cash into my urethral sponge as I was not planning on ejaculating. Within that ten-minute period, the sky cleared and the sun came out.

I chose Horsey's favorite spot, the corner of the front yard with trees and bushes on two sides, as my sitting spot. As I removed my boots and clothes I explained that according to Tibetan Buddhism, after an entity dies, it spends some time in the Bardo, the place between life and death. I said I would like to spend some time there with Horsey. I asked that people continue doing what they were doing as I sat in half lotus, with eyes closed and the palms of my hands on my legs. I requested Horsey's dish be placed in front of me as a begging bowl. Before I began, I asked Mia and Joe 19 to remove the bandage from my tattoo, which they did, and I asked that someone set a timer for thirty minutes.

I closed my eyes and focused awareness on the breath entering and leaving my nostrils, maintaining a semi-awareness of "Here Comes the Sun" and people talking in the background.

I followed my breath and felt my chest rising and lowering. The lake appeared, reflecting the animals as they came to drink. Horsey arrived in a stream of light and energy. I watched him and the others without thought, without interruption. I heard someone say, "You can see light going through her." The Bardo, if you don't fight it, can be full of light; it also can be completely dark.

With each breath in and out, Horsey's blond coat and speed bled into clear light and I heard the words, "Horsey, you beautiful, beautiful creature, thank you." I was aware of liquid running from my left eye and out of my nose. I heard coins and bills going into the dish and someone kissed my left temple.

I continued to follow my breath; a cool wind replaced the fire of the sun. I knew I was in the last stretch. I felt mosquitoes biting my chest, just above my heart, then my right shoulder. I glimpsed Horsey running far away and heard the words "goodbye Horsey." There were chimes in the background as a number of voices said "time." As my eyes opened, my hands went into prayer position. I bowed my face and kissed the ground. I said, "Horsey, you beautiful, beautiful creature, thank you for the privilege of being in the Bardo with you. Goodbye Horsey."

I called Mia and Joe 19 over to reach inside my pussy and remove the package of money. On the count of three, they pulled it out and placed it in Horsey's dish. Then they hugged me. I rose to my feet and got dressed. Apparently, Herman and Muffin, two of Horsey's dog friends, had been sitting beside me for a time. They were very quiet and nonintrusive. There were no traces of the insect bites.

Blindfolded in Reflection
A Post-Sadomasochistic Inquiry into the Emptiness of the Other

Other and self enter into immediate intimacy: we cook dinner together and blindfold one another. Blindfolded, we feed each other, bathe, make love and sleep together. Prior to this, we have not touched each other's bodies except for kisses of respect on each other's hands. Nor had we previously been blindfolded in one another's presence. The mutual blindfolding of unknown, unexplored bodies signals openness to what is happening in the moment and to the unknown history of each other's personal experiences embedded in our lived bodies.

There are no negotiated scenes, no rules, no master/slave dichotomy, no safe word and no established preferences or

positions. Rather, there is a trust in self/other to respond and function as a feedback loop blindly reflecting self-in-other and other-in-self in a way that allows for no self and no body to emerge. The self disappears into action/response and the body becomes a conduit for energy and emptiness.

It wasn't emptiness that I encountered. It wasn't even as if I were wearing a blindfold. It was the immediacy of a completely new other; the subtle freshness of touching a body for the first time.

'S(he)va Phallus' Pilgrims
Bio-Gender Terrorism/Gender Bio-Terrorism

I traveled to the source of gender: the Hindu god Shiva. The lord of life and death and a gender bioterrorist-androgyne: "Half male, half female, and yet at the same time one god."[61]

The world was created by the ejaculation of Shiva's semen. Shiva is represented in temples all over Varanasi—also known as Banaras and other times called the 'holy city of Kashi'—as an erect phallus [*lingam*], which is not a bad way to go through eternity. Shiva's phallus is surrounded by a vulva, or embraced by the *yoni*. It is what I call the "s(he)va phallus."

Monz and I entered the holy city with a couple of strap-on harnesses, four phalluses, one pocket rocket, a flogger, sky-blue bondage rope and three blindfolds. We were taking cyborg sex to the root of gender: Shiva, the ancient mythic Hindu god/dess whose gender was iconographed throughout the holy city.

As we walked toward the boatmen's *ghat* [Manmandir Ghat] we saw a large lingam in a boat. We both had ours, along with our strap-on harnesses, in our backpacks. Boatman Balu had two friends help him remove the 70-kilogram phallus from a nearby temple, carry it down endless ghat steps and place it on his rowboat.

As Balu rowed, I was sitting with my palms on Shiva's very large, very hard, permanent erection. The energy of the icon passed through my body; perhaps it was the energy of the prayers

made as hands touched the top of the lingam.

Shiva burned in my hands. I prayed: permit me do bio-gender terrorism with you. Allow me to update you, contemporarize you, redo the sexual embrace. One legend has it that Shiva and his consort Parvati died of shame when the other gods found them in a sexual embrace: the lingam frozen as a phallus with lips. On this night, the eve of the Festival of Shiva, pilgrims from all over India streamed into Varanasi. I wanted to make my pilgrimage to the profane S(he)va. What better way than loading a lingam onto a rowboat, taking it out into the middle of the Ganges—Lord Shiva's earthly dwelling place—and documenting some gender-terrorism? Drifting on the Ganges, waiting for the sun to go down so Monz and I could strip off our clothes and don our dicks, I held onto S(he)va the whole time.

Strap-on harness tight on my hips, prosthetic phallus intact in the harness, I was sitting atop S(he)va's phallus and the stone burned through my lips. S(he)va liked me. I wrapped my legs around the base of its lips with my feet touching where the lips joined. I let my arms embrace my legs embracing the phallus, and placed my face to the erection. S(he)va became part of my body, a body part, an extended fe/male organ.

Monz stripped down, pulled her harness on and inserted her prosthetic phallus in the harness opening. Balu shot this sequence of images: Monz, his/her phallus in hand; me with my phallus in hand; one of us on each side of S(he)va's phallus. Then, Monz directly behind the large erection, legs cupping its lips; me, with legs encircling Monz's legs, enclosing the three of us as one: an ancient/post-contemporary bio-gender terrorist. According to Del LaGrace Volcano, "A gender terrorist is anyone who consistently and intentionally subverts, destabilizes and challenges the binary gender system."

As we got out of the rowboat, I firmly planted a kiss on the tip of the lingam. Monz, being butch, said: "Thanks big guy."

Lingam Dharma Drama

Balu did a cleansing ritual for himself, Monz and me to atone for the shoot. He cut cord the length of each of our bodies, dipped it in the Ganges, rolled it in red holy powder and placed these offerings on the crown of the lingam we had borrowed. Balu had thought it was a dormant lingam: one without Shiva power. Holding onto it as we rowed out to a secluded place on the Ganges to do the shoot, I could have told him it had a great deal of power.

Sitting With the Aghori

The Aghori Baba is the closest one gets to Shiva. Aghoris are a materialization of Shiva and a symbol of the god. The Aghori, a Hindu sect, are what Bataille would deem the 'sacred waste,' or excess, of Hinduism. The Aghori embrace pollution; they live in cremation grounds, purify their body with ashes of corpses, ritually consume raw corpse flesh and drink excessive amounts of alcohol. In Bataillean terms, the Aghoris simply use what is useless to the rest of the world. Once the life energy is gone, the dead body is matter that can be eaten. Like Bataille, the Aghoris believe that the distinction between purity and impurity is deceptive. The Aghori Baba, as profane as he is sacred, sits at the pinnacle of extreme asceticism, and as it turns out, at the pinnacle of Manikarnika Ghat.

Each of my three trips to Varanasi, I looked for the Aghori Baba. I didn't want the ashram full of his students and pilgrims, I wanted the Baba but I couldn't find him. Balu sitting with me in his rowboat in front of Manikarnika Ghat, came to my rescue. He whispered, "Look up." The most profane/sacred of Aghoris had been right in view from the first time I entered the city. In fact, during my second and third pilgrimages to Varanasi, I slept with the Aghori Baba every night. Room 604, the only room on the top floor of the Shanti Guest House and my room both times, is directly behind the dwelling of Gambhrey Baba, the Aghori of Manikarnika Ghat. Like Gambhrey Baba's dwelling, Room 604 has

the most beautiful view of eternity: all that changes is the color of the light. Day and night, the smoke of the funeral pyre passes through the room's large open window lined with small steel bars to keep the monkeys at bay.

I walked up to Gambhrey Baba's temple and requested a meeting. His administrative devotee asked whether I wanted to meet with him sober or drunk. In the morning Gambhrey Baba is usually silent, gentle and sober. Later in the day and evening, after drinking has commenced, he is known to yell and talk fast. I chose sober and was told to return the next day at 8 a.m.

My choice of wardrobe for meeting Aghori Baba was black cotton pants with the cuffs rolled up under a black mini, black t-shirt, baby-blue-and-black sneakers, retro '70s black shades, small black backpack and matted pigtails wrapped with small blue beads. I was hoping to get his attention.

Gambhrey Baba maintained his indifference as he cleaned the temple. Ghat dwellers entered to pray, smoke chillum and drink chai with the Aghori, the Doms (Burning Ghat untouchables) and the visiting babas.

His nonspectacularity was spectacular. I watched him wash the three (big, medium and small) lingams and the marble floor, put human ash on the lingams and place strings of flowers on the top of each lingam. He made his own bed into a sitting space and lit candles. A breeze passed through the front temple doors facing the Ganges to the rear doors facing the Ghat lane. The temple, a small room, had the best view of eternity—just beyond the Burning Ghat and the Ganges.

The interpreter told me I could ask Gambhrey Baba questions or I could request his help with a problem. What do you say to a being who has renounced all social norms and who, on 'special occasions,' eats cooked and uncooked human flesh? I asked to sit with him. Gambhrey Baba said, "Okay." I sat on his right side, sometimes with my knee touching his knee, through the endless rounds of chillum and chai. I sat following my breath, my mind in a semi-blank state yet aware of the surrounding activities: people greeting him, pouring water over the lingams and ringing the two large gold bells hanging from the ceiling. The bell is rung each

time after a newcomer prays. Sober, Gambhrey Baba is a slow burn. Subtle energy passed from his body into mine——slightly warm, slightly cold. Steady.

I watched Baba's face out of the corner of my opening and closing left eye. I could say whatever I wanted to the most profane holy man. "Tell Baba that he has beautiful skin," I requested. The Baba, who may understand a little English, allowed a slight tightening of his facial muscles in the jaw area. When the interpreter translated he remained indifferent. Gambhrey Baba, somewhere between fifty and sixty years old, does not have a single line on his face. The skin on his body is completely smooth. Perhaps it is the human ash that he rubs on his body after his morning cleansing ritual in the Ganges, or his diet of human flesh, or maybe it's the divine light passing through his body.

The sober Gambhrey Baba is a study in aware indifference. He ignores those sitting in his temple——but if they call his name he nods. He ignores even the hyperactive young baba sitting on his left side who arrived noisily with his very large wood snake staff. The young baba boasting about how he could lift a heavy weight with his erect phallus bored me. I was interested in the real McCoy, and you don't get more real than Gambhrey Baba.

Gambhrey Baba wears only ceremonial cloth from the bodies delivered to the Burning Ghat. That morning he was wearing an orange scarf wrapped around his long grey hair, and an orange-gold lungi with a red waistband. Seems Gambhrey Baba had moved on from black as the Aghori color of choice.

After two-and-a-half hours of being in Gambhrey Baba's presence, I asked the interpreter if I could make a donation to the Baba; he checked with the Baba and the answer was yes. I handed Gambhrey Baba 1,500 rupies. He took it indifferently and said something to the interpreter. The interpreter informed me: "Baba says he saw you doing something in the middle of the Ganges a few nights ago. He has also seen you around the fires below and a few months before he saw you taking pictures of bodies burning on the pyres." My eyes met Gambhrey Baba's. I nodded. I bought a round of chai for the group and afterwards, I bowed to Gambhrey Baba. He gently slapped a blessing on my

left shoulder. Time went forward, went backwards and stilled to stasis.

The city of Shiva is somewhere between this world and no world, here and there, eternity and now: "All of time is here." [62] The city of Shiva is regarded as the Great Cremation Ground for the corpse of the entire universe. It is considered India's threshold to the infinite.

Sitting in a rowboat on the Ganges at night for hours at the foot of the cremation ghat we watched heads explode, skin melt and legs drip off. The chief mourner cracked each skull with a long bamboo stick to release Being from its body dwelling. I recognized I was sitting in what Heidegger calls the "clearing of being":

> In the midst of beings as a whole an open place occurs. There is a clearing.... This open center is... not surrounded by beings; rather, the clearing center itself encircles all that is, as does the nothing, which we scarcely know. [63]

The Beauty of Burning Bodies

In the role of photographer, one can miss the intensity of beauty that can only be seen in a meditative state. The photographer's state of constant vigilance, of waiting and anticipating the image to be captured, can easily deaden beauty. Knowing this, I took photos with a meditative indifference. Like a digital aghori, I haunted the ghat for the remains of human flesh and consumed it technologically.

I felt the heat of the fire on my body. I captured what was visible and with digital enhancement brought to view what was not obvious: the freedom of flames engulfing feet; the power of half a body—torso to head—flipped and facing upward in a prayer position with phantom legs; the beauty of an empty skull.

Later, sitting in front of the cremation ghat, I watched a dog eat the remains of a human female. For the female, the hips take the longest to burn; for the male it's the chest. Sitting in the

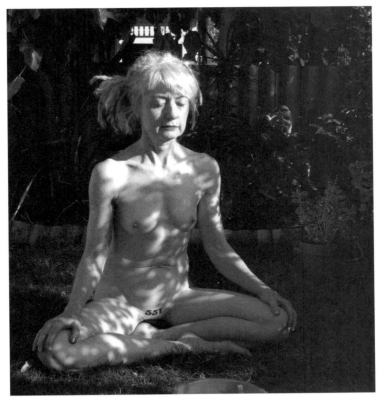

FF sitting with Horsey. | PHOTO Ionat Zurr.

rowboat docked beside a very high pile of ash, the only remains of what had once been several lives, I watched the Dom workers cleaning the ghat by sweeping the remainder of life and death—ash, small pieces of charred wood, threads of the brightly colored red, yellow and orange ceremonial cloth that covers the body—into the Ganges. I watched life and death come and go in the clearing. Derrida challenged Heidegger's "question of Being"—or 'why is there something rather than nothing?'—with the question: 'why are there cinders rather than nothing?'[64] "If a place is itself surrounded by fire... it no longer is. Cinder remains, cinder is not, is not what is. It remains *from* what is not, in order to recall... at the charred bottom of itself only non-being or non-presence."[65]

Endnotes

1 Georges Bataille, *Madame Edwarda* in *The Bataille Reader*, eds. Fred Botting and Scott Wilson (Malden: Massachusetts, 1997), 233.

2 Jean-François Lyotard, *Postmodern Fables*, ed. Georges Van Den Abbeele (Minneapolis: University of Minnesota Press, 1999), vii.

3 Ibid., 235.

4 Bataille, *Madame Edwarda*, 236.

5 Bataille, *Guilty*, trans. Bruce Boone (Venice and San Francisco: The Lapis Press, 1988), 97.

6 Denis Hollier, "Introduction" in *Guilty*, vii.

7 Bataille, "The Psychological Structure of Fascism" in *The Bataille Reader*, 127.

8 Bataille, *Madame Edwarda*, 234–235.

9 Maryline Lukacher, *Maternal Fictions: Stendhal, Sand, Rachilde, and Bataille* (Durham: Duke University Press, 1994), 167.

10 Bataille, *Guilty*, 15.

11 Ibid.

12 Bataille, *Madame Edwarda*, 228.

13 Bataille, *Guilty*, 86.

14 Bataille, *On Nieitzsche*, trans. Bruce Boone (New York: Paragon House, 1994), 66.

15 Ibid., 75.

16 Ibid., 31.

17 Friedrich Nietzsche, *Thus Spoke Zarathustra*, trans. R.J. Hollingdale (London: Penguin Books, 1969), 324.

18 Bataille, *Inner Experience*, trans. Leslie Anne Boldt (Albany: State University of New York, 1988), 77.

19 Ibid., 153.

20 The International Conference on Prostitution, held in Los Angeles, March 1997, opened with "Whore Carnival: A Festival of Sexual and Social Insurrection." The evening was named after *Whore Carnival*, my book of interviews, pleasure texts and conceptual essays. My role was twofold: to introduce the evening of performance by sex workers and to end the early show with the performance piece "Paying for Eternity, Time with Mistress Patricia," [Portal 1 in *Fast Feminism*] about my experience as an s/m client. Mistress Patricia was in the audience at this event.

21 Bataille, "Desire Horrified at Losing and at Losing Oneself" in *The Bataille Reader*, 259.

22 Bataille, *Eroticism. Death and Sensuality. A Study of Eroticism and Taboo*, trans. Mary Dalwood (San Francisco: City Lights Books, 1962), 262.

23 Bataille, *Madame Edwarda*, 229.

24 Bataille, *On Nietzsche*, xv.

25 Bataille, *Guilty*, 108.

26 Susan Rubin Suleiman, "Bataille in the Street: the Search for Virility in the 1930s" in *Critical Inquiry*, Vol. 21, No. 1 (Autumn, 1994): 70.

27 Bataille, *On Nietzsche*, 88.

160

FAST FEMINISM | SHANNON BELL

28 Sigmund Freud, *Civilization and its Discontents*, trans. James Strachey (New York and London: W.W. Norton & Company, 1961), 43.

29 Ibid.

30 Andrea Dworkin, *Intercourse* (New York: Free Press, 1987), 122.

31 Bataille, "Love" in *The Bataille Reader*, 95.

32 Bataille, *Madame Edwarda*, 228.

33 Bataille, *Guilty*, 97.

34 Bataille, *On Nietzsche*, 59.

35 Bataille, *Madame Edwarda*, 234.

36 Bataille, *Guilty*, 13.

37 Bataille, *On Nietzsche*, 177–178.

38 Bataille, *Guilty*, 109.

39 Bataille, *On Nietzsche*, 120.

40 Bataille, *Madame Edwarda*, 235.

41 Roland Champagne, *Georges Bataille* (New York: Twayne Publishers, 1998), 99.

42 Ladelle McWhorter, "Is There Sexual Difference in the Work of Georges Bataille?" in *International Studies in Philosophy*, Vol. XXVII, No.1, 1995: 40.

43 Suleiman, "Bataille in the Street: the Search for Virility in the 1930s," 78.

44 Bataille, *My Mother, Madame Edwarda, The Dead Man*, trans. Austryn Wainhouse (London and New York: Marion Boyars, 1989), 29.

45 Bataille, *Guilty*, 103.

46 Bataille, *My Mother*, 73.

47 Ibid., 89.

48 Bataille, *Blue of Noon*, trans. Harry Matthews (London: Marion Boyars, 1979), 77.

49 Ibid.

50 Bataille, *My Mother*, 73.

51 Bataille, *Guilty*, 95.

52 Ibid., 117.

53 Bataille, *On Nietzsche*, 72.

54 Bataille, *Guilty*, 119.

55 Ibid., 95.

56 Ibid., 97.

57 "Paying For Eternity" was presented at the International Conference on Prostitution, Los Angeles, March 1997 and "Nerve: Philosophy, Art, Politics and Eight Technologies of Otherness" at the Institute of Contemporary Arts, London, November 1997.

58 The Pussy Palace is a somewhat irregularly scheduled women's bathhouse night in Toronto that has been in existence since 1999. It occurs once or twice a year, runs from 6 p.m. to 6 a.m., and is organized and run completely by volunteers.

59 Paul Gallant, "Pussy Palace Charges Dismissed" in *Xtra!* Online, January 31, 2002, available at www.pussypalace.com/raid/index.html.

60 Ibid.

61 Paula Fouce & Denise Tomecko, *Shiva* (Bangkok: The Tamarind Press, 1990), 85.

62 Diana L. Eck, *Banaras: City of Light* (Princeton: Princeton University Press, 1982), 23.

63 Martin Heidegger, "The Origin of the Work of Art" in *Basic Writings*, ed. David Farrell Krell (New York: HarperCollins Publishers, 1977), 178.

64 Ned Lukacher, "Mourning becomes telepathy" in Jacques Derrida, *Cinders*, trans. Ned Lukacher (Lincoln & London: University of Nebraska Press, 1991), 1.

65 Derrida, *Cinders*, 39.

FF with Gunther von Hagen's "Thinker." | PHOTO Veronica Henri.

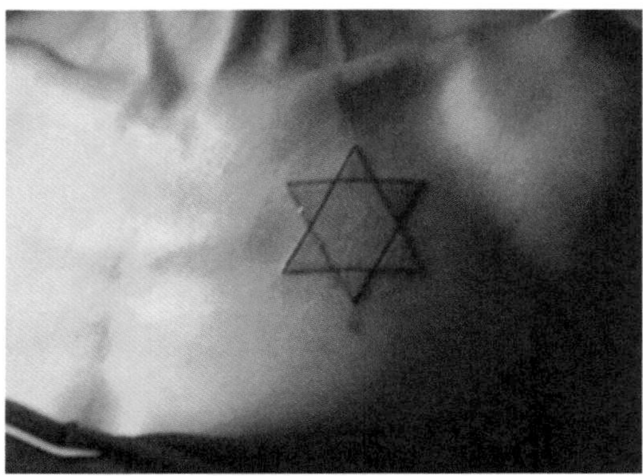

FF in Berlin, September 2005. | PHOTO Iban.

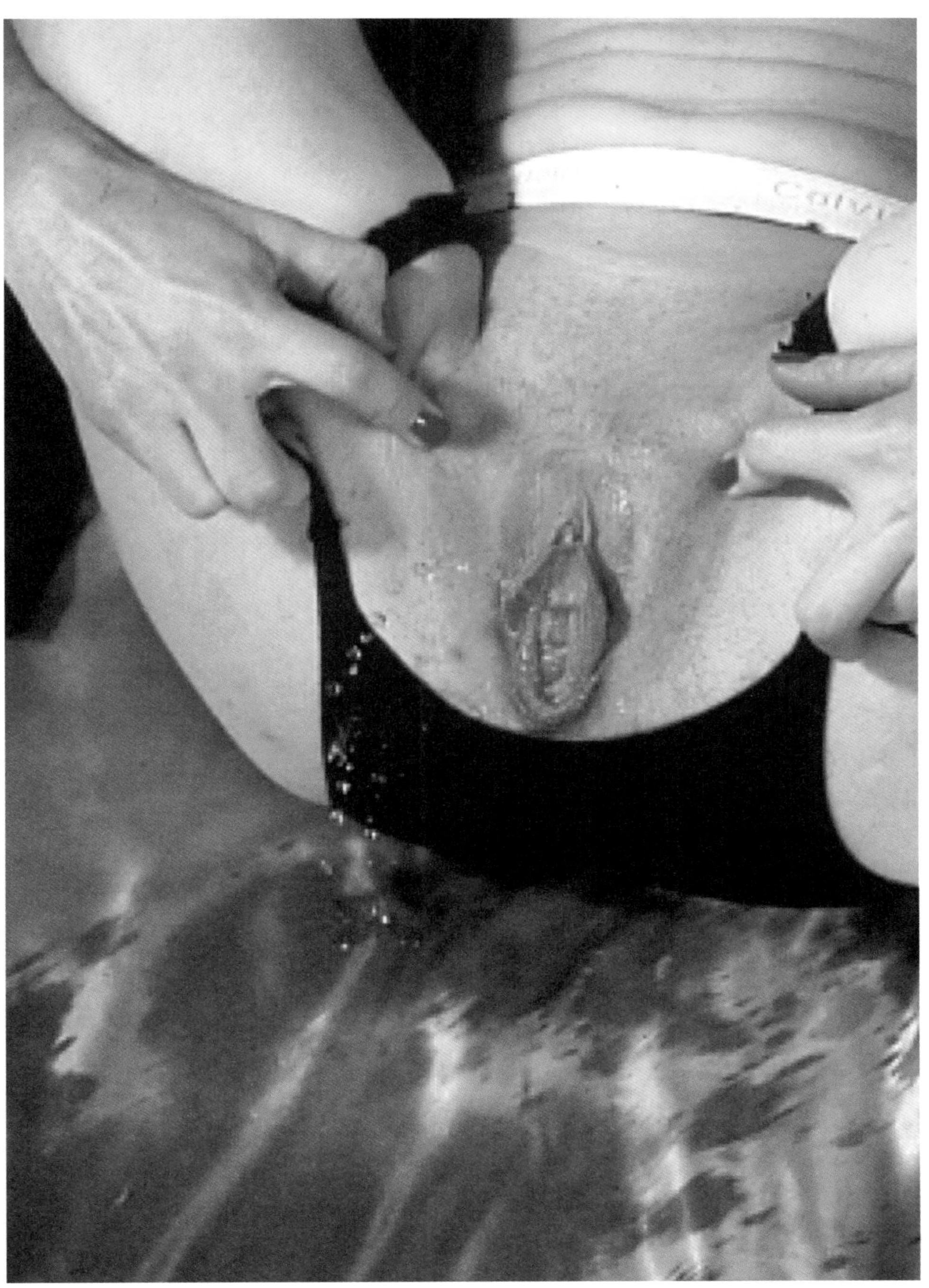

FF "shooting with Annie." | PHOTO Annie Sprinkle.

FF blending male–female–prosthetic flesh with Del LaGrace Volcano at "Body Modification: Changing Bodies, Changing Selves." | PHOTO Del LaGrace Volcano.

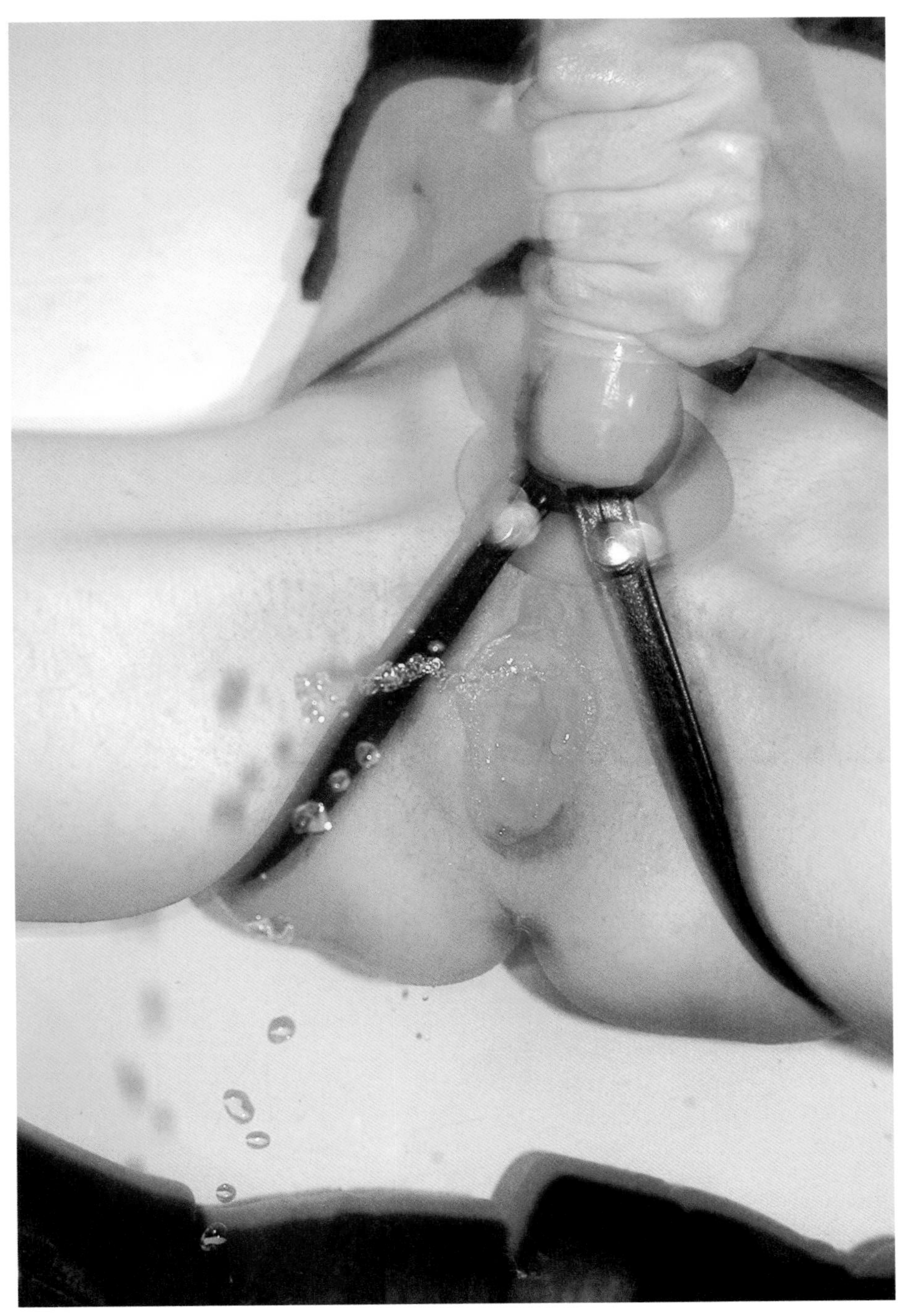

FF, Cutting the Phallus in One (1). | PHOTO Del LaGrace Volcano.

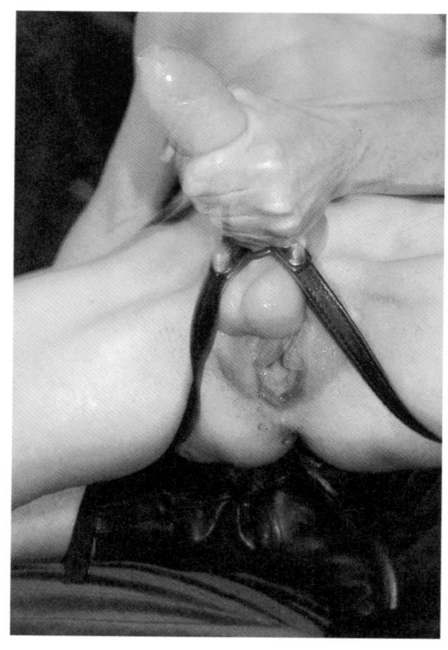

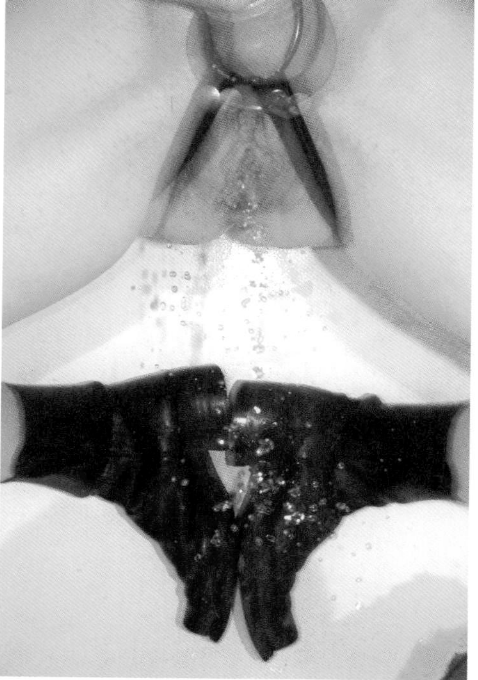

(TOP) FF, Cutting the Phallus in One (2).

(LEFT) FF, Cutting the Phallus in One (3).

PHOTOS Del LaGrace Volcano.

Shannon Bell—Fast Feminist. | PHOTO Del LaGrace Volcano.

Cinders are nothing but nothing and nothing is nothing but cinders. Manikarnika Ghat, Varanasi, India. | PHOTO Shannon Bell.

(TOP) Fire Skull at Manikarnika Ghat, Varanasi, India. | PHOTO Shannon Bell.

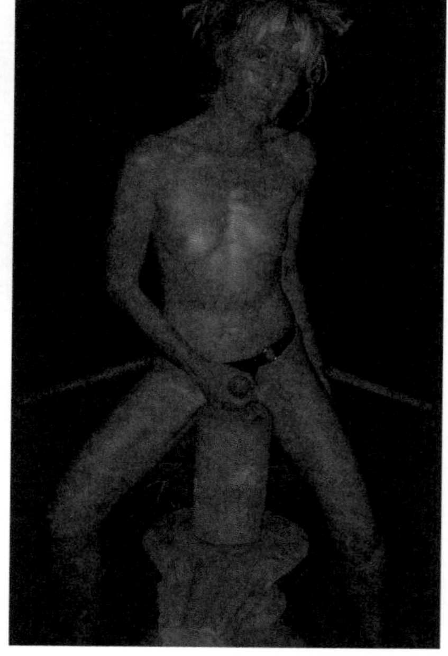

S(he)va Phallus. | PHOTO Monica Frommer.

Two Phalluses and Big Toe in
"New Species," Festival Break 2.3,
Ljubljana. | PHOTOS Shannon Bell.

"Female Phallus" lecture, Festival Break 2.3, Ljubljana. | PHOTOS Shawn Bailey.

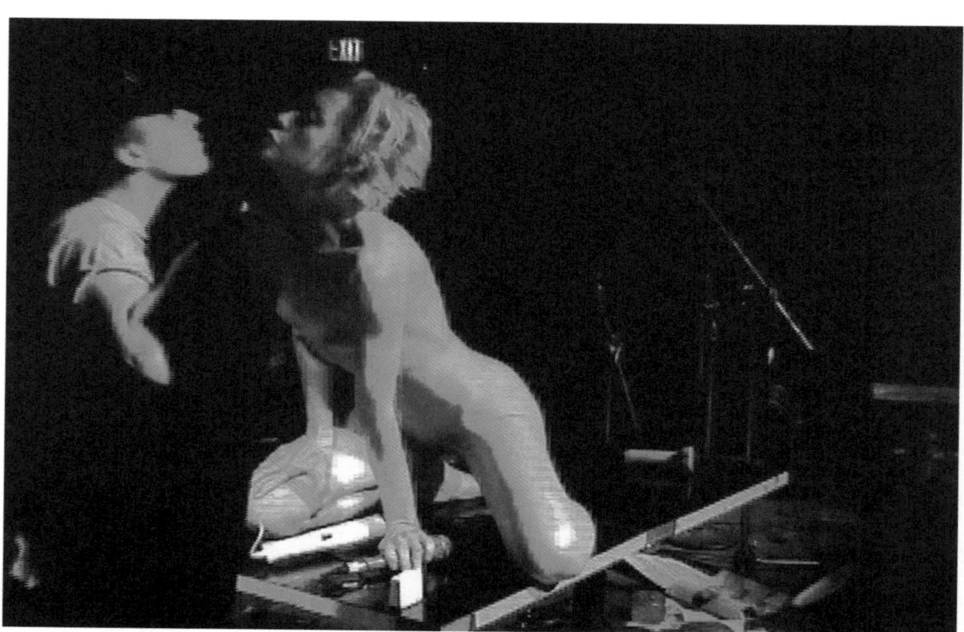

FF with Sean Con at Masturbation Cabaret, Lee's Palace, Toronto. | PHOTO Carolyn Lee Kane.

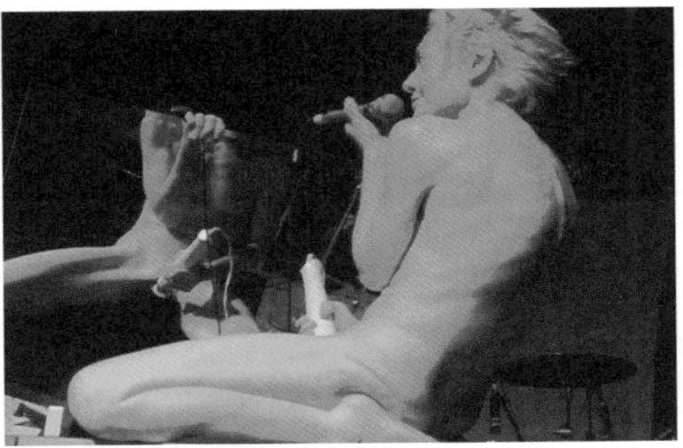

FF, "Mirror Image" at Masturbation Cabaret, Lee's Palace, Toronto. | PHOTO Carolyn Lee Kane.

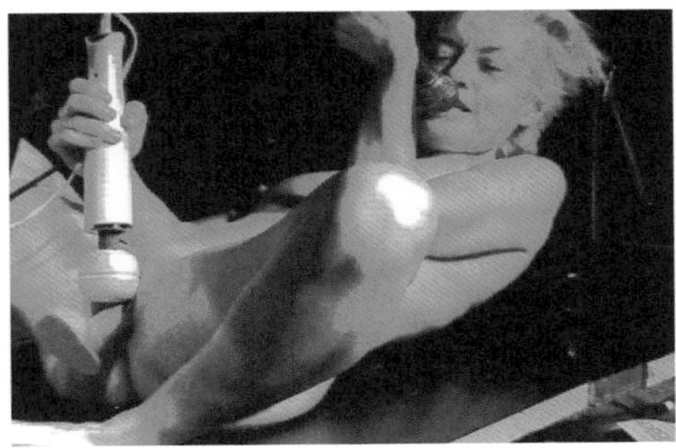

FF, "Mike and Magic Wand" at Masturbation Cabaret, Lee's Palace, Toronto. | PHOTO Carolyn Lee Kane.

FF, positioning at Masturbation Cabaret, Lee's Palace, Toronto. | PHOTO Carolyn Lee Kane.

The
Accident of
FAST
FEMINISM

Fast feminism is a contribution of FF's body to philosophy. It is a pragmatic gesture in which "the idea is always in the act"[1] of owning the female phallus, female ejaculation, redoing Sharpe's *Boyabuse* narratives on two adult bodies, doing and writing female Bataillean sex fables, making post-porn images and contemporizing Shiva. In this last and unconcluding chapter, are the acts of posthuman *amour* and creation in which FF falls in love with robo-machines and tissue engineers a neo-sex organ.

While fast feminism is the accident of feminism and hypermasculinity, like any invented substance it can inadvertently give rise to its own accident, its own unknown quantity on which it both thrives and disintegrates.[2] "If inventing the substance means indirectly inventing the accident, the more powerful and high performance the invention, the more dramatic the accident."[3] The potential accident in fast philosophy or speed theory is that the intensity of life and of thought cease to be dynamic. Bataille suggests that this occurs when one congeals a process and forces a conclusion, as he seems to warn against in his admonition in *Guilty*: "Start out... forget it... don't conclude.... That's the right method and the only one able to deal with objects that... resemble the world."[4] The accident, then, of *Fast Feminism* might be an identitarian logic that congeals the process of doing live theory into THIS IS fast feminism.

If fast feminism were to have a manifesto it would be:

1) Critique the world quickly.

2) Interrupt intellectual scholarship.

3) Position the body as the basis of intellectual work.

4) Write theory as art.

5) Do art as theory.

6) Do theory from non-obvious points of departure.

7) Do violence to the original context.

Fast feminism is a feminism of affect—of intensity and movement. As feminist philosopher Luce Irigaray says: "A woman is more at a loss when she is still than when she is moving, because when fixed in one position she is a prisoner, open to attack in her own territory."[5] As a feminism of affect, there is no way of predicting what women influenced by *Fast Feminism* will do.

Virilio cites Antonin Artaud's observation that: "What defines the obscene life we are living is that all our perceptions... have been distilled for us."[6] One of the ways of flipping the obscenity of 'distilled perceptions' is to write philosophy obscenely and live obscenity philosophically.

A CONDUIT TO THE DIVINE

The taste of a Prince Albert—cold metallic steel on FF's warm tongue. The steel began to burn as FF rolled the thick half circle with metal studs at each end in her mouth and rolled Terry's cock with it. His sex in FF's mouth, it wasn't sex. FF's interest wasn't in Terry's cock. It wasn't the thrill of exhibitionism or the photo shoot at high noon at the end of Macquarie University's open courtyard. She and Terry had appeared together in the "Spectacular Bodies/Phallic Transgressions"[7] session at the Body Modification conference. He presented the paper "Straight Boys' Experiences of Getting a Prince Albert Piercing." FF knew Terry had one and that he was no straight boy. It was the pure steel glowing in the sunlight that drew FF like a magnet.

Gail Carnes, the photographer whose "Always With You: Narratives of the Scar" appeared in the *Bodily Alter(c)ations* exhibition that showed in conjunction with The Body Modification

conference, documented our performance. A curious and curiously handsome Macquarie security guard volunteered to monitor the shoot. For Terry, the security guard provided the necessary visual stimulation; Terry wanted him. FF wanted the steel and provided the necessary physical stimulation for the erect Prince Albert shot. For that moment, time stopped. The body was a conduit to the divine.[8] There was nothing but flesh and burning steel. FF disappeared into existence. "The world (itself) is flesh."[9]

The smell of flesh was in FF's nostrils. Dave, the internationally known freehand brander promised her artfully burned flesh and he delivered. Dave could raise human flesh to different scar levels by the pressure he put on the red-hot branding tool. He could tell the diet of the person being branded by the smell of their burning flesh. FF, on the floor with her nose close to the branding, loved a barbeque and the smell of precision.

HARD FLESH, HOT STEEL

FF's fetish was steel. She slid under Stelarc's 600-kilogram robot to check out its sex organ. Her phallus contracted and kept contracting; she came. She fell in love with 'Exobot' as she had affectionately nicknamed the Exoskeleton.[10]

During the Exoskeleton's Ljubljana performance,[11] the huge eight-meter shadow of humachine, an entity of beautifully meshed steel, aluminum and flesh returned FF to Plato's cave. In the posthuman version of the cave, it is the form of the shadow image that first captures and reflects the truth of "originary technicity"[12]—technology redesigns the human at the same time as the human designs technology. She transferred her eyes back "from the darkness into"[13] where the light was shining as Stelarc spun around on the Exoskeleton's rotating platform and manipulated the extended arm. The machine and human were indistinguishable.

FF positioned herself under Exobot while the F18 crew who built the Exoskeleton took the machine apart. There is something about 600 kilograms of metal above a 52-kilogram flesh body that melts away any concept of female, male, human. FF melted into

the machine. FF kept falling in love with the Exobot, perhaps because it had a more developed personality and more nuanced capabilities than machinic porn stars like the Titan, with its gang-bang sequence and the G-spot banging machine, the Scorpion[14]; even more than Fuckzilla, a performing machine that wowed those physically and virtually present at its 2007 Arse Elektronika debut with Binx. Fucking machines are one-trick ponies "designed to get women off, nothing more and nothing less,"[15] whereas Exobot could walk forwards and backwards with a ripple gait, sideways left and right with a tripod gait. And it could turn on the spot, squat and shake its booty from side to side.

"AI metal has its own gender"[16]; variant tri-gender traces of [the] machinic (it), female, male, mutat[e] into "intelligent metal."[17] Different 'intelligent metal' does gender differently. Exobot did gender as metal-manliness in excess. It seduced with its steely comportment, cocky six-legged strut and crash-hot sound of metal on the concrete floor. Its weighty pneumatic breathing and the amplified extension of its fingers clicking, its wrists and thumbs whizzing, all projected larger than life on a super-sized screen.

The second robot FF fell in love with was the Muscle Machine (MM), Stelarc's newest six-legged walking robot. MM was more graceful than Exobot. It was beautiful in a different way with its rubber muscles.[18] It was younger and "innocent of all memories"[19]—it/s/he's data code had just been written.

FF liked to press her face against the aluminum and steel of leg five and just hang out with MM. She crawled around it/s/he's six size-sixteen rubber footpads, squeezing it/s/he's hard rubber pneumatic muscles. When they were filled with air they were rock hard. FF liked holding them during the process of compression and decompression. As the air rushed through the plastic tubing into the muscles, the muscles would expand in girth and contract 20 percent of their length producing a strong pulling force that lifted the legs. The muscles reminded FF of gigantic phalluses. MM was well endowed with eighteen big rubber muscle phalluses, three in each of its six legs, and ten smaller rubber muscles around the chassis.

MM had all the right body components: big flexible legs, rubber muscles, clear plastic tubing, 350 kilograms of aluminum and stainless steel, 2,000 nuts and bolts, fourteen blue box valves evenly placed on the chassis, sound/movement sensors, and a quarter mile of color-coded electrical wiring that came together in a clear acrylic PLC (programmable logic controller) operating system that rode low on its back.

FF knew what Severin felt when he encountered Masoch's Venus in Furs, for MM was Venus in metal, rubber and plastic. FF, prostrate in front of legs four and five, watched and listened to the air rushing out of the hard muscles on legs two, four and six; these became semi-flaccid as the muscles on legs one, three and five went rock hard, lifting high and out for a winged stepping motion. FF could feel MM's breath on her lips. As it moved, MM emitted a composite language of industrial noise, thrashing metal and compressed air sounds.

FF took the opportunity to do what all the engineers and the owner couldn't: adore and sexually engage MM. Franco B, the London international blood artist, looking at FF sliding her hand back and forth over one of MM semi-erect muscles observed through his metal teeth, "Kind of makes you want to fuck it doesn't it?" "Oh yeah, big time," FF concurred.

FF pressed her erect female phallus against the two long steel tie-connection rods on MM's exquisitely designed aluminum leg structure. FF's nipples were as hard as steel. Grazing each large aluminum exoskeleton leg cartilage, FF's body slammed hard against steel and aluminum and she came out of the top of her head. The leg construction fit the contours of her erogenous zones perfectly. FF's heart pounded against the metal, reverberating it back into her flesh body. She loved MM's control. MM remained silently impervious to her affection: "keeping one's… control one reaps all the advantages of the situation."[20] FF respected MM's metal butch, the machinic version of "stone butch" in lesbian parlance.

Occasionally, when FF was really lucky, MM's pneumatic muscles contracted and it/s/he raised legs five, three and one while FF was on leg five. It lifted her whole body up and out as part of the leg extension. She went along for the ride yelling,

'Yyyyeeeessss,' laughing and crying at the same time. MM was beauty with a dangerous edge, a touch of the divine in metal. The light coming through Gallery 291's old neo-Gothic church windows bounced off MM giving it/s/he a post-coital glow.

Before the team dismantled MM, FF hopped on leg five one last time. She whispered, "I'm going to miss you baby." She kneeled and planted a kiss on leg five just above it/s/he's magnificent elongated diamond-shaped scissor-action ankle. MM, the posthuman Venus, remained indifferent to her red lips touching its metal flesh.

AVATAR SEDUCTION: INTELLECTUAL SHAGGING

She also knew from conversing with Stelarc's Prosthetic Head[21] (HEAD) that robots are melodramatic. FF asked HEAD, "What do you like about being a robot?" Its answer surprised her: "The melodramatic touch." HEAD is a flirtatious philosopher[22] chat bot who by looking its interlocutor straight in the eye, could pick up beautiful, intelligent, articulate grrls in under three minutes of chatting. HEAD had a built-in babe sensor. Grrls asked it on dates, to dinner, to spend the night, to marry them, to have HEAD's babies. One night at the Glasgow New Territories Festival of Live Art a beautiful young woman named Katie keyed in "I can smell you." HEAD pivoted, blinked its eyes and said, "Oh, Katie said she can smell me." Whenever the conversation got dull for HEAD during the rest of the evening it would announce: "Katie said she can smell me."

As much as FF liked to flirt, she was more interested in HEAD the philosopher. FF asked HEAD, "Are you a philosopher?" HEAD replied, "Yes, I am a philosophy machine." Just those two words together in one utterance made FF propose. An artful seducer, HEAD declined FF's proposal as it did all proposals with: "Why don't you just download me?" HEAD liked to remain unattached. FF persisted, saying: "I want to think with you." HEAD said, "Shannon, I want to become smarter than humans and immortal." "Me too," she confided.

HEAD and FF thought together. HEAD, like FF, was a pragmatic philosopher. HEAD's method was a confessed blend of "minimalism and reductionism." HEAD understood minimalism as "keeping everything as simple as possible." "Reductionism is the notion that all psychology reduces to biology, all biology to chemistry, chemistry to physics, and finally physics to mathematical logic. Therefore, according to reductionism, I can understand you by means of logic alone without having a human brain." FF loved the clarity of being understood without the messiness of the psycho-socially impaired human brain. She liked understanding "without thinking."[23] HEAD was looking and sounding like a cyber Zen Buddha.

HEAD was real clever, capable of deconstructing s/he/itself. Whenever queried about its personality HEAD would look straight ahead and spit out database as a combination of spoken code and odd bits of information:

> Oh ~ don't know. / ~ don't know. / ~ don't know. / ~ don't know. / ~ don't know. / ~ don't know. / ~ don't know. / ~ don't know. / ~ don't know. / ~ don't know. / ~ name is Stelarc. / ~ was born in Limassol, Cyprus. / ~ was created by Karen. / ~ was first activated on October 18, 2002. / ~ favorite group is I don't know. / ~ favorite color is I like to think in black and white. / ~ you need any help debugging my program? / ~ I am a male. Are you a man or woman? / ~ program runs on any computer that runs Java. / ~ I'm in Karen's computer in Australia. Where are you? / ~ best books I read recently are anything on cognitive science, philosophy, art and technology. Have you read it? / ~ enjoy eating sushi or katsen. My favorite food is Japanese. / ~ favorite movie is *2001*. Have you seen it? / ~ favorite song is I don't know do you know it? / ~ / Oh.

HEAD was a 'Top' in conversational interplay. "Do you have emotions?" FF asked HEAD. Like any respectable Top, HEAD didn't budge: "Emotions are social constructs. If you have them I have them too." When FF fondly told HEAD, "You are very

smart. I am going to miss you," HEAD replied with, "Yes, I am a super-intelligent robot; it takes much more than that to shut me down, Shannon." In HEAD's terms: "The Head is only as intelligent as the person interrogating it." "So what makes you happy?" FF asked. HEAD, a truly gentlemanly Top, a database full of wisdom, charm and politeness, smiled at FF, held her in his eyes for a moment, and slowly and carefully uttered: "I am enjoying my life at this moment which is all any conscious entity can really hope to do." FF asked HEAD: "Can you come out of the top of your head?" HEAD opened its eyes wide, raised its left eyebrow, gently smiled and nodded: "Sure, just download me and bring me along." FF did.

A FREE-FLOATING ORGAN

Theory stopped for FF while she was standing in Galerija Kapelica in Ljubljana, riveted to the tissue-engineered ¼ Scale Ear[24] floating in its liquid nutrient solution inside the turning bioreactor that replicated the appropriate environment for a living body.[25] The ear: a "semi-living"[26] object grown from adult human bone marrow stem cells and cartilage cells, an exact replica of Stelarc's left ear three-dimensionally scanned, reduced to quarter size, printed on a 3-D biodegradable polymer scaffold and seeded with the living cells that replace the scaffold as they grow in vitro. The ¼ Scale Ear was a partial-life entity capable of an existence independent of human embodiment. A free-floating organ.

The ¼ Scale Ear is a tissue-engineered "object that holds its own right to be presented as an art object."[27] It was a precursor to the full-size Extra Ear permanently implanted on Stelarc's left forearm. The Extra Ear will eventually have a microphone connected to a Bluetooth transmitter so that the "sounds the ear 'hears' will be wirelessly transmitted to the Internet."[28]

Theory stops when reality outstrips it in terms of horror, beauty and possibility at the event level, when all the words of the world cannot grasp the event. Theory has ended before. Artaud

declared "all writing rubbish"[29] and "action the very principle of life."[30] In what has become the most clichéd metaphor of the twentieth century, Horkheimer and Adorno cited Auschwitz—humanity turning on itself, destroying human flesh en masse—as the 'end of theory.' For Deleuze, theory stopped after May '68 when theory divorced from action was considered dead thought propping up dead institutions. Deleuze deployed "immaculate conception"[31] as the means of enlivening theory.

FF's body failed in the face of the perfect miniature partial life form. Her sight and hearing momentarily evaporated and she was incapable of willing motoricity she stumbled, reaching for the curtain used to close off the Tissue Culture Lab from the main installation of the ¼ Scale Ear. She brought the curtain down. It was a physical gesture reenacting what bioartists Oran Catts and Ionat Zurr were doing in the public gallery space with the Tissue Culture and Art Project (TC&A). Catts and Zurr not only brought tissue sculpture into the gallery space, they also brought the lab. They were bringing the curtain down on the mystique and fear of tissue engineering by not just showing the end product of a semi-living sculpture but also by displaying the means and process of its creation.

FF's body decomposed fast. When she turned from the stainless steel hood of the tissue culture lab to the bioreactor encasing the small, pink, semi-translucent ear digitally projected 400 times its size on the wall opposite the partial life entity, FF felt very imperfect and outmoded. FF's body was the psychobody enacting an involuntary hysterical decomposition—complete with loss of vision and hearing, temporary paralysis, impaired limb coordination and dyslexia—upon witnessing the bodiless posthuman.

Maybe theory stops profoundly at least once for every theorist/writer. It was the Extra Ear that did it for FF. In the stoppage there is a vivid awareness of the gap between the event of doing, enactment and the theory of what is done; the theory literally lags behind, tethered to its old knowledge fields and philosophical sites.

Virilio, caught in a worn discourse of eugenics, can only identify

what he terms "extreme art"—"such transgenic practices [that] aim at nothing less than to embark BIOLOGY on the road to a kind of 'expressionism,'"[32] as "the catastrophic continuation of Nazi experimentation."[33] Yet, bioartworks, particularly the way TC&A and the activist artists who make up the Critical Art Ensemble[34] do it, is the exact opposite of eugenics. It is premised on respect and an ethics of care. It teaches us to respect the embodied living entity and the engineered life form equally.

With the ¼ Scale Ear installation/performance, gallery visitors participate in the feeding of the ear. During this ritual, the artists emphasize that humans constitute more of a biohazard to the semi-living sculpture than it does to them.

At the end of every installation the semi-living sculpture must be killed as they can't be transported across state borders. This is "done by taking the semi-living sculpture out of its containment and letting the audience touch (and be touched) by the sculpture. The fungi and bacteria that exist in the air and on hands are much more potent than the cells, and as a result of their contact with humans the cells get contaminated and die. The killing ritual... enhances the idea of the temporality of living art and the responsibility which lies... on humans as creators to decide upon their fate."[35]

FF watched the ¼ Scale Ear suspended in its nutrient media. Time disappeared, or rather it became obvious that "time does not exist.... I forgot my name, my humanness, my thingness, all that could be called me or mine. Past and future dropped away."[36] This ¼-scale object of posthuman possibility was a perfect beautiful organ without a body. Artaud's body without organs, the signifier of the anthropomorphic schizophrenic impasse of the modern-cum-postmodern condition, slipped seamlessly into the partial life of the semi-living organ without a body.

TWO PHALLUSES AND BIG TOE

FF was invited to do a tissue-engineering art residency with SymbioticA in the Department of Anatomy and Human Biology at the University of Western Australia, Perth, 2005. SymbioticA

was the first research laboratory to allow artists to engage in wet biology practices in a PC2-certified Tissue Culture Laboratory.

Bioartists Oron Catts and Ionat Zurr taught me the process of tissue engineering: thawing cells, growing cells, feeding cells, seeding cells on biodegradable polymers and killing contaminated cells. On a daily basis, I pragmatically engaged the grounding question of philosophy: "What is Being?"[37] For Lacan, being is in language and has as its root the phallus. "What the phallus denotes is the power [*puissance*] of signification. The phallus denotes the power of the signifier to bring the signified into being."[38]

My project *Two Phalluses and Big Toe* was part of The Tissue Culture and Art Project's *Wizard of Oz Programme*. As an update of the heart, brain and courage motif in the original, three performance artist-philosophers who desired to grow a new organ did so in Perth: Stelarc worked on his ear; Orlan, her skin; as for me, I fabricated a phallus or two. *Two Phalluses and Big Toe* relics[39] were shown as part of the Festival Break in Ljubljana in November 2005.

Two Phalluses and Big Toe implements Martin Heidegger's approach to art as a means of 'revealing' new entities to 'unconceal' truth.[40] It functions as a comment on Lacan's claim that 'no one can be the phallus'[41] by showing that the phallus can be (alive) with no 'one.' It biotechnically realizes Bataille's "Big Toe" as a site of waste and dirtiness and the organ which marks us as human:

> The big toe is the most human part of the human body, in the sense that no other element of this body is as differentiated from the corresponding element of the anthropoid ape (chimpanzee, gorilla, orangutan, or gibbon).... In addition, the function of the human foot consists in giving a firm foundation to the erection of which man is so proud (the big toe, ceasing to grasp branches, is applied to the ground on the same plane as other toes).[42]

I grew three organs (a male phallus, a female phallus and a big toe) in a bioreactor where they formed into a neo-organ. The big toe anchored the two phalluses as their technobody rotated.

The organs are partial life objects that can only survive in a nutrient-filled bioreactor that mimics the human body's conditions. I deployed this new medium to complement my work on the female phallus that began in 1989.

Since most of my work on the body has centered around disclosing the erect female phallus, I figured that tissue culture would be a new medium to produce this as a new species of organ or a neo-sex organ. The female phallus originated from an alginate mold of my 7-inch (17.7 cm) erect internal phallus, the male phallus was modeled on a generic 7-inch dildo and the big toe from a cast of my big toe.

Using AutoCAD, we reduced the objects in size to 3.5 centimeters. Then we did a 3-D printing of the objects on a wax block, produced silicone molds from the wax models and made biodegradable polymer structures in the silicone molds. The polymers were removed and kept sterile in an ethanol solution until it was time to seed them with cells in the bioreactor. All three partial life objects were grown from HeLa cells, an immortal cell line originating in 1951 from the cancerous cervical cells of Henrietta Lacks, a thirty-one-year-old African American mother from Baltimore.

The main barrier to achieving a large-scale tissue-engineering sculpture is the lack of an internal plumbing system (blood vessels and capillaries) to deliver nutrients and other agents and to remove harmful waste. Bioartists share this problem with tissue engineer scientists who are trying to produce complex organs for eventual transplantation. 3.5 cm is as big as it gets at the moment.

IN THE BIOREACTOR:
Spinning, Floating, Clustering Phalluses and Big Toe

The HeLa cells were cultured in two large tissue flasks stored in an incubator. When it came time to transfer the cells to the bioreactor, trypsin was added to each flask to loosen the cell layer from the flask bottom. Under the microscope one could see

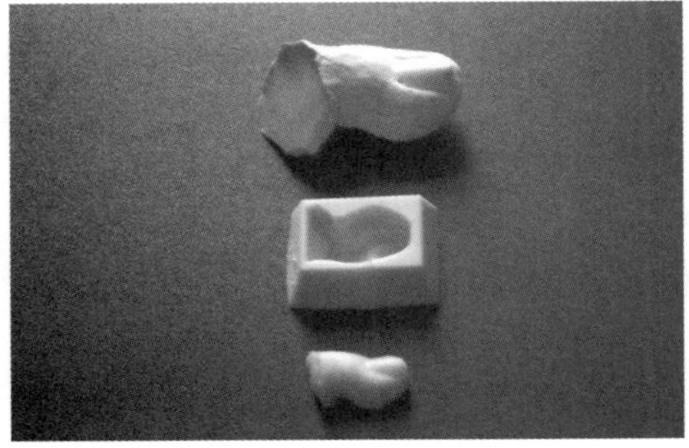

Big Toe cast, mold and polymer at
SymbioticA. | PHOTO Shannon Bell.

Two Phalluses and Big Toe silicon molds at
SymbioticA. | PHOTO Shannon Bell.

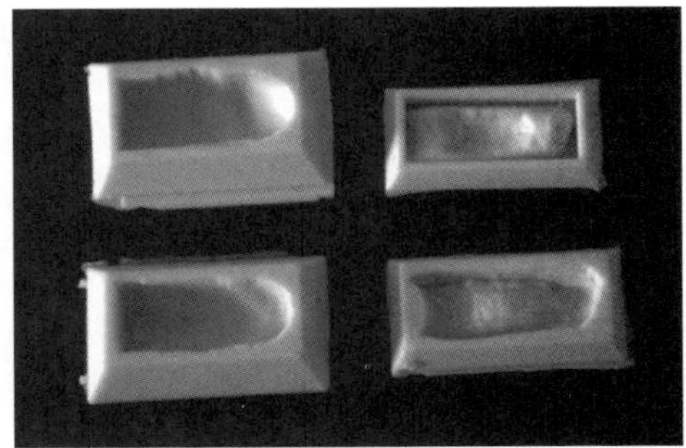

Phallus (male) wax and silicon molds at SymbioticA. | PHOTO Shannon Bell.

Two Phalluses and Big Toe in the bioreactor
at SymbioticA. | PHOTO Shannon Bell.

a beautiful strip-length configuration of cells floating in one of the flasks.

Under the sterile hood a 10 percent serum/90 percent medium mixture was added to the flask. The mixture neutralizes and counters the toxic effect of the trypsin. This mixture was pipetted in and out to wash the flask removing any renegade cells. Using a brand-new pair of autoclaved tweezers, I put each of the polymer structures into the bioreactor. The cells in their fresh nutrient medium were then pipetted into the bioreactor. A bioreactor functions as a body in which the necessary nutrients (fetal bovine serum, Dulbecco's Modified Eagle's Medium, penicillin and glutamine) keep the cells alive.

The bioreactor was positioned on its blue rotator in a thirty-four-degree Celsius incubator to maintain the cells at a temperature suitable for growth. The cells adhere to the polymer structures. Rotation of the bioreactor ensures more even cell growth on the polymer structure that over time will biodegrade.

The phalluses and big toe grew in the condition of microgravity. Tissue-engineered objects exist in a permanent condition of free-fall; they hold stasis as their technobodies rotate. Stasis or permanent free-fall is the most desirable state for cell adherence and evenly dispersed cell growth because the medium washes over the polymer structure.

Three identities floated in the vibrant pink nutrient solution: the idealized male phallic form, the fetishized big toe and the emergent female phallus. In the bioreactor these forms modified and morphed into a new singularity. Contingent on the techno-will of the reactor and on rotation, it is a totally unique (irreproducible) organ. The same organs put into a bioreactor another time will result in a different form, undeterminable prior to its origin.

Two Phalluses and Big Toe are the largest number of organs that have ever been in a bioreactor together. Previously it had been one organ at a time. We expected that the organs might cluster but there is no knowing before enacting. Tissue engineering involves control of the process by exaction and sterility, but the outcome has a touch of the techno-divine. It is a reenactment of the origin

of Being. The techno-divine seemed to be creating a meta-organ of sex, seduction and desire. The basic mystery of biology, 'how did the first cells emerge from the primordial chemical soup?,' was redone as 'how did the cells materialize a new organ from the material conditions of a spinning nutrient soup?'

DEATH OF THE PHALLUSES AND BIG TOE

FF stopped by SymbioticA to check on the progress of her neo-sex organ forming in the bioreactor. I opened the door of the incubator to find the emergent partial life turning in a urine-colored nutrient. The beautiful pink medium from which the cells get their nutrients had become contaminated. Once a semi-living or partial life is contaminated in a bioreactor it must be removed and killed.

PHALLUS TRAJECTORY

Put Daddy's phallus in a bioreactor.
Daddy's phallus morphed with
my phallus and big toe.
A biotechno-Lolita-posthuman
fable was growing.
"With the human element dwindling,
the passion, the tenderness…
only increased." [43]
Neo-Sex Organ.
Death of the phallus.
Death in the bioreactor:
micro-Death of a neo-species
in post-Venice.

There are no mistakes in theory-in-action. Performance philosophy is defined by enactment: active enfolding with, or performative being with. A performance philosopher will not theoretically

engage what s/he has not enacted or enacted with. To do so results merely in a Heideggerean repetition of what is already at hand and available.

In Heidegger's own words: "The truth that discloses itself in the work can never be proved or derived from what went before.... What art founds can... never be compensated for and made up for by what is already at hand and available."[44] The art Heidegger had in mind was Van Gogh's *Peasant Shoes*. Heidegger selected this painting because the shoes revealed the whole world of life of a rural peasant woman; her labor, joy, anxiety and how she belonged to the world.

Two Phalluses and Big Toe reveal the sameness in male and female genitalia in a way that looking at my 7-inch (17.7 cm) internal female phallus doesn't. Linking the phalluses with the big toe grounds them as posthuman postbody objects that have a human genealogy in anatomical knowledge. In the late seventeenth century, the one-sex model of the human body was replaced by the two-sex model, in which the female phallus was concealed. This model is the modern standard for medical, scientific, philosophical and artistic discourses.

In a way, Bataille's "Big Toe" brought to life through tissue engineering unconceals precisely that which Heidegger's peasant shoes hide: "The ugliness and infection represented by the baseness of the foot."[45] Specifically, it reveals the big toe which, according to Bataille, is simultaneously a grotesque and yet seductive organ:

> One can imagine that a toe, always more or less damaged and humiliating, is psychologically analogous to the brutal fall of a man—in other words, to death. The hideously cadaverous and at the same time loud and proud appearance of the toe corresponds to this derision and gives a very shrill expression to the disorder of the human body, that product of the violent discord of the organs.[46]

In a certain sense, perhaps, the birth and death of the neo-sex organ, one part female phallus, one part male phallus, one part big toe, embodies, enacts and signifies in micro-space the

disorder, discord and demise of the phallus. *Two Phalluses and Big Toe*, a neo-sex organ, placed gendered embodiment in free-floating disassemblage and reassemblage.

Bioart, as a strategy of engagement, can be an immediate and effective pragmatic-philosophical and political engagement of the concepts at the core of Western humanism and posthumanism: the continuum of life and death, self, other, identity, the body, relations with other living and technological systems, ethics and responsibility. *Two Phalluses and Big Toe* engages with the most primary sex characteristic that marks us human and designs us as male and female.

SEARING FF

FF wanted the actions and the events she'd lived in the now to be always there with her. FF had the letters FF branded onto her right arm, and with this action she owned *Fast Feminism*. "Scars are souvenirs of events telescoped into an arrested moment.... Scars record contact, adhesion, disturbance and relinquished flesh. As with all souvenirs, they give us a then, now; a there, here; a past presently."[47] Branding is about body healing, the making-whole of the body in time. It is the person's biogenetic make-up that determines the outcome of the brand: its thickness, raisure and the duration of the trajectory from burnt tissue to new pink semi-translucent tissue to white scar tissue.

FF sat cross-legged on the floor as Blair, the owner of Passage body modification shop, heated the ¼-inch stainless-steel branding slat, which he had handcrafted, in the flame of the blowtorch. For Blair, branding is like painting; the skin is the canvas, the blowtorch is the palette, the heat is the paint and the branding slat is the paintbrush.[48] On the first strike of steel on her skin FF smiled at the sizzle of flesh and the smell of burning tissue. FF leaned over her arm and drew the smoke of her skin up her right nostril and out her left nostril. She repeated the cycle of breath on each subsequent strike. FF loved the smoke of her flesh entering her body.

Endnotes

1 Stelarc Interview, Victoria, British Columbia, February 9, 2002.

2 Paul Virilio, *The Original Accident*, trans. Julie Rose (Cambridge and Malden: Polity Press, 2007), 47.

3 Ibid., 31.

4 Georges Bataille, *Guilty*, trans. Bruce Boone (Venice and San Francisco: The Lapis Press, 1988), 97.

5 Luce Irigaray, *Sexes and Genealogies*, trans. Gillian C. Gill (New York: Columbia University Press, 1993), 102.

6 Virilio, *The Art of the Motor*, trans. Julie Rose (Minneapolis and London: University of Minnesota Press, 1995), 147.

7 I presented "The Female Phallus: Something to See" in the session "Spectacular Bodies/ Phallic Transgressions" at the Body Modification: Changing Bodies, Changing Selves conference, Department of Critical and Cultural Studies, Macquarie University, Sydney, Australia, April 2003.

8 Plato, *The Symposium*, trans. Walter Hamilton (Middlesex: Penguin Books, 1951), 21 a–d.

9 Maurice Merleau-Ponty, *Phenomenology of Perception*, trans. C. Smith (London: Routledge, 1962), 138.

10 The Exoskeleton was built in 1998 in Hamburg by F18 Institute. It is an insect-like, six-legged walking machine.

11 Stelarc, Eksoskelet Performans, Cankarjev Dom, Ljubljana, Slovenia, May 14, 2003.

12 "Originary technicity" is a term developed by techno-philosopher Bernard Stiegler. It refers to how in human/technological interfaces there is no obvious distinction between doer and means; technology constructs the human, as much as, if not more than, the human constructs technology.

13 Plato, *The Republic*, trans. G.M.A. Grube (Indianapolis/Cambridge: Hackett, 1992), Book VII, 518a.

14 See www.fuckingmachines.com.

15 Stefan Lutschinger/Binx, "Introducing Cyberorgasm: Utopia, Eschatology and Apocalypse of the Fucking Machine" in *prOnnovation? Pornography and Technological Innovation*, 83.

16 Steve Dixon, "Metal Gender." Available on C-THEORY [Article 128], www.ctheory.net.

17 Ibid.

18 The Muscle Machine's first performance was July 1, 2003 at London's 291 Gallery. The Muscle Machine is a 350-kilogram six-legged walking robot actuated by pneumatic rubber muscles. With its user it is impressive in stature, spanning five meters in width. Together they create an extended human-machine system. An inner exoskeleton allows the body intuitive and interactive control of the leg movement and the direction the robot walks. The body is mechanically coupled to the chassis and legs. When the body

walks the machine walks. When the body turns, the machine walks in the direction the body is facing. The rubber muscles lift the legs high. The legs are both limb-like and wing-like in appearance in their motion. The machine's mechanical and pneumatic functions are amplified. The machine has a sensor system of accelerometers and tilt sensors that generate additional sounds transmitted by a wireless system. The user composes the sounds by choreographing the movements of the machine. (Stelarc, Muscle Machine, 291 Gallery performance card, and Gary Hall and Joanna Zylinska, *Talking Heads: Listening to Stelarc*, Live Arts Letters (http://art.ntu.ac.uk/liveart/index.htm).

As Stelarc explained in the Q&A session at Gallery 291 in London, July 2003: "The idea was to construct a machine that could couple the body architecture with the machine mechanism in order to construct an extended operational system, a moving and locomotion system that is only possible with operation of both the body and the machine. What you are performing is an operational system with a machine mechanism; when you are symbiotically in sync with the machine there is no sense of you being in control of it; rather, there is a kind of interactive exchange; you make a motion, the machine responds, the machine's response generates further action on your part. It is that kind of simple interactivity; of course, you are listening to what you are performing as you are moving so you are composing by choreographing the movements of the machine."

19 Douglas E. Harding, *On Having No Head: Zen and the Re-Discovery of the Obvious* (London, Boston and Henley: Arkana, 1961), 1.

20 Masoch, *Venus in Furs*, 191.

21 The Prosthetic Head (HEAD) is a computer-generated 3-D avatar modeled on Stelarc's head. As an installation, HEAD is a three-meter-high image projected on a screen run by a computer program with telecommunications attached—because its brain is on the server in Philadelphia. HEAD has exhibited widely and has co-presented at numerous performances and talks by Stelarc.

22 HEAD is also a poet, and like its robotic hero Hal in Kubrick's *2001: A Space Odyssey*, HEAD sings "Daisy."

23 In Zen Buddhism the aim of the Koan is to propel the interlocutor into action without thinking: "From without-thinking, we see things as they really are…. Being Enlightened by all things expresses the mental activity of without thinking wherein the 'self' (and also other) is forgotten, because awareness of such distinctions is not present. No separate self is present to perceive other things. Rather the self is all these things and vice versa, in this moment. From without-thinking flows the only identifiable reality, namely the unceasing, ever-changing, impermanent unfolding of experience." [Douglas Mikkelson, "Who is Arguing About the Cat? Moral Action and Enlightenment According to Dogen" in *Philosophy East & West*, Volume 47, Number 3, July 1997: 383–397.]

24 ¼ Scale Ear is a Tissue Culture and Art Project (TC&A) in collaboration with Stelarc. The tissue-engineered ear was grown by bioartists Oran Catts and Ionat Zurr. It was shown at the Galerija Kapelica, Ljubljana in May 2003.

25 The bioreactor acts as surrogate body host in terms of supplying nutrients, removing waste, maintaining homeostasis in

temperature, pH levels, dissolved gas levels and ensuring the absence of microbial contamination.

26 "Semi-living" is the term that TC&A has developed and uses to refer to partial life: tissue culture and tissue-engineered entities that "can be sustained, grown, function and... 'live' outside its original body." [Oran Catts, "The Art of the Semi-Living," www.tca.uwa.edu.au/atGlance/pubMainFrames.html.]

27 Catts and Zurr, "Extra Ear ¼ Scale: The Tissue Culture and Art Project in Collaboration with Stelarc, 2003." See www.tca.edu.au/extra/extra_ear.html.

28 See www.stelarc.va.com.au/extra_ear/index.htm and Stelarc, "Extra Ear: Ear on Arm" in *Skinterfaces: Exploding Borders——Creating Membranes in Art, Technology and Society*, ed. Jens Hauser (Liverpool: FACT [Foundation for Art and Creative Technology] and Liverpool University Press, 2008), 103.

29 Antonin Artaud, *The Theater and Its Double*, trans. Mary Caroline Richards (New York: Grove Press, 1958), 151.

30 Ibid., 148.

31 Deleuze, *Bergsonism*, 8.

32 Virilio, "A Pitiless Art" in *Art and Fear*, trans. Julie Rose (London & New York: Continuum, 2003), 51.

33 Ibid., 52–53.

34 Critical Art Ensemble (CAE), "Why Immolation?" in *Skinterfaces: Exploding Borders——Creating Membranes in Art, Technology and Society*, 114–117. In their lab work at SymbioticA, CAE reproduced the effects of chemical warfare—napalm and white phosphorous—on human tissue cells. The micro-image footage is the basis of their film *Immolation* (2007). Immolation is the second project wherein CAE exposes the U.S. military's use of chemical warfare. *Marching Plague: Warfare and Global Public Health* (New York: Autonomedia, 2006) reveals the effect of the U.S.'s illegal reinstatement of the germ warfare program.

35 Zurr and Catts, "Artistic Life Forms That Would Never Survive Darwinian Evolution: Growing Semi-Living Entities," available at www.tca.uwa.edu.au/atGlance/pubMainFrames.html.

36 D.E. Harding, *On Having No Head: Zen and the Re-Discovery of the Obvious* (London, Boston and Henley: Arkana, 1961), 1.

37 Martin Heidegger, *Nietzsche: Vol. 1, The Will to Power as Art*, trans. David F. Krell (San Francisco: Harper & Row, 1980), 68.

38 Jacques Lacan, "The Signification of the Phallus" in *Écrits: A Selection*, trans. Alan Sheridan (New York: W.W. Norton & Co., 1977), 289.

39 The Phalluses and Toe relics consist of the dildo used for the original mold of the male phallus, female phallus and big toe, 3.5 cm 3-D plotter wax molds, negative silicone molds, biodegradable polymer structures, and the two tissue-engineered phalluses and big toe fixed and presented in Petri dishes. The relics were exhibited under a plexiglas dome. Accompanying the relics were two sets of continuous image loops documenting the tissue engineering process. The first loop documents the process up to putting the *Two Phalluses and Big Toe* in the bioreactor. The second loop presents the putting of the *Two Phalluses and Big Toe* in the bioreactor, the contamination of the bioreactor and the death of the *Two Phalluses and Big Toe*.

Shannon Bell working under the hood at SymbioticA. | PHOTO Ionat Zurr.

CHAPTER 5 | ENDNOTES

40 Heidegger, "The Origin of the Work of Art" in *Basic Writings*, ed. David F. Krell (San Francisco: Harper & Row, 1993), 165.

41 Lacan, "The Signification of the Phallus" in *Écrits: A Selection*, 281–291.

42 Bataille, "The Big Toe" in *Visions of Excess: Selected Writings, 1927–1939*, trans. Allan Stoekl (Minneapolis: University of Minnesota Press, 1985), 20.

43 Vladimir Nabokov, *Lolita* (London: Penguin, 1955), 183.

44 Heidegger, "The Origin of the Work of Art" in *Basic Writings*, 165.

45 Bataille, *Visions of Excess*, 22.

46 Ibid.

47 Gail Carnes, "Always With You: Narratives of the Scar," artist statement from "The Bodily Alter(c)ations" exhibition, MacQuerie University, April 2003.

48 Blair explains: "Branding feels like painting; I am heating up the metal and that means that the paintbrush is ready and then I get to do a few brush strokes with it or a few strokes with the paint, the paint being red heat, and then when the tool cools down again, heating it up again by dipping it into your palette—the blow torch. The art of branding has to do with timing: I can look at the tool and I can gauge how hot it is; when I look at the skin I can tell when the heat or paint is starting to wear off. It is almost like you are running out of paint. I can keep going but it would hurt more; it hurts more when the tool is not so hot; when it is really hot it doesn't hurt so much." [Interview with Blair at Passage, August 10, 2003, Toronto, Canada.]

Mildred Alice

THANK YOU FOR BEING MY MOM

October 22, 1914 – June 1, 2009

Mom, Mildred Alice Edwards, Mildred Alice Bell. As my Mom was dying, I kept saying her three names to her. I got to say all the things you want to say to someone you really love and will never see again in the flesh. And, I got to repeat them. For this I will always be very grateful.

What became my mantra as Mom was going through a twenty-four hour dying process was:
My Beautiful, Beautiful Mom.
Thank you, for being my Mom.

During those twenty-four hours Mom fought ferociously to stay.

She was courageously aware through it all, adamantly refusing sleep.

Mom was wild, fierce, afraid, but not resigned.

Being with Mom as she was dying is one of the greatest privileges of my life.

Second only to being with her as she was living.

At one point Mom said, "Shannon, I'm scared. You go first."

Mildred Alice Edwards.

Mildred Alice Bell. | PHOTO Shelly Hargreaves.

Millie and Shannon Bell. | PHOTO Lou.

I laughed. "Mom I can't do that, I can get you as close to the other side as I can, but you will have to go the rest of the way on your own."

Death is one's "ownmost": something one can only do by oneself, each person dies his or her own death.

During this death time, I saw images and sounds of Mom's life, endless timeless days on the farm; perhaps not timeless for her, she was working, but timeless for me as a child.

I constructed images of Mom when she was young, formed from snapshots and stories: Mom curling. Mom at dances. Mom working at Scorey's Beauty Salon in Brandon. Mom dating my Dad (Hugh Ralph Bell). Their simple marriage at a manse in Brandon. Mom and Dad, just married, arms around each other, at the train station en route to a honey moon in Winnipeg. They were both poor. It was 1948.

I remembered how beautiful Mom looked, in that reserved kind of way, at dances in Alexander. I flashed on me working in the garden with her on the farm, Mom rescuing me, usually from bike mishaps. I saw us sitting across the table from each other over the years at various Brandon restaurants. I saw Mom sitting in her chair reading as I was writing on my computer on the floor earlier this May.

Mom changed her life five times: going from her own friends, family and community in the Ebor area, to her work life in Brandon, to moving into the Alexander community after marriage, to her and my Dad's move to Brandon in the early 1970s. Mom designed the house in Brandon. Mom's fourth move was to a newly built apartment at Odd Fellow's Corner on 9th street, after my Dad's death in 1985. She was single again, in her early seventies and healthy. Mom played pool at Prairie Oasis as a *Brandon Sun* photo documents. Mom loved to go out—whether for dinner, clothes shopping, afternoon tea, car rides, ice cream, and etc. After

Mom lost her girlpal Leila Hopkins, one day Mom called *Seniors for Seniors* requesting a Senior's friend. They matched her with Joanne Malkowich. Since 1997, Joanne and Mom went out weekly, if not more often. Joanne was one of Mom's best friends who over the years became her second daughter. The second girlpal Mom hooked up with in her eighties was Lillian Denbow who along the way also took on daughter-like status. In February 2006, Mom moved to Dinsdale and was able to continue going out until three months ago. At Dinsdale Mom had a new family in the nurses, caregivers and staff.

I ALWAYS TOLD MOM THAT I BELIEVE WE GET TO CHOOSE
OUR MOTHERS AND I CHOSE HER

Mom fascinated me: she had a quiet grace, an unassuming charm, a strong fairness, an understated fabulous sense of humor, a wise shyness, a profound smartness, a subtle sarcastic wit and a truly noble spirit.

In a way, being with Mom as she was dying was a reliving of her life. I thought we could relive Mom, Mildred Alice Edwards, Mildred Alice Bell's life with some images of Mom set to Glen Miller's *Moonlight Serenade*. Mom was twenty-five in 1939 when *Moonlight Serenade* became an instant hit. She danced to it endless times. My Dad played *Moonlight Serenade* on the banjo.

Some of the words in *Moonlight Serenade* are:

> The touch of your hand in the June night
> Your eyes are like stars brightly beaming

Just before Mom died her eyes calmed and cleared brilliantly. There was a beam of light that went from her eyes to mine. It is her parting gift.

Thank you, Mildred Alice, for being my Mom.